ZORN

BOOKS BY JONAH JONES

Fiction
A Tree May Fall

Non-fiction
Lakes of North Wales

ZORN

Jonah Jones

'Es gibt nur eine Einsamkeit, und die ist schwer zu tragen.'

Rainer Maria Rilke

HEINEMANN : LONDON

William Heinemann Ltd
10 Upper Grosvenor Street, London WIX 9PA
LONDON   MELBOURNE   TORONTO
JOHANNESBURG   AUCKLAND

First published in Great Britain 1986
Copyright © 1986 by Jonah Jones
SBN 434 37734 1

Photoset by Rowland Phototypesetting Ltd
Bury St Edmunds, Suffolk
Printed in Great Britain by
Butler & Tanner Ltd, Frome and London

In Memoriam

Rosa Yaroslavska
Florence Harrison
Jeremias Grossman
Norman Jones

*All the characters in this story
are imaginary, except Cloragh,
whose stone still stands in a
once private demesne.*

I

'Who is he that cometh
Like an honoured guest . . .'

Alfred Lord Tennyson

If anybody knew the origins of Zorn's presence in the area,
it was Mrs Flood. She either knew, or was likely to know,
or was responsible for the origins of quite a lot in the village.
For one thing, she often sold 'cut-price' goods in her shop,
but since there was no rival emporium to establish the norm,
the more querulous of her customers were puzzled to know
what that price had been cut from in the first place. Mrs
Flood's answer was to reveal the source of the goods in
question as relayed by Victor the delivery man: 'Fell off the
back of a lorry.'

As to origins, Mrs Flood only hinted, if she felt like it.
Otherwise, it was sealed lips. And although Mrs Flood knew
a lot about Zorn, or 'Thorn', as she translated it for respectability, she was coy when asked about him. She wished to
keep the white stranger to herself, and only in extremes of
want of gossip (for the village, being a dead end, was the last
to receive news and generated very little of its own) would
she expand over a cup of tea.

Mrs Flood, as owner of the only shop, was in one sense at
the centre of village life. But in all other senses she was
isolated. Her shop was the last building in the long-drawn-out

row that comprised the village. She was a war widow, which might seem a matter for regret or even sorrow. But Flood, who had brought her to Nentend in the first place, had never been liked, and his widow would be the last to display any sorrow over his absence. Mrs Flood was a Catholic, which tended to compound an isolation from the rest of the village; Nentend would never have admitted to anything as foreign as Catholicism. Finally, to make matters even more difficult in a place as peripheral as Nentend, Mrs Flood came vaguely from the Midlands.

As for Zorn: 'Well, he just came, like,' she would declare in her weaker moments, 'all skin and bones, and the clothes nearly off his back, I tell you. Another cup?'

This to Miss Willis one day, who was proving persistent. Miss Willis was not so easily deflected. 'All skin and bones, you say? But people must come from somewhere, mustn't they, Mrs Flood?' Which was meant to reprehend, for skating over.

'You could say we all came from somewhere, Miss Willis. It all depends on your way of looking. Sure you won't take another?' Which in turn was meant to dismiss the subject, or Miss Willis, or both.

Yet where Zorn had come from, even Mrs Flood genuinely did not know. Except that, judging by the generally bleached look of him, it was the sea. What she would not divulge, yet, was how he had first arrived at the shop. The police might press her too hard, but so far, on that momentous arrival, she had not declared a word that could be construed as actually meaning anything.

It was shortly after the VE celebrations, when Nentend had laid on its own festivities, having conquered the Nazis but then been unable to reach agreement with its ally, the larger village of Crosstrees (which aspired to township), six miles further up the one road connecting the two communities. Nentend had settled back into its customary torpor when on a fine evening late in the May of 1945, at about eleven o'clock, Mrs Flood had just switched off the wireless and at once was aware of something scrabbling at the bin in her back garden. The village boys had long since established Mrs Flood as a target for raids during apple time, but blossom time was hardly over. However, she took up the poker, more as a badge of office than as a weapon.

When she opened the back door to give them the rough edge of her tongue, there was still light in the western sky. At first she could see no one, and then almost under her feet there was a man, sitting in the new grass that was sprouting out of the old bleached tussocks of winter. He was sitting there, cleaning out a jar of raspberry jam with his finger. She had earlier thrown it out, the one damaged item of a carton Victor had delivered that day.

Standing over him with her poker, Mrs Flood felt, as ever, in total command, but for once was lost for words. It was the sight of a grown man with his fingers in a jam jar in her garden at eleven of a May evening.

It was he who got in first: '*Ich bin hungrig, sehr hungrig.*' Then, so politely: '*Herzlichen Dank.*'

And he made to hand back the jar with his sticky fingers.

'Ach! What the divvel! I don't want it!' she answered, correctly as it happened, for the idea of taking the jar from his outstretched hand struck her as the last straw. She was trying to weigh up the situation. Above all, this man seemed not in the least frightening, still sitting there with his jam jar. She saw how white he was in his faded clothes. The upturned soles of his boots looked so pathetic, she felt inclined to probe them with her poker. But forbore.

'Ah, English!' he cried, too loud for comfort.

'Ssssh!' she beseeched him, for already he seemed something out of the way to keep to herself. 'People'll hear you.'

'Ah, so. People, yes,' he whispered hoarsely. 'I speak also English. Thank you . . . what is this?' He pointed with his free hand to the jar. It sounded so foreign, she had to smile. She decided this was no tramp, since tramps never penetrated to Nentend anyway. Tramps kept to roads that led to somewhere else.

9

'Jam. Raspberry jam,' she replied. 'One and a penny a jar, I'll have you know, mister.'

'Mister Zorn. I have no money, you know. Here.'

Again she warded off the proffered jar.

'Mr Thorn?'

'Zorn, *ja*.' He waited for her name, saw her shift her ground as though thinking out the next move.

'Well, Mr Thorn, I don't know what you're doing here in a person's back garden this time of night, but you'd better get out of here quick.' Not shouted, but half-whispered, so that he caught the mood. This was strictly not for the neighbours. He was aware of lights over the way.

'I do not eat for many days,' he replied. 'I'm very hungry, you understand.'

Did she detect a slight threat in his voice? If so, she was unimpressed, for to be so hungry (raspberry jam, God bless him!) implied a certain helplessness.

'You can keep it. Now go away – and don't come pestering a body this time of night.'

She retreated slightly as he tried to rise, but he seemed stiff from the damp grass. Then he stumbled, and dropped the jar. He fumbled so anxiously, she sensed his desperation.

'You *must* be hungry to get to these straits,' she murmured absently, for she was trying to work out the next move. 'Wait here. Don't move, mind you. I'll bring you a bite.'

She was gone, locking the door behind her. After ten minutes she reopened the door, a tray in her hand. He was still there, sitting weakly on the grass.

'Here, take this.'

On a plate there were two baps filled with butter and boiled ham. Beside the plate was a steaming mug of tea.

Eagerly he took the tray and laid it reverently on the grass. At once he began to wolf the food. Halfway through he said, in their conspiratorial whisper: 'Thank you. This is so good. Mistress . . .'

'Mrs Flood.'

'Ah, Mrs Flewd.'

10

'Well, just get that down you and leave the tray where it is. I'll get it in the morning.'

With beating heart she turned inside and he could hear her slamming the bolts home.

Contentedly he addressed himself to this benison of baps and cold ham, then scalded his lips on the tea in his eagerness. He was just cleaning up the crumbs, nipping them between thumb and forefinger and sucking them in with his lips, when he heard her drawing the bolts.

'Here, take these,' she said. 'You can have them on tick.'

She handed him two labelled cans.

'"Tick"?' he asked, all suspicion before he took the articles. 'What is "tick"?'

'Some other time. Pay when you can. Call again with it. But before half-past eleven. A body might be in bed.' And she was gone with a clash of bolts.

'"A body"?' he wondered as the late warm evening folded back over him.

Only Mrs Flood knew how he came to be there in the first place. Nobody else knew, and Mrs Flood was close about it. She wouldn't say, being Mrs F., not if it didn't suit her.

Pritchard the poacher, on the other hand, was prepared to speak, or rather speculate. But the trouble was the other way round – nobody would speak to Pritchard if they could avoid it. Pritchard would hint that he knew a lot more about people than they would give him credit for. But people were generally loath to give that credit. Talking to Pritchard was not likely to improve your social standing. He smelt of game, very high game.

Of one thing everybody was in agreement, and nobody would accuse Pritchard of it. Zorn (if that was his name) was so white it hurt your eyes. According to the word, he hadn't gone white with years. He had been white from the beginning, the beginning being when he arrived, from nowhere, or out of the blue if you can agree the sea is blue. But beyond that, nobody knew, *really* knew anything about Zorn, except

11

Mrs Flood. But that is how the word is formed, a bit here, a bit there, a rare sighting (like a marsh harrier) reported, an inspired guess. Nothing that would help the police.

Over the years there had been disagreements. Was he short, tall, fat or thin? Worst of all, was he foreign, was he a power for good or evil? Because not quite knowing, or not knowing at all, made it now important. There were even years of silence about Zorn, years when he was forgotten, when he meshed in discreetly, years when he simply did not matter, for there was so much else going on. A lot had happened since the war, people had come and gone and the village wasn't nearly the same as on that first, secret advent. Not even his name, which was peculiar, found agreement. But on one thing everybody agreed – on his whiteness: everybody agreed from beginning to end, his whiteness. And until Angela Watkin had been interfered with, there seemed general agreement, if only by silence, that Thorn, or Vaughan or whatever, was harmless, even likeable in a funny sort of way, the sort of way that sees a presence in a remote peninsular woodland as benevolent, as a sort of presiding genius of Nature – even a sort of Green Man, if he hadn't been so white.

Now, Miss Willis had the satisfaction at last of assuming (she didn't *know*) that of one thing Mrs F. was ignorant: of how Thorn had disappeared, and where to. Mrs F., as usual, wasn't saying, but Miss Willis risked a wry smile, on the chance that Mrs F., for once, didn't know.

Nobody would quite say, either, that Angela Watkin had been more than 'interfered with'. The girl had indeed been 'interfered with', but she was also dead, only nobody could bring themselves to say the word. Her knickers were found under a bush on the outskirts of the village, way beyond the end council house, and half buried for some reason. Her brassière, its cups still with their suggestive foam-rubber firmness intact, was found hanging on a low branch over the girl's body.

The more righteous would point to that as a token of her

12

willingness. But until she was decently buried, nobody would say she was dead. The general agreement was simply that she had been 'interfered with', following her eighteenth birthday party, and that she was no longer, so to speak, present. Which was true, since Angela's lovely form lay prone, white and frozen, in the morgue thirty-five miles away, awaiting the inquest.

Given Angela's reputation, the entire male population of Nentend was questioned, excluding such venerable figures as Miss Willis's father, who was ninety-four and rumoured to be still continent if otherwise beyond the call of such as Angie. But the finger pointed naturally, 'it stood to reason' that that odd character, living out there alone without a woman, could no doubt provide a few answers. The news of Angela Watkin's fate had hardly rippled through the village, like a stone thrown in a pond, than it rippled back towards the centre, embellished by the mention of Zorn's name.

An overriding problem for the police was not only the history, but the geography of Zorn. What everybody surmised (for they did not know) was that he was settled somewhere in the Gwildy, a wild and deserted peninsula that reached out beyond the golf links.

As far as police surveillance went, this was indeed a problem. The police station was situated at Crosstrees, about six miles inland from Nentend, a nodal point for farmers and villagers around, so quite important in its way, as important as Nentend was unimportant. The road in from Crosstrees carried on towards the county town, but the awkwardness, as far as the police were concerned, was the road outwards to the peninsula.

It was a narrow country road, mostly between high hedge banks, leading to this isolated village of Nentend, where the last building, set apart, was Mrs Flood's shop. There the road petered out, except for two tarmac parallels, a wheelbase apart, leading to the nine-hole golf course beyond Mrs Flood's.

In normal times a constable cycled down from Crosstrees

once a month or so. He would have a quiet sniff round the village, especially in the region of Pritchard's noisome yard, and perhaps call on Mrs Flood, if only to show he had completed the beat.

So the police could hardly claim an intimate knowledge of Nentend and its people. Crime of any sort to interest the police simply did not occur. The villagers were too busy watching one another to allow any crime, and passion could not be said to run high in Nentend.

The place had its own particular social stratification – three large detached houses (one of which housed Miss Willis and her ancient parent), two rows of undistinguished dwellings either side of the road, and at the landward end a small estate of council houses built in the 'thirties for no reason anybody could think of, except that, there being little else in the way of leisure (no pub, no cinema, no church and only one small Methodist chapel), the birthrate was unusually high.

But the case of Angela Watkin presented a further difficulty. For that twin track that led into the golf links covered what had once been a drive into an isolated estate on the peninsula, established in the early nineteenth century by an eccentric landowner, a Major Furnival, returning from the Napoleonic Wars and determined to put as great a distance as possible between himself and his family.

What was now the golf course had been farmland. Beyond that, a high stone wall guarded the estate proper, which then reached to the tip of the peninsula and was interrupted only by one gateway with a pair of high cast-iron gates. These had been severely chained and barred for more years than anybody could remember. Beyond that nobody had penetrated, and certainly not the police. For in 1884, the last of the major's brief line, a surviving spinster daughter, her cook, estate man and maid had barely escaped when the house burnt down in an October gale. The story was told of how sixteen dogs of various breeds had perished in the flames.

From that night in 1884, the gates had remained chained and nobody had since set foot behind the wall, excepting, probably, Zorn. The posse's nearest access had been by Land Rover to the end of the golf course. The chained gates had proved unavailing, and they had scaled a broken portion of the wall. Beyond that, it had been scrub, head-high bracken in what space there was, trees, mostly gnarled sessile oaks that had flourished here since geological time, and the cursed rhododendrons. For after Miss Furnival's demise, nobody had ever wanted to take up the headland; no shepherd, woodman or huntsman had ever wanted to make anything of the estate's two miles of rough woodland scrub. Only Pritchard might have chanced his arm at the initial barrier of bracken and blackthorn, because a poacher knows no bounds. Besides, the golf course protected it all too well, and to cross a golf course for the doubtful reward of game (even assuming there were any) was more than Pritchard cared to face. Crossing a golf course, even at night, unauthorized, would be like walking up to the altar in church with your hat on. Zorn, of course, being a foreigner, was unlikely to feel any such inhibition.

The difficulty for the police lay behind the wall, for the man rumoured to live beyond it had to be apprehended. It all appeared to be impenetrable jungle, and if this hermit of unknown origin was in there, they would have to tackle an intricate mass of bracken, brier, scrub, blackthorn and a profusion of rhododendron and azalea that the major had planted and which now twisted and twined in dark tunnels, impassable to all but the red squirrels that on this outlying tip of the peninsula had survived the intervention of the grey. A tangle of brier, nettles and ivy actually pushed through the gates themselves and all but consumed them in a mosaic of greenery.

To bring Zorn in was not going to be easy. He had simply disappeared, which both solved the mystery of Angela Watkin's death and yet compounded it. For why should the man hide if he wasn't guilty? Yet how does one ever know the whole truth until the criminal is taken, alive and talking?

The police, of course, had scaled the wall, which was

15

broken in parts, and tracker dogs were brought in. But though a lot that was mysterious was found, not least a great tower of metal taking its place among the trees, Zorn or Thorn or Vaughan was nowhere to be seen or scented, judging by the dogs' indifference.

Sergeant Helliwell was relieved to find that tall structure. After the hard work of combing the wilderness with nothing to show, this thing, this mast (he supposed) was a positive find. It pointed to *something*, if only to the sky. He was relieved too, when he radioed, to hear that the superintendent was more than interested and would send in an expert as soon as he could raise one.

'Where are you? Over,' came his voice, like a sheep with a strangulated hernia.

'Oh, I'd say about a mile and a half in from the links. Hard to say with all this stuff. You can't see the gates. We've scaled the wall and we've hacked our way here. But where I am it's cleared. *He* must have cleared round the old house. And the mast, or whatever it is, is in this clearing. Over.'

'OK. Just hang around till I can send an expert in.'

The sergeant wondered how the super planned to get a radio buff into this jungle without a guide. The sergeant had a posse of four constables and two dogs, and they had had the devil's job hacking their way thus far.

But he had not counted on the superintendent's initiative – and power, when it came to a man-hunt for murder. After only forty minutes the sergeant and his men heard the uneasy roar, more a bellyaching, of a helicopter. It was quartering back and forth over the trees by the sound of it, getting nearer all the time, obviously under orders to do its own combing before delivering the expert. Then the roar was deafening and the thing was whipping the tree-tops into a frenzy with its down-draught.

A man was sitting in its open door, signalling to the pilot that he had spotted the sergeant and his men. He was winched down unceremoniously into a cabbage patch.

'Sergeant Helliwell,' the sergeant shouted, and stretched

16

out a hand, half in salutation, half to help the expert find his feet, for he stumbled in the unfamiliar terrain.

'Alley – Corporal. Royal Signals.'

'Spot anything on the way in, Corporal?' the sergeant asked.

'Like what?' The corporal clearly had not been briefed.

'Well, a man hiding or running, or something.'

'Oh, you're after a man, then. I thought it was something wrong with one of the sets the air-sea rescue wallahs have.'

The sergeant waited for an answer to his question. The corporal merely mumbled, as he pulled himself together after the trip: 'No, nothing. Nothing but bloody trees.'

The sergeant turned away, guiding Alley towards the metal structure set almost against the surrounding trees at the outer edge of the clearing.

'Rummy thing, isn't it?' was all Alley had to say as they looked up at the structure. 'All scrap by the look of it.'

It was an odd structure by any account. Several kinds of metal of all sizes and shapes joined together ingeniously but without welding. Although only about twenty feet high, and therefore dwarfed by its attendant trees, it had an undeniable presence. Bits of it branched out for no apparent reason, though each extension seemed to obey a certain mad logic. Sometimes a branch would be finished with a delicate mesh of wires, woven across the skeleton of aluminium, steel or brass elements like a web. Other branches were left skeletal, some only half-meshed, as though it were some sort of work in progress.

'Well, it might be "rummy",' the sergeant replied testily, 'but what's it for?' He looked Alley in the eye. 'Isn't it a radio mast or something of that sort?'

'Not a clue,' replied the expert, just as anxious as the sergeant to be off. 'If this chap you're looking for was some sort of radio buff, I can tell you definitely this thing wasn't part of his equipment.' He kicked the structure's base; the thing shuddered cyclically to the top, but remained firm.

The potential 'radio mast' having proved a red herring,

17

Sergeant Helliwell decided it was time to show Alley the 'holy of holies'. Across the clearing, which was neatly divided by grass paths into vegetable patches, was the ruin of 1884.

It was quite apparent that the man had worked hard over the years to clear the encroaching wilderness from the immediate environs of the house. But otherwise it was as the fire and subsequent nature had left it, a tumbled profile of ivy-covered walls, interrupted only by door and window apertures. But somehow the settler had rendered it from chaotic to picturesque. Paving in front of the house and a balustrade had been cleared and kept in order.

The sergeant dawdled, not to hurry Alley towards the most intriguing item of all.

They went into the roofless hall. The whole foundation, in fact, was open to the sky. They turned right. And there, on the floor of what had once been a spacious kitchen, stood a hut, a home, exploiting the sound surface of quarry tiles, but attached only to one wall of the old ruin.

'Well, strike me!' was all Alley could think of.

'I reckon this used to be the kitchen in the old days,' the sergeant said, as though guiding at an archeological site.

It was a wooden shack, more a bungalow, though the timbers were a random lot, probably beachwrack brought up from the shore.

'Well, now you've written off the radio mast,' the sergeant said, 'you'd better check inside this place before you go.'

But before approaching the door of the hut, the sergeant felt a sudden burst of irritation at the sight of his four constables standing quite content, having a breather after the day's effort.

'All right,' he addressed them, 'carry on as far as you can. Pick up anything you might think likely to help.'

They could not have shown less willingness. The trees were tall round the ruin. Here they were mostly ash, whose open foliage allowed a dense undergrowth to flourish. The men were tired.

'Just another hour, eh?' the sergeant pleaded, for he could

see he was asking too much. 'Find anything you can, then we'll call it a day.'

The men strode off into the wilderness beyond, idly flailing their sticks. The sergeant then turned to Alley.

'All right, now let's see if there's anything in your line inside, eh?'

The fabric of the beach timber imparted a delicate mosaic to the walls of the hut, which rose straight from the quarry tiles of the original kitchen floor. It was about twenty-five feet long, which had surprised the sergeant, for the sheer scale indicated habitation over a number of years.

That could be construed as negligence on the sergeant's part, for despite rumour and gossip, and especially the epithet 'foreign', the sergeant had never ventured beyond the club-house of the golf course. Where was the need? What harm was the chap doing, even if he was a foreigner? The sergeant could be flushing out strays, hippies, tramps and gypsies for ever and a day if he listened to village gossip.

The front door of the hut was a fine panelled specimen of mahogany, beautifully varnished. There were one or two meticulous repairs to it, the mark of a fine craftsman, good matching, good joins and finish.

Windows too – they were an odd assortment, all shapes and sizes, but in each case, like the door, meticulously repaired and finished, except that not every pane was glazed. Some panes were filled with plywood or hardboard, even select bits of plastic. But most were glazed. That pointed to patience. Obviously, what windows had arrived from the sea had come without glass, and this man had set about getting his glass elsewhere. Doors and windows along the front presented random but neat apertures in a quite handsome frontage. Beach timber did not come in critical lengths and thicknesses, but somehow the man had achieved an admirable evenness of texture in the timbers. It was intriguing how he had managed weather-proofing on the roof with odd bits of tarpaulin beautifully overlapped and pinned down.

The shack was in three sections. He had started with

something no bigger than a wide garden shed against one wall of the old kitchen and then gradually extended further into the room. According to rumour, he had been there since the end of the war. How he had arrived, from where, how he had started, how subsisted in this outlandish hermitage, were all questions the sergeant might have asked long ago. Or rather, his predecessor at the station might have asked in the beginning and handed on a file. But no file existed, and the rest was no more than gossip and speculation, not worth investigating until the rape and murder of Angela Watkin. The sergeant surmised that he himself might well be under investigation after this lot.

'Yes, you've got to hand it to him,' he condescended. 'Whoever he was – is – he knew how to run a home. And all on his ownio – as far as we know.'

The floor was paved with the old quarry tiles, but here inside they had been polished to their original red oxide glow. He had filled out the pattern to perfection, obviously exchanging damaged tiles with better ones from outside the structure. To the right, the newer end, he had established a workshop, separated from the living quarters by a partition. Through the opening, they could see the beautifully wrought tools hanging from individual brackets along the rear wall.

But the living quarters held their eyes. An ample bunk, large enough for two, and on the other side, a child's cot made up with loving care. A chair he had made for himself, an austere structure which nevertheless looked perfectly fitted to the vagaries of the human spine. The table-top was made of selected planks of pale matching wood, scrubbed and pristine. There was a simple dining chair, a carefully restored original he must have picked up somewhere.

'D'you know something?' the sergeant mused aloud. 'If it wasn't for the walk, I wouldn't mind taking this place over myself.'

But Alley only shrugged his shoulders.

'You're sure there's nothing in your line here?' the sergeant persisted, frowning with displeasure.

20

Alley was all too evidently unimpressed by anything the sergeant might say. No sign of even a portable receiver. The question irked him: 'I thought this was a murder hunt, not a spy hunt.'

'It *is* a murder hunt. But then, as far as we can gather, he was a foreigner, so I was told to check, that's all.'

The sergeant reflected that nothing actually pointed to this Thorn so far, except that he was there – or had been – and had no right to be there all these years.

'Well, you can be satisfied, believe me. There's nothing here in the way of transmitter, receiver, nothing. In fact, from the look of it, there's nothing electric either, no batteries, nothing. So how could he be a spy? See what I mean?'

'All right. I take your word,' the sergeant said mildly, but desisted from thanking the man, who seemed not to mind anyway. 'You might as well go. Can you find your way?'

But the expert had seen enough from the air to have no appetite for the bush.

'I'll wait for your men,' he said.

The sergeant took out his pocket radio, drew out the aerial, pressed a switch.

'Hello there, Roger. Any sign of a boat, any sort of craft, or anything like that? Rubber dinghy marks maybe? Over.'

'Not a sign. No moorings, ropes, anchor stake – nothing. Just footprints, plenty of 'em, mind you. Nothing else that I can see. Looks like he collected any timber washed up. There's a neat pile above high-water mark, waiting for transport, I suppose.'

'How far do you reckon it is?'

'No more than three hundred yards, I'd say.'

'OK, Jim. Thanks. When you've combed the rest of the shore, you'd better come in. Over and out.'

A hush like velvet settled over the place as the day began to die. It was high time to think of getting out of their wilderness.

The sergeant, satisfied that the task was nearly over and that no superior was likely to approach this improbable

21

terrain, risked another cigarette. He sat on Zorn's chair, comfortably.

Alley touched the ash in the grate. 'Quite cold,' he said. 'Must've been gone some time.'

'Cold when we first arrived,' the sergeant replied, just to quell any suspicion that he might have neglected such an elementary procedure.

Pots and pans were random, but it looked as though Zorn had insisted on quite a cuisine. Everything was clean and polished. Alley moved past the sergeant, who puffed philosophically at his cigarette. Helliwell was tired by the day's exertions and ignored the expert's restless movements. At the workshop end, the man had been working on yet more timber from the shore. In a vice was a battered and weathered hatch-cover. It was all too clear how this man's mind worked. The wood was a write-off, but not the brass handle that he had been in the process of prising off when he was disturbed – or whatever happened to him.

'What's all this about then? The man's definitely done it, has he?' For Alley was already impressed enough by the fugitive's ingenuity to have a sneaking sympathy for him.

'Nobody's definitely done anything at English law until he's been tried and found guilty.' Three days of this had stretched the sergeant's patience.

But the corporal did not see, did not recognize signs and portents in people. 'Well,' he retorted, 'I know that, don't I? But what do *you* think?'

'I don't. Not that way anyway. My job is to search out evidence, not judge it.'

'Oh, so you think he might be innocent?'

'I didn't say that, now, did I?' The sergeant was suddenly roused. He wished the expert would dismiss himself and leave him in peace.

But it was all lost on Alley, who continued exploring the hut. It was an experience beyond him. Everything here bore the imprint of a man who had lived for and unto himself alone. It was as though the rest of humanity had been closed off. No photograph, no newspapers, no cuttings, no radio, above all no television. How could a man live?

'So what's it all about?' Alley tried again.

'It's about the Watkin girl, that's what. What d'you think it's all about?'

'Yeah. But what's this bloke got to do with it?'

'He's got to be a suspect, that's what. We've got no other lead.'

Alley scratched his head. 'But what lead is there to him? He's interested in tools, chisels, this lathe. Making things, like . . .' The corporal was picking up various utensils, pots and pans, wooden spoons, many hand-made. 'Look at this knife. Lovely bit of steel picked up somewhere, handle box-wood, I reckon. Beautifully made. Made it himself, you can tell. He's got his mark. Looks like he either found or made everything himself. But not a single pin-up in the whole place. Not natural somehow, is it?'

'Well, that's maybe why we've got to look at him. What happened to Angie Watkin wasn't natural either.'

And with that, the sergeant had had enough, looked round for somewhere to extinguish his cigarette and decided on the bars of the grate, thought better of it and took it outside to stamp underfoot.

'Come on,' he said, 'we'll meet the rest coming from the beach.'

They found a well-defined path behind the house. Zorn had obviously spent much of his time treading this path between home and sea, while leaving the rest, the landward side, practically undisturbed.

He had alternative routes out, none of them easy. The dogs had traced them, but each track was so difficult, involving much stooping under tentacles of rabid rhododendron growth and sweeping aside the head-high bracken in a few open areas, that it seemed Zorn had every intention of keeping it inaccessible to outsiders.

Sergeant Helliwell and Alley had gone no more than fifty yards when they heard the sound of men and dogs. Two

23

thoughts occurred to the sergeant as he saw the men approaching. First, what was the best and quickest way out of this place – overtime for the weary constables had to be considered – and second, although he had no instruction about it, should he not leave a couple of men behind at the shack, in case the fugitive might still turn up from some hiding place?

As to the first question, the dogs would be hungry and could be trusted to find the quickest way home. And as to the second, the sergeant tried to think. It would be dusk in less than two hours. There were no rations. It was no occasion to leave men behind, hungry, facing the dark and possibly a frightened homicidal maniac.

Then, inspiration – he would propose a tactic. If they left the ruin unguarded overnight and this Zorn fellow was still about somewhere, it was odds on that he would steal back to his lair. If so, by one sign or another, they would know the following day. To this end, the sergeant led the group back to the hut, but told his men to stand back from the entrance. He picked up the cigarette stub he had earlier stamped on, and to the fascination of all put it carefully in his tunic pocket. He then went inside the hut, brought out Zorn's home-made birch-twig besom, and swept the quarry tiles all round the entrance to the hut. He did the same at the back door. The unsuspecting Zorn was bound to leave prints, however vestigial, to confirm any new scents the dogs might pick up. They would then know that the fugitive was still about. As it was, there seemed no way of knowing.

This clean sweep seemed the logical conclusion to a most tiring and frustrating day. The sergeant, who had started without any particular feelings about Zorn, now hated him, not only because of what he might have done to Angela Watkin, but because he was troublesome. A man is innocent until proved . . . it was no use. The sergeant felt a deep resentment against the man. He turned to the senior constable: 'No definite track, I take it?'

'That's right. His prints are all over the place.'

'Could he have swum somewhere?'

'Not that we could make out. I mean, surely the dogs would have picked him up if he'd holed up somewhere else on the peninsula. We've just about covered the lot, Sergeant, I can tell you.'

'What about the next headland? That would be Kern Point, wouldn't it?'

'He'd have to be a bloody good swimmer, that's all I can say. If you reckon he's there, then you'd better alert the coastguards, don't you think?' Anything to shed or share the burden of Zorn. It was all beyond them in their present exhausted state.

'OK. Let's hit the trail,' the sergeant concluded. 'Provided the dogs can find one!'

With a last look, to check the brushed area round both doors, the sergeant indicated to the dog handlers to lead the way.

The effort of following the dogs through tangled tunnels of feral rhododendron proved too much for conversation. But after scaling the wall and descending on to the end rough of the golf links, Alley broke the silence yet again:

'I wonder why he lived in there. Damned difficult, don't you think?'

The sergeant, brushing filaments of bracken off his uniform, thought about this. 'I'll tell you what I think,' he said. 'I remember an old farmer, Willie Protheroe, who once dug out an old vixen and her cubs and shot them all bar one. He kept this cub and reared it, just to see how it would turn out. He cosseted it, took it for walks on a lead, treated it like a proper pet. But as soon as the thing was adult, off it went one night and they never saw it again. Couldn't stand the smell of humanity, I suppose. I reckon this fellow must've had something of that in him to live out there on his own all these years.'

'But what did he live on?' It seemed Alley was never satisfied.

The sergeant considered his answer had been philosophical enough to be final.

'Well, until you just wrote off my radio theory, I'd have said he lived by monkey business.'

'Monkey business?'

'Espionage, Corporal, espionage. But you say not. So we'll have to find out how he lived. From what I've gathered, he was open to casual labour in the village – when he wasn't building masts!'

But Corporal Alley was not a man to let a subject die.

'It sounds as though you know nothing about this character,' he said provocatively.

'You could say that,' the sergeant conceded, albeit reluctantly. 'I suppose everybody in the village knew *of* him, even knew him, if you like. Depends what you mean by "knew". He did odd jobs, painting and decorating, that sort of thing – casual labour. I gather he was a first-class joiner. Oh yes, everybody thought they knew him. But nobody actually knew who the hell he was – if you get my meaning.'

'And nobody bothered to find out?'

This was clearly below the belt, a blow from hindsight.

'Look here!' the sergeant replied with unconcealed irritation. 'The police are no less fallible than any other public service. There might be chinks in our armour. We all know things after the fact, don't we? Anyway, this fellow Thorn wasn't important. He wasn't doing anybody any harm, or at least not till lately. And even then, how do we know? Even you can find nothing of any interest, can you? Not in your department anyway. So, naturally, he was just left alone, so . . .'

'He's a foreigner though, isn't he?' Alley went on, still probing at weak spots.

'So what? You've just ruled out spying, haven't you?'

'Yes, I have. But you haven't. All I've done is rule out any radio communication on the available evidence. And you still haven't a clue as to who he was,' Alley said ironically, as if suggesting the sergeant had been neglecting his duties.

'You're right,' the sergeant went on wearily. 'We don't know who he was. That's all we have against him at present

26

– unless we establish that he was responsible for the Watkin girl, of course.' The sergeant revealed a rare constabulary pessimism in the way he took off his helmet to scratch at the few hairs left frontally. It quite startled Alley. 'To be honest, we've got nothing definite to connect him with Angela Watkin, except that he's disappeared, and yes – that we don't know who he was.' But Alley knew he was clutching at straws, and whether from service rivalry, or from common suspicion of the law, he was as satisfied with his day's work as the sergeant was not.

II

'. . . but to myself I seem to have been
only a boy playing on the sea-shore . . .'

Isaac Newton

The Welck is not one of Europe's greater waterways. But it does impart its name to most features along its course. It flows out of the Welcksee, one of the hundreds of lakes that spread over the northern plains of Germany, and glides over a weir, where the village mill of Welckdam grinds the rye harvest from miles around. The Welck then flows on, its slow-moving surface almost level with the broad, flat fields. There is good duck-shooting: mallard, teal and pintail. After breaking through the low morainic hills of the Welckwald, an area of lean, stunted oak, beech and pine subject to the bleak winter winds, the Welck meanders, then gathers momentum and reaches the Baltic at the small seaport of Welckmar in characteristically undramatic style. This is the southern Baltic, where to be undramatic is obligatory. The flat earth and grey Baltic waters dampen even the most ardent spirits, except in midsummer, when a sunny calm settles over the area. Winters are long, grey and distinctly unpleasant, with the harbours freezing up for weeks on end. A damp mist can settle over the flat, inner littoral, and an icy north-easter sweeps down from the Finland Station and clamps the low, off-shore islands, sandspits and estuaries in ice and sea fog.

28

Welckmar has been there since the fourteenth century, taken and retaken in wars with Swedes, or between East and West. But all that remains dates from the eighteenth and nineteenth centuries. Welckmar is now burdened with some rather unprepossessing suburbs, mostly five-storey community blocks that seem part of the Cold War heritage. But between the wars, Welckmar still rested on the glories of its past, a weak strain of vernacular Baroque. The town was no more, and no less, than one of those self-contained little seaports that were strung along the coast from Lübeck to Gdansk.

After the First World War, only half a dozen trawlers tied up alongside Welckmar's fish-quay, mostly plying the North Sea. There was a fish-processing and canning factory, employing twelve men and thirty-two women, and there was an agricultural depot in the port area, where butter and cheese were produced for export, and where sugar-beet was collected and processed. The one abiding characteristic of the area was the smell, above the horse-droppings, of that slightly nauseous, sweet air that goes with pig-rearing and sugar-beet, with the fish-creels on the quay adding a certain pungency. And, of course, the timber yards.

These were significant. The top-heavy coasters negotiated the shoals, spits and islands off Welckmar, bringing in raw logs of softwood from Sweden and hardwood logs from Africa and South America, and taking out bagged sugar, fish products and processed timber.

All this, with its wide hinterland of farmsteads, was Welckmar's lifeline. Welckmar would always survive. Its people were dour, hard-working and stoical. The saw-mills never seemed to flag, though the years of peace and depression after the Great War nearly finished them off. But the mills survived. The chug-chug-chug of the old steam-engines was as characteristic as the smell of sawdust and the bitter burnt-wood smell of tough hardwood logs being pushed through the circular saw. The Zorn yard could turn out massive green-heart piles for harbour works, stanchions and staithes all along

29

the coast. Tides are no problem on the Baltic. The level of this inland sea hardly changes at all. Only in a persistent north-easter on a long fetch all the way from the Gulf of Bothnia, would the waters pile up against this north German coast and create some semblance of the ebb and flow of the tide. At its worst, there could be flooding, for which the natives always seemed as unprepared as the British are for the first snow of winter.

The trawlers and tramps tied up along the wharf or moored out in the harbour would then bob and yaw, and the stout rope fenders would creak against the quay wall with that magical sound that quickens the step of any man with the sea in his blood. Welckmar had many of those, not all of them plying any trade at sea, but sailing their 'double-ender' ketches and gaff-rigged sloops for pleasure.

In those Versailles days, the town was still compact, if not stagnant. Away from the quay with its distinct life and smells, the town extended into one main square, where the eighteenth-century high-gabled houses looked down on a pattern of granite setts. At the farthest end from the harbour stood Welckmar's chief claim to civic pride, the 'Neapolitaner' Opera House, which kept a small repertory theatre company barely alive and was host once a year to a short season from an itinerant operetta company.

But to keep a toe in for virtue and propriety, St Pieterskirch stood at the north side of the square, built to accommodate a whole province, but more usually echoing with a resounding emptiness as the citizenry tried to live up to its expectations, and at best failed to occupy more than half its pews. Pastor Stentewik, with his stentorian, censorious address, hardly helped.

On the south side, the Hotel Ystad catered for travellers from Sweden and beyond, and like St Pieterskirch, was rarely more than half-full in the 'twenties now that Germany was defeated.

And there was the hospital, which again was intended to answer the needs of Welckmar's extended farmsteading hinterland and did. It also fulfilled the needs of those for whom good works were a more reliable passport to salvation than Pastor Stentewik's doctrine of predestination.

Narrow streets struck out from the square, full of character, with Oststrasse in particular catering for the vice that customarily goes with seaports. Then the streets grew wider, tamer, marked by the stern sobriety of their occupants.

On the south and landward side of town, in high-walled gardens, stood the large houses of the few burghers who elected to live apart from Welckmar's public sounds and smells in private worlds of their own; the Schinklers who owned the trawlers and other ships; the Grohls who owned the fish factory (the Grohls and the Schinklers spoke to each other only when a third party was present); or the Zorns, who owned one of the timber yards at this time. By 1923, the rival Tadziewicz yard was practically out of business, barely surviving in that way *Ostseefolk* have of keeping their heads down when the wind blows from a hostile quarter.

A single-line railway joined Welckmar to the outside world, with the terminus just off the square. The whole community was linked by a horse-tram route. Later, when Germany began once again to flex its muscles, Welckmar saw tangible benefits when this tram route was electrified in 1936. But at the great defeat in 1918, horse traffic predominated, mostly the long, four-wheeled farm carts with a pair of horses or mules yoked to a central shaft, driven by men whose blank faces bore the mark of unremitting toil, hard winters and dull domestic lives. The years of Versailles offered little enough hope of change for the better.

Certainly, 1923 was not the most propitious time for Dieter Zorn to be born in Welckmar. The stars were not consulted, not having the power over lives that they have today. Yet the signs were there for anybody to see. Thorvald Zorn, the father, was blond, a true Nordic *Ostseeman* if ever there were. He had had a good war, having distinguished himself on the Somme in 1916. But there was one impediment to a wholly satisfactory horoscope, for Thorvald Zorn was not really

German, but Swedish. Enough to mess up the chart: Thorvald Zorn was a naturalized German.

But he had his luck, his star, which was constantly to steer him into situations that offered no alternative. Returning from the war had in some ways been more difficult than the war itself. The Versailles Treaty was not intended to make life easy. Germany, if not in the wrong, had nevertheless lost, and that was that. Life could not be easy, it was not in the stars, influenced as they were, surely, by a vindictive French government, intent on exacting the last ounce in reparations.

Thorvald Zorn, whose presence in Welckmar was wholly due to the timber trade, found business extremely difficult. From 1919 to 1922, he found it so grim that he was planning to return to Sweden. But when he sailed over to Gothenberg and travelled inland in search of softwoods, he found little to encourage voluntary repatriation. The effects of the war were contagious, even to those who stayed clear of it. On the other hand (Thorvald was fond of postulating alternatives) – on the other hand, should things turn up (and only the French were holding things back), the import and processing of timber in Germany might be very rewarding some day. But the time it was taking! How many permutations of fraud, blood-sucking and downright theft could the French find? 1922 was distinctly bad.

Until a certain 'conjunction' presented itself. Then there was no alternative. Marriage! An alliance! Since Welckmar could now support only one timber business, Thorvald must marry into the rival firm.

But here the stars would have troubled the astrologer, because the rival mill was owned by Josef Tadziewicz, a Jew of emancipated disposition. How Josef had managed to ease himself into such an unlikely business as timber was a matter of conjecture. But by September 1922, he was in even worse difficulties than Thorvald, because where there was a choice, contractors would turn away from Josef and do business elsewhere.

Friends were scarce for Josef at a time when business refused to move. In fact, both yards seemed destined to fold up. An alliance would save them both. And since marriage offered an even stronger bond than a cold merger, the stars pointed ineluctably in the direction of Josef's daughter, Etta.

Since Josef was eccentrically secular in his attitudes and not in the least outrageous by good Baltic moral and social standards (which could be very exacting), there would be no undue difficulties over religion. The final plunge was influenced by Etta's beauty. She had a well-shaped face, and great, dark orbs for eyes, all crowned by a fine coif of black curls.

After a lightning but careful courtship conducted along the lines of an international treaty, the alliance was sealed by a marriage in St Pieterskirch, the final submission by baptism of Etta being Josef's one regret. But times were hard, and the various terms of the contract going against him, Josef, like Thorvald, was faced with no alternative. The conjunction of stars seemed at last to be easing in everybody's favour, given the times – and the French.

The honeymoon was as revelatory as most honeymoons. It was spent in the snows of Sweden in January 1923, where Thorvald had the advantage of a decent ski technique. Two items marred what promised bliss: first, news of the French occupation of the Ruhr, which might well cancel out Thorvald's expansionary plans in business. And second, the acerbity of Etta's tongue in response to Thorvald's less patient words at ski instruction.

But the marriage contract, once sealed (and it was), must be observed. Against anything the French could muster in the way of impediments to trade, 1923 did indeed see a slight improvement in Thorvald's business. The combined assets of the two yards coped easily with an export order to the new Russian republics, which might own more standing timber than the rest of the world put together, but had not yet learnt how to process it to keep pace with a much-promised house-building programme for their emancipated proletariat.

And Etta was pregnant.

Even speculations as to the sex of the unborn child were a matter for rather tart exchanges – if it was a boy. Thorvald almost prayed it might be a girl, but there was the future to think of, and there were enough Tadziewicz males ripe for any future inheritance that might be going free.

But if it was a boy – 'You promise, on your honour,' Etta insisted.

On his honour! Was it not enough simply to promise?

'I promise.'

'On your honour!'

'God in heaven, Etta, isn't it enough to say I promise?'

'No, it isn't. It matters enough to seal your promise with the only thing that matters to you Germans – your honour.'

'You're the German, not I,' Thorvald retorted, with some strength, more to deflect the drift than for vanity.

'You can call me what you like,' Etta replied, 'but when it comes to honour, you're a German.'

In her condition, he thought, perhaps it was better to practise a little patience.

'I promise, on my honour.' Spoken so quietly, it might have been taken for submission – but was meant, rather, to be passed over, forgotten.

'You promise, then, on your honour,' said Etta in clear, impeccable German, so that the occasion should be remembered, recalled at the appropriate moment – should it, as she hoped, be a boy.

Thorvald had major preoccupations beside which honour paled. The Mark fell to 160,000 to the almighty Dollar, then to 242 million, and, by the birth of his firstborn, to an unbelievable four billion. It needed a barrow-load to buy a newspaper.

And the Russians were finding it difficult to pay – and a child on the way!

Thorvald found solace only in long strolls round his yards, where the logs were stacked high, ready for drying and planking – should there be an upturn.

* * *

34

When the little innominate creature, red, wrinkled and unbelievably ugly, first thrust his head into this world, Herr Zorn was hardly delighted, but felt satisfaction on two counts. First, it was white-haired, and second (when the midwife paused a moment in her important cavortings with the child), it was a male. That noted, Herr Zorn stooped to his exhausted wife and kissed her on the brow, where the sweat still stood in beads.

'A boy!' was all he could think of saying.

She had come not to expect any thanks, for anything, but managed to catch his arm.

As for the child, his eyes opened wide, and swivelled in a glazed, unfocused way from one end of his brief world to the other. The midwife took him in her capable hands, hitched him safely and professionally in the cushion of her left arm and bosom, while with her bared right elbow she tested the temperature of the water in the large enamel bowl. It was the sort of thing to reassure nervous fathers.

The babe did not protest as the midwife plunged him into the water. His eyes closed, that was all, as though the better to hear, for he was already, at ten minutes old, witness to a pattern of acrimonious debate between his parents that would be with him always. He whimpered as the midwife washed and probed his folds, not at the water, which was familiar enough, or at the big hands, but at the noises coming in to him from his parents.

'And you will? You promised, since it's a boy . . .' his mother whispered, trying to impress her husband, while excluding the midwife.

But having done his duty as he saw it, Thorvald Zorn removed the detaining hand.

'There now. You must rest,' he said, turning to leave, for the general clinical goings-on were more than he could stomach.

But still, she found strength to detain him with her dark eyes. The black curls, he saw, clung damply to her brow. The

35

shadows under her eyes bore witness to the night's labour.

'But you will see to it? On the eighth day? Please?'

'Will what?' he asked with calculated cruelty. But he saw that she was not to be denied. 'Oh, that! Yes, all right. I'll see to it. I don't suppose it matters one way or t'other.' Dismissively. But as the midwife towelled the infant, she wondered at the thin mat of white hair that covered his little skull like swan's down. As it dried out under his own warmth, it glowed.

'Oh, thank you, Thorvald. You're so good . . .' (which he took more as blackmail than gratitude).

He knew he wasn't, had not the least ambition to be 'good'. Turning towards the little creature in the midwife's arms, he scrutinized the tiny penis, no bigger than a hazelnut, and wondered what the doctor would find to cut.

But it was done, clinically if not ritually, on the eighth day, and the child was so sore that at the christening in St Pieterskirch he howled throughout the ceremony, till Thorvald wanted heartily to disown the brat.

Etta, if uncomfortable under the soaring vault of St Pieterskirch, was quietly satisfied. It had been done, whatever this sprinkling of water meant. Whatever expiation might be required for her marriage to a goy, the boy was sanctified and enfolded to her people, the boy's people, chosen of God. Not by oath, or laying on of hands, or by signed declarations, all of which could be undone by man's own perfidy or others' persecution, but by a tiny surgical snip.

For Frau Zorn was never to feel wholly secure after the advent of her firstborn. 'Will what?' Thorvald had asked, and in asking had intimated that she had asked too much. He would concur, but with an ill grace, and then only on the grounds of hygiene, which was an obsession with him next only to his business and his yacht.

That was the boy's first memory, aged four. Standing by his father's side in the bathroom, his little white head just up to the edge of the wash-basin, scrubbing at his teeth with such vigour that the inevitable happened. As, according to instruction from above, he stood on tiptoe and spat the frothy pink of his own blood into the basin, he looked up beseechingly for reassurance.

'It's nothing. Nothing! Don't whimper, now. That's for women. You'll see plenty of blood in your time, so buck up.' And his father bade him rinse again. 'There, you see, it's gone already.'

He was to do the same daily, by his father's side, until the gums hardened. And after a week, the task was delegated to his mother. Except that, from time to time, his father would ask, just as he was leaving for the sawmill: 'Have you scrubbed your teeth, boy?' Always 'scrubbed', never simply 'brushed', 'washed' or 'cleaned'.

It was among his first lessons in life's ironies that, at nine years of age, he had to submit to the ministrations of Doctor Ziegler, who plugged the first of several gold caps into Dieter's new but erring molars.

His mother was in attendance. The boy's tears moved her to ask Doctor Ziegler if there was anything to be done to prevent or deter dental caries.

'Oh, no!' the good doctor replied. 'It's only natural. Nothing to worry about. Let him chew a raw carrot from time to time. If it doesn't work, it'll always help to keep his bowels open.' In a world of perfect molars, he would be out of business.

For such a question, he added 100 Marks to the bill. But his work enhanced an already charming smile. It worked wonders on all but his parents. The boy would stand below them, head moving from side to side, as he watched them sparring and chopping at one another with a venom he clearly found unacceptable, for there was no smile, only his lips puckering in the effort not to cry. It was not so much the violence of their language, for each, patently, was enjoying the cut and thrust, it was an outlet of some sort, till they sometimes shouted. No, it was the fact that he was excluded. He might not have been there.

One summer day over breakfast, and as though he did not

exist at the table, his parents had reached a stage which he had long recognized, and which made him slump in his chair, his head just level with the dish of bread and milk. The cause of the crisis was his mother's whims about colours, which fascinated Dieter. For the exterior of Frau Zorn's physical life was supported, as far as she could devise or choose, by colours in the 'warm range', by yellows, browns, and only certain reds – ochreous colours in fact. Crimson, with its infinitesimal shift towards purple, rather frightened her, while any yellow that might suggest green, like lime, set her teeth on edge, she declared.

Outside, a haze verging on mist drifted through the shrubbery like a wraith, and Dieter had noted the droplets on a spider's web that stretched across the corner of the French window.

Inside, Frau Zorn sat down to the coffee and viands beautifully set out by Berthe, and beseeched Dieter to eat his bread and drink his milk. Herr Zorn breezed in and looked out of the window.

Dieter prayed earnestly that he would not open the window, thus destroying the spider's web. He didn't, and Dieter pawed idly at his breakfast.

Herr Zorn came to the table, where his wife, while pouring coffee, tried to weigh his mood.

'I rather enjoyed last evening,' she attempted, by way of remembering the previous evening's dinner party as a topic for breakfast, 'but I do wish Esme Doenische would learn how to dress. . . .'

'My dear, Esme seemed perfectly dressed to me.'

Which at once set out the ground for battle. If Etta had unwittingly provided the ground, nevertheless she would give no quarter once challenged. The coffee pot came down a little too firmly on its stand, all of which Dieter noticed with bated breath.

'Thorvald, you know perfectly well what I mean. All those powder blues positively exhaled halitosis! I confess I could hardly bear her near me.'

'Would that be why you turned most of the time to Victor? I suppose the spots on his tie didn't disturb you?'

'Let's stick to the point, since you seemed to have eyes only for Esme.'

'Did I?' Herr Zorn adjusted the napkin under his chin, a sign of firm grasp of the situation. 'Well, as far as I'm concerned, if that is so, it only shows my good taste.'

'That's as may be. I know those goo-goo eyes. Just like carriage lamps. Moths do fly into them so. Darling Esme spreads love like Gideons scattering Bibles – it's no great effort and seems like a splendid activity!'

At which Herr Zorn's face went quite red, Dieter saw, distinctly red. 'You have such a genius for spoiling breakfast!' Herr Zorn shouted harshly. 'I've no appetite for it now, thanks to your tongue, it's as keen as cheese-wire – fit only for garrotting!'

Dieter's eyes swivelled as he noted with a sense of symmetry that his mother's face was just as red as his father's now.

'Thank you!' his mother spat. 'If it matches your temper, I'm more than satisfied.'

Herr Zorn snatched his napkin from his breast and tossed it down on the floor. 'Sit up, boy, and eat your breakfast!' he shouted at the child – and flung out of the room to his study.

'There now, Dieter, don't cry,' Etta crooned.

But he was not in the least crying, only his eyes were large. His father had already taught him that boys do not cry.

'If you don't wish to eat,' his mother went on, ruffling his blond hair across the table, 'just leave it. We'll give it to Katya, she'd love it. Watch her licking her whiskers when she's finished. Come.'

While Berthe cleared the table, Dieter's white head nestled in the concave warmth between his mother's breasts as she mulled over the scene in her mind and moved her lips in unison with the vengeful words she would fling at Thorvald when he returned to forgive. For she had never known him to acknowledge guilt on his side.

Dieter had come to recognize the bitter exchanges, the apparent reconciliations, and to await the reward, which as often as not would include him. On this occasion, his father reappeared after only half an hour, but that was long enough for Dieter to have become detached from his mother's arms and therefore from his father's disapproving eye. Herr Zorn had the folded newspaper under his arm.

'I'll forgive your words, Etta. Shall I say I didn't hear them?' Then, pointing to the foot of the column in the newspaper, the reward, before his wife could think of a suitable riposte, Thorvald continued: 'I see the weather experts forecast an end to this mist outside. There's an anticyclone stationed over the southern Baltic and the sun is promised, sunshine without a cloud once this stuff lifts.'

Herr Zorn rattled on quickly, leaving no opportunity for his wife to interrupt: 'Things are running well enough at the yard. I see no reason why we shouldn't take a day by the sea and cool our feet. What about it? How long will it take Berthe to prepare a hamper? Nothing elaborate. We needn't be there all day. But I do think a cooler is indicated.'

There seemed nothing Etta could do but submit with good grace. She resolved, as usual, that next time he would really not get away with it.

And indeed it was cooler by the sea, and so pleasant that both parents settled peacefully for once into their deck-chairs. Dieter scuttled off a sufficient distance to start digging into his own world of work. The Baltic strand, being unaffected by tides, does not always provide sandy expanses for children's castles. But young Dieter would be the last to be deterred by that. He was a builder. Here were scores of sawn ends from the timber yards left beached on the shoreline, and soon he was building an elaborate structure of these ready-made blocks. Half of the fun was in searching for the right shapes and sizes.

40

After half an hour he felt secure enough in his labours to seek approval. 'Look, Papa!' he shouted shrilly. 'Come and see my castle!'

Herr Zorn was too deep in his deck-chair and in *Buddenbrooks* to do more than cock his head inquiringly in the general direction of his son's work. 'Where?' he called.

'Over there. Can't you see?'

'Ah, yes, splendid! Now build another wall round the first. Sometimes castles have outer walls, so that they can attack the enemy between the walls. Splendid, splendid!' And he returned to *Buddenbrooks*.

It was enough to satisfy Dieter. His father had seen, albeit at a distance. His mother was asleep, and in any case not to be impressed by castles. With care (another trait his patience had imposed on him) he started the outer wall. No moat this time. The enemy could be trapped in the flat area between inner and outer walls. After another half an hour, Dieter had completed the outer wall. Taking a sly look in his father's direction, he ventured further afield and selected some sticks and straws from the beachwrack, and began to place them on the turrets of his castle and along the ramparts at intervals.

Dieter was just finishing the last of his flagstaffs and imagining some way of designing cannons, his lips moving with his thoughts, when a foot crunched into the outer wall. It was a boy of about ten. He wore only a shirt. He stamped round the wall, systematically crushing it back almost to ground level.

Dieter raised his head slowly. Should he cry? Should he bring Papa, who was so absorbed in his book and never liked to be disturbed? Mama? She was still asleep.

The older boy then shogged off, as though well satisfied. But Dieter, in an agony of despair, watched him turn, then return to the remains of the castle. Only the keep remained.

Checking that Dieter's parents were still oblivious, the boy kicked down the castle, lifted his shirt and, holding his penis, which to Dieter seemed enormous, directed a jet as systematically as he had stomped, until the keep was a pile of sodden wreckage.

Dieter watched, half-horrified, half-fascinated by this colossal feat of manhood. He had never seen anyone pee before and was amazed at the amount the boy could produce. Then he howled. He shrieked at the horror of it all, shrieked as his father had always forbidden, a high, wounded note. He was beyond help.

His father jumped. His mother woke with a start.

His father was quick, decisive. In one flash, he saw what was happening. He leapt towards the boy, who started to run, and caught him by the shirt-tail, then the ear.

'What d'you think you're doing, lad? Spoiling the child's castle!' A strong twist of the ear. 'What, eh? Come out with it!'

The boy just wriggled, shivering. Herr Zorn gave another twist, until the boy was on tiptoe with pain.

'I won't leave go till you answer. What's your name?'

'Willi – ow!'

'Willi what?'

'Willi, sir!'

'No. Your surname.'

'Willi Vogel.'

'And where do you live, Willi Vogel?' Another twist of the ear.

The boy wriggled, beat Herr Zorn's hand with his fist, and extricated his ear in one twisting movement. He was off before Herr Zorn could recover.

It was all too undignified for Herr Zorn. People were beginning to notice. As the boy once again lifted his shirt and held his penis as though to pee, Thorvald saw his wife had been wakened by the brouhaha. He returned to his deck-chair, dusting his trousers.

'Whatever's the matter?' she asked.

'Oh, nothing.'

'Has something upset Dieter?'

'You know it takes very little to upset him.' Which was not strictly true, for the child had learned from his parents to hide his feelings. His shriek was a lapse. In utter revulsion, he now just sat, his back to his parents, trying to absorb his despair by repairing the broken handle of his bucket.

Frau Zorn was so enervated by the sun and sea air that she was soon asleep again. Herr Zorn returned to *Buddenbrooks*. When he decided it was time to take their picnic luncheon, Dieter simply wouldn't eat, and although this irritated both parents, it was much too hot to bother trying to persuade him. Willi Vogel, however, had left his shadow.

As a boy, Dieter was much given to thinking. He could sit for as long as an hour, just thinking, but he had soon learnt that this not only irritated his parents but worried them.

He could tell by the way they looked at each other, a rare look of collusion meant to exclude him as an errant object. If in front of them he found himself thinking what he was going to do, he would break off and do something, anything, however trivial, like wiping his nose with great deliberation.

But sometimes he could not help himself. He would be planning something, and they would catch him out.

'What's the matter with you, boy?' his father would say. 'You just sit there. Haven't you got anything to do?' – the suggestion being that he was not quite normal.

But he did have things to do. He had built a caterpillar house of cardboard, with choice, succulent cabbage leaves in the main traffic areas which the creatures surely could not miss. But they did. They seemed determined only to crawl over the wall and escape. He was thinking out why this should be so, how it might be remedied, when his father jolted him.

Then, as his parents bickered over how best he should be occupied, Dieter retired to his room, to pick moribund caterpillars off the floor and return them to their house, where they formed little furry coils as they gave up all ambition to become butterflies.

43

Nevertheless, between sessions of parental bickering, he learned about life and the world in his own way. A word would be heard, and linked with others. It was like managing a jigsaw puzzle without help.

In the autumn, Dieter and the pastor's son Gerhardt Stentewik joined a string of boys and girls wandering over the Welckwald in search of mushrooms. When Dieter proudly emptied his knapsack on the kitchen table, Berthe smiled knowingly, and once his back was turned, threw out most of them. But the day had not been totally unrewarding. When Nelli Pfeiffer bent down to pick up a mushroom, they saw her knickers, and Stentewik nudged him. Nelli was, it was said, an orphan and lived with an 'aunt', or was it a 'grandmother'? Dieter thought it was an attractive alternative to parents, because Nelli always seemed to be happy.

Paterfamilias – so called because when he was not taking Latin he was liable to take any other class that was wanting a teacher and thus would turn up anywhere – Paterfamilias was filling in for Herr Zorblatt at Geography.

As usual, it would not be a country or an object that would spark off Paterfamilias – indeed, he would not only be ignorant of the whereabouts of Madagascar, but of its very existence. It would be a word that animated him, and he could be very animated.

That day being tranquil and blue, he sprang upon the word 'anticyclone', like a hound at a hare.

'"Anti-zyklon" – "anti", from Greek,' chalking incomprehensibly on the board while the boys chuckled behind cupped hands. '. . . Quiet! Your specious humour is too wet for a day like this – *humour*, from the Latin *humor*, moisture . . .' He could go on like this for hours.

Paterfamilias rambled on. Erratic circles and arrows, wind directions and atmospheric pressures gradually filled the board.

'Zorn!' Paterfamilias shouted across the room. 'You're incorrigible. You sit there in smug complacency, your eyes out of the window. You're so rarely with us, Zorn . . .' – walking up the aisle with the textbook in his right hand at the ready for a clout. 'Zorn!' – applying the clout carefully at the rear of the cranium, for complaints had been received about damage to the delicate mechanisms of the ear. 'Zorn, you're last in all things: Zorn, Z – for the Greek *zita* – the Latins deigning not to favour such a barbaric sound. If we're to judge by our absent friend Zorn, then clearly they were right . . .'

Pater could go on and on in this vein, obviously enjoying punctuating a dull hour's conjugation of verbs with speculative diatribes on a name, an address, or even an appearance, so long as they exercised his academic wit and were personally offensive.

'And whither are we wandering this sunlit afternoon, Zorn?'

Dieter's mind would leap at some word or problem all his own, to the present exclusion of the world. He might accept a note of instruction from outside, as when, after the failure of the caterpillar house, he realized from a subsequent nature lesson that the creatures lived off live vegetable matter and that his limp offerings were obviously not the correct culinary blandishment for growing things at the most voracious stage of their brief lives.

This tendency to find out for himself and even to admit error in his search was his real education. It extended to both his mind and his hands. It came from the self-sufficiency induced in an only child by parents whose animus was each other, practically to the exclusion of all else, most of all himself.

His room was his world. There he thought in peace, read avidly, and made things. Gradually, his skills grew. He even made tools to make things, such as a sharp blade attached to a pair of compasses for cutting perfect cardboard circles.

At school, the subject of Physics appealed to him for non-academic reasons – the problems and solutions of manipulating matter. The Chinese pulley fascinated him by its very simplicity, the way a horizontal cylinder, one half a narrow girth, the other wide, could be made to lift weights by winding in the cord from the narrow girth on to the wider. The particularity and practicality of things attracted him.

When, at eleven, he was left almost completely to his own devices (there was some crisis impending between his parents), he often wandered down to the harbour, where winches and the tackle and gear of trawlers held him in thrall. Beyond his room, which was gradually evolving into a workshop, the harbour came to fill his life, in so far as things at school rarely went in, while everything in the harbour did.

There, at its moorings from Easter till late September, lay his father's yacht, *Donner*, its halyards whipping and singing to the least zephyr, music in Dieter's ears. In 1935, during the first modest voyage with Herr Zorn and Herr Schinkler over the choppy waters of the Welcksee in a flighty little four-metre craft, the lad's white poll had nearly caught the boom – or the boom it – as his father tacked deftly back to shore after running goose-winged across the water under billowing sails.

'You'll have to be sharper than that, my boy, if you're to make a sailor!' For, whether from the conditioning of the early sailor suits, or simply from the constant presence of the water, Dieter dearly wanted to be a sailor. He flushed scarlet before Herr Schinkler, not only for rising when he should have ducked, but for the tone of his father's voice, which seemed to dismiss him with contempt from this manly sport. All of which made him more determined to succeed.

But the first voyage out over the Baltic in his father's nine-metre ketch only confirmed his disabilities as a sailor, for as soon as they reached the bar where the Welck's fresh waters met the breakers, he was violently sick and remained green and prostrate for the rest of the trip, withered by his father's look and somehow perpetually under the feet of the crew as they tackled the sheets. He could only lean disconsolately over the rail, heaving as the yacht dipped and rose on the green Baltic swell.

★   ★   ★

46

The whiteness, the barleycorn hair and the pale skin persisted, though the eyes were those of his mother, hazel flecked with black, and dark lashes that recalled her kohl-black gaze. Dieter might be a sport, oddly un-Aryan, but he was beautiful in his whiteness. So he passed unremarked, for Frau Zorn kept herself to herself. In everybody's eyes, he was his father's son. Yet sailing was the only thing to bring father and son together. Dieter had gone a long way in his room towards completing a model, *Donner II*, and he sensed his father's approval when he brought him in for advice on some final detail about securing the shrouds to the hull. It was one of the rare moments when both parents and child came together, and his mother launched *Donner II* with an egg-cup of Schnapps over its bows into the harbour.

Thorvald Zorn liked to show Etta off occasionally, for beauty like hers – 'bizarre' was the word he had heard and approved – should be seen from time to time by the right people: people in business or in office, with contracts to dispense to the right firms.

In 1935, what could be less remarkable than a wife born Jewish, but Lutheran by ascription, so long as she kept out of the public eye? Who would suppose the Nuremberg Laws applied to a small Baltic port like Welckmar? Nuremberg was another place, another time, best forgotten. It did not affect Herr Zorn whose capital, wrapped up in prime timber, had survived inflation with comparatively little harm. He had ridden the tides of inflation and recession and finally bought out his failing father-in-law's shares. Old Tadziewicz's dealings had always veered towards paper-money when the squeeze came, since the first to be denied viable raw materials would be the Jew.

Josef Tadziewicz's name was carefully excluded from the document sealing the bargain, despite protestations from Etta. Thorvald was adamant:

'I have an instinct that if we're to survive these difficult times,' he said, 'your father's name will not help.' He promised that Tadziewicz would be kept off the streets, which, given the times, was in his opinion extending charity as far as he could.

Thorvald flourished again, while his parents-in-law moved to a small flat, tightened their belts on Thorvald's charity and prayed that Berlin would remain indifferent to little Welckmar.

Inflation, the Reichstag fire, the meteoric rise of the Führer might give Thorvald pause for thought. But then the upturn of the economy, and the people's pride in their leader and the Third Reich were good business. Welckmar lived its own life, kept its own rules and social patterns and went its own way, albeit with a token march or two by a thin column of fanatics with a liking for uniforms, brown shirts and armbands bearing the Swastika. It all seemed a trifle theatrical for the staid townsfolk of Welckmar.

None of it touched young Zorn, who first in a succession of sailor suits, then in the almost mandatory *Lederhosen* with braces, had charmed his way round everybody but his father.

But Dieter, at fourteen, had other worries.

Whiteness was all very well, but the hairs on his chest, if any, were barely visible. Diving into the harbour waters in high summer, he tended to wear a formal bathing costume rather than the brief triangle kerchief of his companions.

This formality in dress he tried to conceal by adopting a strict crawl stroke when he swam. No fooling about – he dived meticulously, then struck out, his arms observing the correct windmill precision: in, out – his feet paddling at the correct speed, his body flat on the water, and his head almost under and just appearing for the necessary breath. Thus he concealed his major worry while enjoying the aquatic pleasures of Welckmar harbour with his friends.

Paterfamilias poured scorn over certain extra-mural activities of his charges – the rallies and marches that some of them subscribed to all too willingly.

'Gertler!' he shouted, for Gertler was dozing audibly. 'Gertler, if you devoted as much time to your Latin as you do to stumping around the streets in your Hitler *Jugend* ranks, we'd have a scholar on our hands. . . .'

He was about to expand, but the class had broken out into uncontrollable laughter. Pater was not used to such generous applause. He read, correctly, that he had erred somewhere, to a ludicrous extent. Both morals and manners had deteriorated lately, in spite of the talk from on high about cleansing Germany. Of what? Pater could only raise his hands.

'May I inquire,' he said, 'what is so very risible about my remarks to Gertler?'

'Not Gertler, sir!' was all he could elicit amid renewed guffaws.

'Not what?'

'Gertler can't join *der Jugend*, sir.' More callow howls, no longer sincere, but coldly calculated.

'Enough, enough!' Pater shouted.

This he hated. He had committed the unpardonable error, if an understandable one. But he had been unwise to pick on Gertler – or rather, to pin that particular label on him, for *der Jugend* was unashamedly anti-Semitic – why, he never understood. Could anything be more innocuous than the somnolent Gertler? He now saw how ludicrous the thought was – Gertler, in that particular wolf-pack. But seeing and understanding would not mend matters.

Pater was furious, both with the mockers and with himself. Angrily, he strode down the aisle, book in hand, and in one movement dealt such a blow over Klingel the ringleader's head that the youth went reeling.

That was the end of Pater's career. Nothing was heard of him again. The following day he was called to Herr Schellenborg's office and dismissed forthwith. Whether it was that he had aimed badly and caught Klingel's ear, or whether it was simply that he had picked out Klingel did not matter. Pater had transgressed where it was dangerous to transgress. He had struck at German youth. At a time when the carefully staged rallies and marches were taking on the reality of war, Paterfamilias had been careless. Hitler now strutted among his serried ranks like a cock over a midden, and was already being vindicated by his successes as commander-in-chief. The straighter the outstretched arm, the more Europe bent to his will. But even more so did the German people. There was no denying the man. Dieter, a mere stripling in all this, looked to his parents for guidance, for he guessed, judging by words he heard off-stage, that it was all of particular moment where they were concerned. But no guidance came. His father preached strength, integrity, abstractions that were insinuations, even accusations, rather than advice. His mother now spoke little. While his father hardened perceptibly, his mother had retreated into a fearful silence. Thorvald seemed to grow stronger every day, to exude strength and to require strength around him.

As they passed through the house towards the dining room, Thorvald stroked the door panels for the benefit of visitors, murmuring fondly, '*Pinus Palustra*,' with a reverence that set his guests looking at one another furtively.

'*Pinus* what?' Herr Grohl asked diffidently, by way of keeping conversation going, for there had been unendurable silences round Etta. One had to be so careful lately.

'*Pinus Palustra*,' Thorvald roundly declared. 'Pitch pine, finest pitch pine. Look at the grain, the finish it takes. It will never move, you know, never move . . .' He went on and on, still stroking the reddish brown grain, '. . . not even if Berthe throws a whole forest on the stove and roasts us out!'

'Move?' Zorn Junior imagined doors in pairs leaving their hinges to dance a gigue outside on the lawn, as Berthe piled offcuts on the stove.

Then the cabinets, the shelves, above all the great chamfered beams exposed across the high ceiling – all these Herr Zorn took in with a sweep of the arm.

'No, no timber like it. It's the making of Europe. *Pinus Palustra* . . .' How he stroked the Latin. 'Integrity, that's what

50

it's got – integrity. Look at those beams. Tensile strength of steel, you know.'

It was always about strength, steel, integrity. Young Zorn wondered if there were room in the world for such as he alongside the palpable virtues of *Pinus Palustra*. Diffidently, he asked Herr Grohl if he would care for a portion of *Käsekuchen*.

'Not now, my boy,' his father interrupted gruffly. 'Do go and find something to do.' For he had not yet become accustomed to the fact that his son was now all but a man. And where German sons were concerned, the state was calling for sacrifice.

Dieter by now felt quite excluded by his parents, who had distanced themselves from each other to an extent which distressed him. But he dared not speak. He left the room, and was not missed.

In Berlin the Führer preached 'strength', 'integrity', 'the virtue of valour in war for the Fatherland', and the perfidy of anybody, inside or outside the country, who dared raise a voice against him.

People accepted this. How else could they, short of seeking some haven of peace elsewhere, some *Bruderhof* on the un-adulterated plains of the North American continent?

But now, as the party paraded its brown uniforms, dis-tinguished in particular by that armband and the flags, it was different. This you did not accept. You joined, or were suspect. And nobody could remember how things had mutated from choice to compulsion. It had become dan-gerous, in a new indefinable way, even *en famille*, to talk about it, to speculate, to be seen or heard debating any sort of choice.

As the marches, rallies and pronouncements increased in order, so did discipline and cumulative nastiness, till even Welckmar became infected; it became clear that there were not only political impediments but social, even racial ones – blood!

As the words 'strength' and 'steel' echoed off his tongue, Herr Zorn might just remember, for one instant, that his wife might be marked down in some dreadful black book, come the day.

Only for an instant. For had not her origins been expunged by the extravagance of the shade of her child's hair, so very fair, so white, so unmistakably Aryan?

But now, a large timber contract for constructing submarine pens at Bremerhaven had been lost. Now it mattered a great deal that Etta was not what she ought to be. Indeed, the loss of the Bremerhaven contract could be attributed to her in Thorvald Zorn's mind. He was at a loss to understand why the Zorn yard had been overlooked, for surely every government contractor knew that if Zorn softwoods for concrete shuttering were no better than anybody else's, nevertheless only Zorn had an adequate stock of prime greenheart baulks for the piles that must be driven into the river bed.

In retrospect, Dieter remembered that the paternal proscription, as he saw it, took two stages. The first was over the visits to the Tadziewiczes.

Each Friday, Etta Zorn took her son to her parents on the far side of town, to bring in the *Shabat* with the *Kiddush* prayers.

Although when addressing their daughter the grandparents used German, Dieter looked from one to the other when the old people spoke between themselves. It was not the classical Hebrew his mother had taught him for the *Kiddush*.

'Yiddish,' his mother said when he asked. 'It's Yiddish. They brought it with them from the Pale in the Ukraine, my dear.'

Clearly, it embarrassed her. Yet he sensed how much she loved these Friday evening rites as Nanna Tadziewicz, hands over the candles, intoned the *Kiddush* prayer.

It was the only occasion Dieter wore the *kepale* on his white head, and his mother always took care to leave it behind as they left amid the usual valedictions. Dieter knew that she regarded herself as Jewish, but wore it lightly, acceptably, even to her parents, who knew the pressures on her elsewhere and could forgive all, provided she still remembered the

52

Covenant and could be seen each Friday evening. Emancipation was one thing – to forget 'O, Jerusalem', quite another.

Until, in 1938, when Dieter was fifteen, his father one Friday evening in October had scowled as his wife was putting on her coat and calling Dieter to join her. There had been some burning of certain books in Berlin, which had been widely reported.

'You're not to take him,' Thorvald had muttered under his breath.

'Why ever not?'

'Because I say so.'

And such was the force of his expression that that was truly the first proscription, for Dieter was never to see his grandparents again.

The second proscription was more dramatic. War had been proclaimed. The Polish Problem had been solved.

Etta was weeping bitterly one Friday evening. They – whoever they were, and one did not care to discuss it even in the privacy of the home – 'they' simply came and arrested people, took them abruptly away to some undisclosed destination, without naming any crime (for they had not committed any, were too frightened even to contemplate any, except that of being what they were).

Frau Zorn was about to don her coat, to go to her parents for the *Kiddush* meal. Herr Zorn was out of his study in a flash. From his room, Dieter heard the harsh whisperings and agonies of their quarrel. Herr Zorn clearly did not want it heard abroad, but he was adamant in his proscription. His wife was not to visit her own parents. Indeed, claimed Thorvald, it was doubtful if they were at home. They had probably been 'resettled'.

As she threatened still to go, Thorvald muttered something vile – and pointed to the danger to her own son should she persist in her 'folly'.

A darkness was closing over the northern sky of Welckmar. A year later, young Zorn was so excluded that by now he

53

had formed his own life. He was strong, blond, and as prone as any seventeen-year-old to close his eyes to the unpleasant if it threatened the present joys of youth.

Besides, the German forces had so proved themselves that he might not be needed. As to those things that were rumoured by the braver sceptics (and they were few and certainly did not abound in Welckmar), it was better to look to a future when peace in Europe would render them unnecessary. A new millennium was promised, and Dieter Zorn had little difficulty in setting aside unpleasant rumours if they were, in the end, towards a greater good.

But he felt a trace of guilt. The silver lining might be all very well, but there *was* a cloud. And whatever was going on between his parents, clearly his mother was very unhappy these days. Nothing is more closely locked than affairs of husband and wife. He could see his mother's unhappiness, assess it in adult terms, yet could only stand by helpless. He wished to talk, to listen to her, and perhaps, with his emerging strength, to help her. There must be something he could do, some wisdom that only he, from the outside, could contribute. But he was kept strictly apart. His mother kept him at arm's length now. He was conscious of being acceptable in a way she might not be. He was blond, so very blond that he was physically on the wrong side of the fence from her.

Now, beyond husband and son, she had no family to go to, and because Thorvald was responsible for her present misery and ultimately condoned what society could do and had done to her parents, she could not go to him. Indeed, although they lived in the same house, it could be said she had left her husband. Dieter watched it, but was unable to intervene, was not allowed to.

As to Dieter himself, Etta's feelings were two-fold: first, he was, in looks and physique, so very much his father's son as to be physically beyond reach in that Aryan world that was the only safe world these days. But also, she was determined that her personal unhappiness, her possible fate should the SS search her out in spite of her husband's impeccable racial credentials, all this should not touch her son, not bring him down. She would smile ruefully at him, trying to conceal her fears, anxious to show her love in the best light, in so far as Thorvald allowed her, for he was watching every move.

Otherwise, Dieter was distanced from his parents by the more intimate tussles that went on. Unhappiness is infectious, and Thorvald reacted with irritation and occasional bouts of anger. Dieter, a filled-out man in all but a few kilos, was no saint. Whenever possible, he fled. He simply could not help himself. His heart might be heavy as he left the house and its tensions behind, but his feet were light as they led inevitably towards the harbour, where Gerhardt Stentewik and *Donner* offered release from his familial burden. He loved the harbour for the life and the craft that persisted still, in spite of war. And girls too gravitated in the same direction. Pastor Stentewik would have blenched had he known how and where his son kicked over the traces. 'Sailing *Donner*' covered a multitude of sins, in both houses.

Now that his father was completely absorbed in war contracts and had no time or even thought for *Donner*, the ketch was Dieter's to use as he wished. His seamanship was well enough established by now. *Donner* was free. The girls loved it.

The war was going well. There was national euphoria in the air, and actual admiration of the triumphant Führer. He had proved himself. Germany's past was being expunged from the record like a bad dream. The future promised everything. It was a time for hardships, effort, unity, but not for unhappiness, unless you belonged to the dissident and disaffected minorities. Those people were being dealt with.

So Dieter Zorn came more and more to live in two distinct worlds, or rather three, since he was reaching the climax of his secondary education. There was home with its tensions, there was the *Gymnasium*, and there was the harbour with *Donner*, Stentewik and the girls.

Stentewik, almost as blond as Zorn, strutted among their circle and never stayed long with any girl. Zorn on the other hand was wrapped up, in every sense of the word, with Nelli Pfeiffer, whose virtue might not be impeccable, but whose capacity to take him out of himself was unquestionable. Stentewik might drift, even 'rest', as he put it in his so adult way. But Zorn and Nelli were inseparable. Zorn knew the liaison would not be approved at all at home. His guilt, if anything, compounded his joy in Nelli's fond company.

Nelli was small, ash-blond to Zorn's white, and, in the austere fashion of the times, wore white 'bobby-sox', which enhanced her shapely legs and made a virtue out of necessity. She was known to enjoy an occasional evening at Nummer Neunzehn, so-called because that was its number on Oststrasse. Nummer Neunzehn boasted the only neon light in Welckmar – '19' – but most nights the One flickered and died, and it was Nummer Neun in consequence. Nummer Neunzehn was notorious by the sober standards of Welckmar. It was the safety-valve: where is the virtue if there is not a little vice around?

Neither Stentewik nor Zorn dared go so far as to be seen anywhere near Nummer Neunzehn. A little horseplay aboard *Donner* with Nelli and perhaps another was one thing, but nightlife of that sort was outside both their experience and their social horizon. Whereas for Nelli, who worked at the canning factory during the day, there was no problem: she was her own mistress from five thirty onwards. She never talked of her origins or background. All that impressed Zorn was that she was free of parental constraints and her 'aunt' (or 'grandmother') had died. In her rare moments of seriousness, Nelli would hint that her parents had been victims of the inflation years. Nelli was free, and far from being sad, exulted in her freedom. She had her own little house, an artisan dwelling near the quay. She earned enough from piece-work at the factory to live comfortably and without need to exploit the evening strollers on the quays. Had the need been there, she would have had few scruples. She liked the thought that the small house with its large divan was there all the same. She had her moments. Men came – and they went.

Zorn, given his more bourgeois background, might have been, indeed was, expected to observe certain standards. The trouble was that *Donner*, almost wholly his now for all the use his father made of it, was in the harbour, and those standards manifestly did not extend to the harbour area. *Donner* spelt release from the tensions at home, so it was to *Donner* that he fled whenever opportunity occurred. Besides, this girl, who loved *Donner* apparently no less, was herself irresistible. Evenings, when Dieter should have been working for his *Abitur*, were sheer guilty summer delight as they sailed *Donner* well beyond the harbour light at the end of the jetty and anchored offshore to consume the delicacies that Nelli could provide. Then a swim, more horseplay, and a return to *Donner*'s moorings.

More and more, as Stentewik roamed and returned, Nelli and Dieter were inseparable. Dieter in his whiteness was so distinctive even by Baltic standards that Nelli felt she had here a Northern god for her special delectation. Not that she gave him all her freedom. The rigours of preparation for his *Abitur* could still claim too many of his evenings for Nelli's taste, so she would spend the latter part of these blank evenings at Nummer Neunzehn. Dieter was perfect. But she had to pass the time somehow till he turned up again. Like nature, Nelli abhorred a vacuum.

'Do you have to study like this all the time?' she asked impatiently when Geometry had kept them apart for three evenings running. They were back on *Donner*. She wished to take him home, extend their play to its logical conclusion. He was so – so fresh. He was strangely boyish in a way that excited her the more she saw of him. Nothing like Zorn had graced her life before. He would retreat that little, held back by the guilt over home and the sheer inappropriateness of these hours spent with Nelli, however delightful they might be.

57

'I must, you know. It is expected of me,' was all he could say.

'Who expects?'

He sensed that nothing, and occasionally everything, was expected of Nelli, who recognized no laws beyond nature's.

'My mother and father, of course . . . and the *Gymnasium*.' A long pause. 'People.'

'But why does it take so much of your time?'

For that was what she wished, to have even more time with him, claim him as her own. And Zorn, entranced by her closeness, her obvious devotion to him, would yield to temptation and leave Euclid undone for yet another day. As for his Latin – Paterfamilias was gone and his successor, old Herr Wundt, brought out of retirement to replace him, possibly remembered less Latin than his pupils had ever learned. Latin, at which Zorn had excelled despite many a sleepy afternoon under Pater's steady drone, was now a matter of even more guilt. How to explain it to Nelli? 'Who expects?' Herr Wundt expected, Herr Schellenborg expected. Above all, his parents expected.

Nelli, this summer of German conquest, sat with her bronzed legs dangling over *Donner*'s side, her arm round Dieter's waist, his round hers. Long sun-soaked evenings bathed them in a peace that kept at bay the tensions of home and of war. It was unbelievable, both would admit, though the contrast was more marked for Zorn. For Nelli, peace and war were all one, provided she could have this boy all to herself. Aboard *Donner* she had her wish, with occasional interruptions by Stentewik who, when not 'resting', re-asserted his claim to *Donner* with his latest girl in tow.

But it all had its dangers. Both Zorn and Stentewik, in a fit of conscience, would reassert their independence as males. They would sail *Donner* farther out and test their seamanship before Nelli and temptation arrived from work.

One evening late in June 1941, becalmed well outside the harbour lights and waiting for a breeze to take them in, Zorn felt for the first time the salacious conjunction of moonlight and the warm emanations of Schnapps, taken medicinally, of course, from the locker reserved for such defence against the sea's wanton exposure.

'*Prost!*' called Stentewik manfully, taking a swig that sent him spluttering.

Zorn reached for the flask, in solemn silence swallowed once, twice, and again, and though he managed not to splutter, felt the world keel over – port – starboard – port – and not settle until, with a deck lamp, searching in the half-light for their moorings, he tied up *Donner* fore and aft with a precision he had not achieved before. At that he felt really good; Gerhardt Stentewik rather less so, for he had the giggles and could not row the dinghy to the quay.

With the blood coursing through his veins, Zorn manoeuvred the small craft over the dark silken waters with unbelievable speed. He had never felt in such good form.

'Another swig, and I'd have passed out,' Stentewik mumbled feebly, his slack torso sprawled over the transom, tipping the dinghy up like a crazy wind-blown feather.

'Here!' Zorn replied, for he had pocketed the flask as he tied up, unsure if the night's exposures were yet over.

'Ach, no. Enough, enough!' Stentewik managed to say, for he was in danger of falling in. His arms trailed in the water up to his elbows. Zorn, on the contrary, was all precision. He helped himself to another nip. Really good! He even saw that Stentewik would require help up the steps. Stentewik's giggles had become a downright menace, for a slight sea was running under a stiffish breeze that had got up from the north-east. Eventually, Stentewik was pushed safely on to the quay. Climbing over his convulsed body, Zorn too got himself ashore and tied up the dinghy.

Arms over each other's shoulders, they reeled off along the deserted wharf, and as though impelled by the moon's deity, found themselves where neither had dared venture in a hitherto almost spotless German youth, at Nummer Neunzehn.

Neither quite knew what was going on. Zorn, half-guilty,

half-fogged, was delighted to see Nelli there. By eleven, the flask had disappeared from Zorn's pocket. There was enough silver about its stopper to attract the eye of the sailors who practically lived there when ashore. Zorn's fingers, searching for it, barely sensed the void, for they had wandered instead to that deliciously soft area above Nelli's bobby-sox.

Stentewik was asleep on the floor, being stepped over. As Zorn's hand closed over the secret moss for the first time in his life, Nelli, all impatience, clutched his hand away and dragged him, half-protesting, outside and towards home. But he protested vehemently suddenly: 'Must get home!' She turned towards him passionately, kissed him fervently, held him close to her in a frenzy of love. 'Now!' she whispered.

But for some reason, perhaps the missing flask (his father's), or the sleeping Stentewik, who must be returned home intact, he failed to rise to the occasion.

'What's the matter? Oh, do come on!' she urged, and eventually coaxed him to proud perfection, till the moon, the water's sibilance against the quay and Nummer Neunzehn's barely heard music closed off in a last fine throw.

'My God!' Nelli whispered. 'Why have you been so long?' She wished it had been at home. But no matter. He was hers.

'All right?' he asked nervously, as the right thing to ask between lovers.

'Mmm! Yes! Slow starter, but worth waiting for!'

And then, suddenly and irrelevantly, Stentewik reappeared, dishevelled but sideways if not upright to the world. His English was that much superior to Zorn's that in his exalted state he could not forbear to display it:

> 'Ven shall ve tree mit agine?
> In sundor, lightening or in rine? . . .'

Zorn struggled to remember and finally dredged it up:

> 'Ven der hoolyboorly iss donn,
> Ven der bettle's loest und vonn . . .'

It seemed inappropriate. There was still a war to win, but

few questions were to be asked for the rest of the autumn, festive with the Wehrmacht's conquest of Europe. Only Russia remained, and the first months of invasion had brought spectacular advances.

Thorvald Zorn was so engrossed with the sheer volume of war contracts that his one great concern was to find raw materials and to corner as much as he could of Norway's mandatory timber export to the Reich. *Donner* was not to be thought of. Where his son got to of an evening or at weekends was the last thing on his mind. A few wild oats were to be sown anyway, prior to call-up.

Etta Zorn, by contrast, was now sunk in a brooding mood of waiting for the worst. All things for her depended on whether and when some bureaucrat in Berlin remembered Welckmar. Her husband's obsession with 'strength' only diminished her. And Dieter now was blind to all save Nelli Pfeiffer.

If Dieter asked his father specifically about sailing *Donner*, he was vaguely dismissed in the affirmative. It was enough for Dieter, such was the scale of distracting business on Thorvald's desk. Dieter was welcome to kick over the traces.

Such was the sport of 've tree' in one another's company that they met nearly every evening aboard *Donner* and sailed across the bay as far as discretion allowed. Stentewik enjoyed the exalted state of helmsman, which left Nelli and Zorn free to roam the deck on a long reach. If on a beat against the wind they needed to haul on sheets and generally behave like sailors, the work was performed with laughter but thoroughness, for Zorn would allow no less. But Nelli and *Donner* – it was too much. A fellow hardly deserved it. Dieter remembered his father once exulting over *Donner* in front of Herr Schinkler: 'The thing about a boat, my friend, is that you can feel the tiller trembling under your hand, like a woman, you know . . .'

Dieter recalled the image as he and Nelli enjoyed their play, he gently exploring, she trembling with delight. He wondered if Herr Schinkler had understood his father. It was difficult to imagine Herr Schinkler . . .

Stentewik connived at Zorn's sport – or Nelli's, for it was she who, having discovered the sheer passion of Zorn's gentler attentions, was well content to devote herself entirely to him, especially with *Donner* always as the added attraction. After that explosive evening, Zorn and *Donner* was more than she had expected of life. The grey waters of the Baltic lapped against the bows of *Donner* with a Nordic indifference. Europe was almost subdued, and the three young *Ostseevolk* were free as air and sea could offer.

Zorn peeled the bobby-sox off Nelli's brown calves, then her skirt, then her shirt, and as she plunged over the side naked but for a demure brassière and knickers, Zorn followed in an ascending arc of bubbles, under her thrashing body and beside her. She was not the greatest of swimmers, but learned to have complete confidence in him.

'Come back!' Stentewik shouted across the water as Zorn encouraged Nelli to develop her breaststroke. It was more of a dog-paddle however, and Stentewik, remembering Zorn Senior, became nervous. This was fine, just fine, but, oh God! . . . let there be no trouble. For in a world of war, this interlude, if that was what it was to be, was too good to be true. Next winter the Russian Front . . .? Who knew? Everything was fine, just fine, but Russia . . .? 'Come back!' he repeated.

Nelli struggled back, Zorn with her, and while she clambered up and over the side, Zorn thrashed away in his confident crawl in a transport of male display. Stentewik, meanwhile, handed a bath-towel to Nelli. She wrapped this round herself and took off her knickers, wrung them over the side, then pelted them at Zorn as he came alongside, but missed.

The idea of this flower of German womanhood going ashore devoid of knickers was not to be contemplated. Stentewik dived overboard to join Zorn in the chase. The two females, Nelli and *Donner*, bore this rumbustious chivalry with patience. It was to be expected of German youth, for the sacrifice later could be great.

'Did you sail *Donner* today?' Thorvald Zorn asked his son, as though the ketch, like a dog, needed exercise.

'Yes, Father.'

'Good! Good! Keep her in trim, will you? I never have the time, as you see. And who'd you have as crew?'

'Oh, old Stentewik, of course – and another chap. We went round the East Buoy and back. Nothing too strenuous.'

It satisfied Thorvald. He might have queried the post-sailing activities, but did not. Much too busy. Besides . . .

Life for Dieter was not always easy. The few occasions when his parents seemed to be of one mind usually concerned their son. There were inevitably moments of crisis, moments when he was arraigned before them as at a court of investigation. Herr Schellenborg's latest report could be said to indicate both progress (from what towards what, his parents wished to know) and failure (which seemed to be writ larger on the page, according to their present indictment).

'But I thought you were good at Latin,' Etta murmured plaintively.

'Leave this to me,' Thorvald interrupted impatiently.

'I was only . . .'

'Women don't understand Latin,' Thorvald persisted, his voice rising. He bore down on Dieter with the report in his fist. 'What's this about Latin . . . "no progress whatsoever"? Explain yourself!'

How could he? 'Paterfamilias has gone and . . .'

But his father silenced him, eyelids closed with pain, hand held rigidly up in protest against such familiarity. 'And who, if I may ask, is Paterfamilias? If my Latin serves me well, *I* am Paterfamilias where you're concerned.' His father latched on to this shred of scholarship, his head held high, waiting with all the patience of the scholar.

'I'm sorry. Herr Holz. We always called him Paterfamilias.'

63

'No wonder you make so little use of your studies if all you can do is mock your betters,' Etta said.

'Please, would you mind not interrupting,' Thorvald pleaded yet again with a show of infinite patience.

'We meant it as a compliment,' Dieter replied lamely. 'He was more friendly. He was our father in a way, he took so many classes, different subjects.'

How could they be expected to understand? He wished he could change the subject, in case they asked why Herr Holz had left. That, he guessed, could prove uncomfortable.

'Sounds more like a mark of disrespect to me,' Thorvald said. 'It still doesn't explain why you've failed so miserably in Latin. I take it Paterfamilias . . . er . . . Herr Holz's departure would affect your colleagues likewise, or perhaps not?'

Would it help to deny this, or to agree? Dieter felt his very inadequacy was the one thing that could unite his parents. He dreaded these confrontations, when the sarcasm and measured acrimony they usually reserved for each other were directed against himself.

'Very well,' his father continued magisterially. 'You've been spending too many evenings out of the house. From now on, you'll stay at home, young man, and I'll see to it personally that you address what brain you have to Latin . . .'

He stamped out, red in the face.

'You see?' Etta said quietly, by way of deliberate contrast. 'You see what you do?'

Dieter feared she was going to burst into tears, and then his guilt would be immeasurable. He had his own worries. He had to see Nelli.

'Ah, dear,' his mother keened on. 'I wish I knew what to do.'

Dieter saw all too plainly that she had worries beyond solving. Was he to blame? Or was it his father? Or perhaps the war and all it meant, the new hardships, laws, requirements, curbs and threats? Perhaps all these things. But he simply had to continue to see Nelli. Of that there could be no question.

His mother's worries so often confined her to her room, and his father was so often out of an evening, that Dieter took the law into his own hands. He laid Virgil aside. 'Omnia vincit Amor,' he sang under his breath, 'et nos cedamus Amori . . .' And slipped out unnoticed most evenings.

His mother, being a woman, would never know. But his father, being a man, might guess. And if he did, Dieter knew he would never live it down, not because he was wasting his time on a woman, but because Nelli, he surmised, would not figure in his father's expectations of him.

Nelli too had her worries, as who would not at such a time, with even fish hard to get? Orphaned and left to fend for herself, she too conducted her own quest for peace, even love. Nothing had so far coloured her life with that feeling she had heard about, imagined, seen on the silver screen, or on rare occasions had heard and seen in Der Neapolitaner when the local repertory company was doing Lehar. Men were so transient, here today, gone tomorrow. Not one liaison had ever come to anything worth considering, despite sincere protestations. None of it had accorded with a vague ideal she clung to, until that first rough night with Dieter Zorn. And she had had him all summer, with *Donner*.

Herr Zorn might have been less than delighted. With an eye to business and a possible post-war boom (only Russia to subdue, and Britain neatly sanitized by a stretch of water), he had already cast a perfunctory glance over the marriage market. There were ways of steering a boy, were there but time. Fortunately for Dieter, there wasn't. But Thorvald kept a weather eye open. A son and heir was an asset not to be wasted. But he was so busy, oh so very busy, he knew nothing of Nelli and her little terrace house by the harbour.

There, after an invigorating sail round the bay, Zorn and Stentewik lounged on the divan while Nelli prepared coffee which, if mostly ersatz, was amply laced with the hard stuff.

Nelli had resources and was ready to share them with those she liked. But there were degrees. Stentewik was politely dismissed after an hour or so.

Nelli's athletic games on the divan launched Zorn into a fullness of life he had not thought possible after the suffocating atmosphere at home. But Nelli tended towards ambition. After a particularly replete evening, she ventured seriously:

'You'll be going soon, won't you?'

Things were going so well, Zorn was quite content to risk his father's inquiries about such late hours.

'Another hour, yes? Who cares?' he asked lazily, kissing her neck where the white down ascended into the abundant tresses, for Nelli, whose origins might be obscure, was unquestionably beautiful.

'No!' she persisted, intent for once in her seriousness. 'I mean, altogether.' It was difficult to be quite specific, and he might have been more helpful. 'To the war, I mean.'

'Oh, that. I suppose so. I'm in no hurry.' It was a thing a man should be casual about, he thought. 'Anyway, it looks as though the war is all but over. Only Russia to mop up, they say. So maybe it'll be finished before my time. Maybe they'll even forget me.'

But as autumn bit quite abruptly with a cold blast from the frozen north, Stentewik was mobilized. *Donner* was laid up, and the problem was to stretch Nelli's meagre intellectual resources indoors.

The onset of winter gripped the harbour outside with an ominous austerity. People queued even for potatoes. Nelli's little house enfolded Zorn in the warmth from the stove, fed by scraps of oily timber gleaned from the boatyards and the quay.

'Just listen to this,' Zorn murmured drowsily from the divan, as Nelli brewed yet another pot of what passed for coffee these days. He read aloud from a volume of Rilke, to see if his own sudden blinding initiation to a new language would convey anything to her. She paused, listened.

Nelli might not understand the words, but she could

66

respond to the meaning. 'Ah, when the war's over . . .' she tried, bringing him a steaming mug and reclining gracefully at his side. She brushed his cheek with her lips in a way she knew met the mood of his reading.

'Do they know?' she ventured, gently wrestling the volume from his fingers.

'Who? My parents?' He did not care to develop this. 'What does it matter?'

Which she took as negative, but persisted. 'Well, don't you think they ought to know?'

Guilt afflicted him whenever she tried this line of thought. Compared with home, he found such peace here, peace from his father's strength and vague disapprobation, from his mother's even more evident insecurity, and from their mutual tension. What was he offering this girl, who so beautifully matched his every mood?

'Oh, the war, you know,' he replied, embracing the immense difficulty of sustaining relationships in such times, and taking up her theme: 'When it's all over, we shall see, eh?'

But did she? He lingered a little too long in the warmth and peace and finally ran home through the darkened town. He knew his mother would be in bed, if not asleep, for she had retreated into a world of her own, of waiting, mourning and constant fearing. With luck, his father might be in bed, or still out on one of his frequent evenings away from the family hearth.

But he was there, waiting, enjoying a rare cigarette in his study. The door was ajar. He heard Dieter creeping by and called him.

'You're late, my boy,' he said.

'I'm sorry, Father.' There was no explanation to hand. 'I was detained.' He had heard it somewhere before. It seemed the decent formula.

'"Detained"? May I ask by whom – or by what?'

'Ah, well, you see, Father, er . . .'

Raised eyebrows on the paternal forehead. 'I see. Oh, yes,

I see . . .' Then the dramatic pause. 'I trust it's nothing serious – only physical, mm?'

Both felt rather pleased with themselves, as between men, though not without a certain shame on the son's part. Was that it – only physical? His father smiled through the curl of the smoke. Barricades were down in mutual recognition of male priorities. Thorvald paused, then thought better of a talk on hygiene. The boy was old enough, probably knew all the ropes. Dammit, the girls these days looked nubile at fifteen, so was it any wonder?

'I'll say goodnight, then,' Thorvald Zorn said by way of dismissal, shaking his head amiably and nostalgically, as though to say 'those were the days'.

Dieter crept away with his secret. There was no way of reconciling these two worlds. But he would stand by Nelli, come what may, for peace and . . . love? Was his father right? Only physical? Ah, surely not. Yes, he was sure. He loved that bright face, the lovely body, the matching innocence under all that experience, he supposed.

Over a drab Christmas, Zorn was held at home by a series of hollow festivals that his father insisted on, mainly to entertain certain business contacts. At Christmastide one was presumed to relax, and his son, as heir apparent, must be present. Even Etta played her heretical part. What was it about Christmas that excited so much anti-Semitism among them? But she would act the hostess, none the less, offer no handle to anyone for the least complaint, least of all her husband, who was so strong.

'Herr Schinkler, this is such a pleasure,' she was bold to say, for of them all, he was her *bête noire*. 'You do look well,' – appraising his ample paunch.

'Not as well as you, Frau Zorn. Dare I say how beautiful you look?'

She looked him in the eye, as though to say 'you may dare', and swept off to break up one of her husband's more extreme expatiations on the strength and integrity of pitch pine with a summons to table. It was the third Christmas of the war, and fare was getting thin.

Dieter fretted about the likelihood of Nelli being entertained elsewhere – or worse still, entertaining.

January froze. At breakfast, Herr Zorn laid down the newspaper with a deliberation that portended trouble. He turned to Dieter:

'It has been reported to me that you have been seeing too much of a girl down by the harbour. While I am prepared to turn a blind eye on casual adventures, indeed might recommend them as, er . . . ('Good for the health,' Dieter wondered) . . . as, er, well, I forbid you to engage on any course that is more than casual. D'you understand?'

And left abruptly, lest Etta bite.

Who had reported him? Did it matter? Zorn now looked right and left as he entered Nelli's humble dwelling. Nelli was independent, an inflation orphan you could say, though inflation is slower, less dramatic than war as death-dealer.

He could not be said to be compromising Nelli. But yet one more paternal prohibition was another matter. Or was it? With a surge of independence himself, he decided that if he was old enough to fight and die for the Fatherland, he was free to do as he wished with his private life. But that, God bless them all the same, meant freedom from parental interference. If, as he surmised, Nelli would be deemed unsuitable, as far as he was concerned she suited him admirably. He was due for mobilization, and if he was not needed, the war being all but won, nevertheless he was of an age when he might be needed, and might possibly have to give his life. Who could deny him Nelli?

Welckmar's hospital had been honoured lately by being designated a *Luftwaffelazarett*, and the point was not lost on him that the daily admissions of the dreadfully wounded could well have included himself.

Zorn felt deeply responsible as he entered Nelli's door, and he could forgive her all if indeed she had been entertaining during his enforced absence. For one thing was certain – he must get away from home, where the atmosphere by now was unbearable. Fathers are not meant for sons to understand – but his mother? Nothing he said or did now seemed to touch her. Clearly, she had other worries, things of another world that she would not wish him to enter or to share. Coming home late, it was his father mostly who would be up, with words of admonition, but never severe enough to deter. Dieter knew exactly how to measure his father's mood. Mostly it was ritual.

It would have been much more difficult had his mother chastised him, had she looked him in the face and said, 'Darling, what keeps you out so late?' But if she happened to be up when he returned, flushed from Nelli's arms, either she would sit in silence, perhaps responding to his greeting with cold, upturned brow for his goodnight kiss, or she would leave silently, as though to say: 'Ah well, I have lost you, and there is no longer a place in this world for me.' He found it cold, a denying he could not fathom.

What was a fellow to do if the general mood in the house was so cold as to freeze him out?

'Do your people speak to one another?' he asked Stentewik, who surely was in worse case than himself with Pastor Stentewik to confront at home.

'Speak?'

'Yes, I mean – well, do they get on? Do they like each other?'

Gerhardt Stentewik considered this. One's people were such an abstruse quantity, not to be assessed, measured, described. They were just there.

'No idea,' he replied at last. 'Hardly ever see them, to tell you the truth. Papa keeps to his study, Mama doesn't give a hoot, one way or another. Why? Do yours?'

'Not at all. I think they hate each other. They're so busy lashing into one another, I might as well not exist!'

'But Dieter, they've got problems, haven't they? My father

70

said the other day that it was high time your father got your mother over to Sweden . . .'

This quite startled Zorn. Then he thought: 'What cheek! Pastor Stentewik discussing my people like that!' And dismissed it from his mind as they approached the harbour, where Nelli was already waiting.

III

'As a feather is wafted downward
From an eagle in his flight . . .'

H. W. Longfellow

Dieter was awaited elsewhere, and ever more conscious of it. If Welckmar faced north and away from any theatre of war and had heard neither a shot fired in anger nor the scream of a falling bomb, nevertheless eyes began to look appraisingly at youths of seventeen and eighteen. In no time at all, the march of the Reich over Europe was complete. In Russia it was at the doors of Moscow, the winter's end only awaited. Dieter was awaited and he knew it.

News of the Russian Front being as bracing as ever in February 1942 – '. . . despite massive Bolshevik troop movements against the Forces of the Reich in front of Moscow, the brave German Army has held all positions . . .' – full mobilization was decreed in March.

For Dieter Zorn, as blond as could be desired, this might have been as uncomplicated, inevitable and disastrous as for any other youth of eighteen. The process would be domestically catastrophic in any case. Quite suddenly, when his papers arrived, Zorn realized with regret there were demands greater than those of Nelli Pfeiffer. In spite of the inevitability, his mother was devastated.

'Oh, Dieter darling,' she keened in his ear as she clasped

him in a tight embrace, rare these days, since his aura of manliness and her own worries had removed him from the tenderest maternal contact.

He was – rather frightening, she thought, this child of her womb, feeling the touch of his clavicle against hers in an attempt to avoid more mammary pressure.

'. . . and your *Abitur* to sit in three months' time. However will you get to university now?' she went on disconsolately. 'You'll keep studying, won't you? If you need any books, just write. We'll send you anything you want. I know you'll write and tell us . . .'

'That's quite enough, Etta,' his father broke in like a boxing referee. 'The boy must go. He's due at the *Luftwaffelazarett* at eleven, and it's already half-past ten.'

'It's just – well, he needn't give up all these years of hard work, just because he's joining the Luftwaffe. He'll surely have lots of time to study. And if not . . .'

Herr Zorn was growing more apoplectic by the minute.

'Nonsense! He'll have his work cut out to learn his new trade. You don't master a Messerschmidt by reading Goethe in your bunk!'

'Messerschmidt? Who said he was to fly?'

'Oh, come now. You don't think he's joining the Luftwaffe to learn how to cook an omelette?'

Dieter was becoming surplus to requirements, as the atmosphere built up yet again. He knelt to attend to his valise.

'There's no need for sarcasm at such a moment,' Etta replied, pushing a packet of sandwiches into her son's pocket. 'In case of a journey . . .'

'He'll get his orders all in good time,' Thorvald persisted manfully. For him too it was 'such a moment'. '. . . I served my time, and if we lost, it was no fault of ours. If we'd had the home support they have now, we'd not have suffered the humiliation of Versailles. Dieter's lot will put that right. So come along, it's time to go.'

Roughly, Herr Zorn parted mother and son, to the latter's

relief, since he knew how quickly they could work up from nothing.

'Got your razor, shaving soap, brush, toothbrush, hair-brushes, Dieter?' his father rattled on methodically, ticking items off on his fingers. 'Hygiene is the main thing in the forces.'

'I'm sure I have. Yes, I checked. I remember.'

'All right. And now, we must go.'

The mandatory but genuine tears fell from Etta's eyes as she kissed her son. His father had his arm, as though making an arrest – and they were off.

It was a short tram journey to the *Luftwaffelazarett* not far from the harbour. Use of the Adler, if not prohibited, was unwise and unpatriotic in view of the shortage of fuel pending the conquest of the Caucasus.

But the process of mobilization was not without its complications. In the first place, though the centre was at the *Luftwaffelazarett*, apparently it did not follow that it was a recruiting centre for the Luftwaffe. In fact, it was for the Wehrmacht.

Thorvald tried to see his son into the building, but was barred at once by two seedy-looking sentries at the door. Dieter walked in with the air of a man entering a casino. The *Rottenführer's* boredom showed through his pebble lenses.

Dieter was passed on to the next room, where his fate was decided by almost idle curiosity. He faced a doctor in a white coat, a stethoscope at his neck.

'Strip, and be quick about it!' the doctor said roughly, a man impatient to return to more interesting duties.

Zorn stripped down to his underpants.

'The lot, boy! Are you cold, or just prudish? Come along, let's see the family jewels!'

Zorn snatched off his vest and pants, exposing his hairless breast and fair pubic area.

The doctor exclaimed in admiration: 'Ah, one so blond – and why so shy?' and palpated Zorn's chest. 'Turn round . . .'

74

Then his back, his finger thumping on Zorn's scapulae like a baker's testing bread.

'Turn round!' The doctor eyed Zorn's penis with what might be relish. He took it in finger and thumb, twisted it bottom side up, as though admiring.

The orderly noted something in his files.

'Are you a full-blooded Aryan?' the doctor asked sharply. Zorn said nothing. 'Well, out with it, Zorn. Are you, or aren't you? *Mischling* perhaps?' the doctor rapped at him.

Still Zorn hesitated, petrified.

'Your father then, Zorn? Aryan? Swedish?' The doctor was more than impatient. He was angry at the slowness. A queue was forming in the next room.

'Yes, Aryan – I think.'

'You *think!*'

'Yes, Aryan, I'm sure.'

'Thank you, Zorn. I'm glad you're sure. I wonder if I am,' said with a curl of the lips. 'And your mother?' The doctor rose from his stool and planted himself directly in front of the naked Zorn. His eyes stared into Zorn's.

'Your mother, Zorn? Is she a full-blooded Aryan mother, fit to perpetuate the pure blood of the German race?' Did the sarcasm refer to Zorn, or to the State?

Zorn froze in his wretched nakedness. But the doctor merely asked him to open his mouth wide. Peering in, the doctor muttered to the orderly: 'Er – left lower four, gold – two, gold. Wider! Right lower, none – upper left three, gold . . .' Thus Zorn's only worldly wealth in gold was recorded. The hours of pain over the years at Doctor Ziegler's were now apparently of some moment.

'Right, Zorn,' the doctor said. 'You will return home, at once, and stay there until further notice, so that we know where you are when we want you.'

'You mean, sir, I mustn't travel until my call-up?'

'No, I do not mean that. Call-up takes place here.' The doctor rapped a finger on the table irritably. 'The Wehrmacht is too urgently in need of reinforcements to send people home after recruitment.'

'So I was given to understand, sir. I've brought my kit with me, as instructed.'

'Well, take your kit home with you again, and stay there until we investigate certain matters.'

Zorn dressed quickly. His head ached. His breakfast threatened audibly. He felt utterly miserable. Physical humiliation (the actual handling of his body) and mental anguish assailed him. As he walked slowly homewards with his unwanted valise hanging over his shoulder, no words formed in his mind except 'pure blood of the German race'. He trailed wretchedly through the streets until home was in sight. He knew then that he could not face his parents and their questions, to which he would have no answer.

He turned away and made for the harbour. He rowed out to *Donner*, clambered on deck, and sat with his legs dangling over the side. Idly, he took out his mother's packet of sandwiches from his pocket and threw bits to the gulls which circled and screamed and fought enough to distract him.

Then, after two hours, he knew he must move, must find answers to questions. He rowed back, tied up the dinghy and trailed homewards again. He would tell the story as straight as he could remember – every detail. That was the only way. He would ward off their questions by starting immediately, leaving out nothing. Then let them work it out. He had said nothing . . . incriminating. Well, had he? No, of that he was sure.

He had taken so much for granted, he had forgotten the import of those early paternal proscriptions. And he wondered yet again what had become of his maternal grandparents. There was simply no news of them. Now it seemed much more important. He was still trying to work it all out as he turned the last corner.

Two men in civilian clothes came up to him. He noticed another standing outside the front gate of his home, as though on guard. He had only a moment to take it all in. The two men were up to him at once.

'Zorn – Dieter Zorn? Your papers?'

He could only nod as he handed them over. It was the last he was to see of them.

'All right, come with us.'

Without ceremony, the men took each arm and marched him off. He tried to protest that he must see his parents. They simply did not hear. They ordered him to get into the back of a van waiting at the end of the road. One man climbed in with him into the semi-darkness, the other got into the driver's seat, and in a few minutes they were at the railway terminus and boarding a train. The two men were dour customers. When one went to the toilet, the other stayed close to Zorn. It was almost as though he were under arrest.

At the end of a seven-hour train journey, one man simply sloped off into the night, with the air of a fellow glad to be at the end of a shift and homeward bound. But his companion bundled Zorn into the back of another small van, locked the door, and then got up front in the driver's seat. After half an hour's bumping over cobbled roads, the van halted. The driver unlocked the door and ordered Zorn to get out. Zorn had never felt so stiff – or so hungry.

As he started to stretch his limbs and to shake out his crotch, like any man after a cramped journey, his escort suddenly thumped Zorn in the back.

'Come on, enough of that. I've got to get home, and it's late enough . . .'

The man marched him across a yard towards a large building which loomed ahead in the night sky. In the black-out, Zorn stumbled, and the man's patience seemed at an end. He practically frog-marched Zorn, handed him to a sleepy sentry at the door, and left. The soldier opened the door.

He was in what looked like an abandoned factory. It was a long building with a cold, concrete floor. In the dark, he thought he saw bodies everywhere.

Zorn bumped into feet and legs. People groaned and cursed

77

him. He wished he had brought a greatcoat, because despite the warmth of bodies sleeping all around him, a chill was descending from the roof.

On receiving his papers, he had begun imagining the best of the inevitable – the uniform, the comradeship, home furlough, possible combat, even a wound (not too incapacitating, enough to earn an Iron Cross Third Class perhaps). He would drive Nelli in the Adler, hobble on his stick to the dinghy and board *Donner* to sail a splendid reach downwind and tack back to shore where, in each other's arms, they would wine and dine somewhere more respectable than Nummer Neunzehn. They would then retire to bed happy and fulfilled.

He felt absolutely bereft as he dozed and started by turns. It was now that his mother mattered, he needed her desperately, he was not nearly ready for this rough introduction to communal life. Even his father would have been a comfort. Their quarrels were nothing to him now; he wanted only to be returned to them, away from this ghastly crowd of bodies all round him and suffocating him.

It was still dark when the doors were opened. Soldiers shouted: '*Raus! Raus!*' and there was pandemonium as bodies rose everywhere. Zorn had difficulty in focusing. Instinctively, he rose with the rest, shuffled with them towards the door, clutching his valise.

'Leave that!' a soldier shouted. And Zorn dropped it.

Outside, men were lining up in the yard. Some were well dressed, two wearing Homburgs and well-cut overcoats. They were all ages, which surprised Zorn, for he had imagined only the young and fit would satisfy the Wehrmacht. Some of the men looked more like labourers in their working clothes. Did he detect a lot of Polish?

Zorn was pushed by a guard into one line, and this tendency to push him around roused in him an instinct to protest. But he sensed too that it would only make matters worse, for he could see one or two of the more recalcitrant receiving worse treatment, as though the guards would be only too happy to bring their rifle butts into play.

78

Looking behind a high perimeter fence, Zorn thought he saw a town, but was not too sure, so much of his attention was required at this lining up, with guards shouting all the time. A sergeant, obviously in charge of the parade, stood in front.

'Any joiners among you?' he barked.

Four men put up their hands. They were told to return to the hut. The sergeant seemed dissatisfied.

'All right. Any of the rest of you slobs handy with tools?' he shouted again.

Zorn, who had always been good with tools, decided he qualified and raised his hand with a few others. This seemed to satisfy the sergeant and he ordered the new group into the hut to join the more experienced ones.

Inside, Zorn found himself in a group of fifteen, not one of whom he would have known outside the wire. They all stood in a huddle, hands gripping their shoulders against the morning chill. Nobody talked. If anything, their common mask was fear. It infected Zorn. He looked from one to the other and decided on an older man who looked the least forbidding.

'Excuse me,' he said in a half-whisper, anxious to conceal his bewilderment. 'Is this the Wehrmacht?' For administrative errors happened, and he might be anywhere.

The man smiled sadly. 'Wehrmacht, son? That's a joke – Wehrmacht! No, son. *That* is the Wehrmacht, those fellows out there with the rifles.'

'So are we all joining?'

'*You* might be.' The man was taking in the blond hair and fair complexion. 'But the rest of us aren't.'

'But what is this place?' There was obviously some mistake.

'What is this? This? This, my son, as far as the rest of us can gather, is a collecting point for undesirables of the Third Reich.'

The sergeant entered the shed, accompanied by a guard. Zorn felt his companions stiffen.

'You, Greichhardt,' the sergeant spat at a tall man in the

79

group, 'you'll be in charge. You'll take this lot into the yard and organize carrying the timber in. You'll start making bunks as quick as you like. It's up to you. The sooner you make the bunks, the sooner you'll get off the floor. Bunks – understand? Three tiers, against the wall. If we get any more guests at this hotel, we can think about building more in the middle of the floor when the time comes.'

'What about tools?' asked Greichhardt, who did not appear to be in the least intimidated by the Wehrmacht.

'What'll you need?'

'Saws, good crosscut saws for a start. Hammers and nails. What d'you think?'

This needled the sergeant, who moved threateningly up to Greichhardt, but then thought better of it. 'I don't know about "good crosscut saws",' he said, 'but if you take one man and call at the stores, you'll probably get what you want.'

But it was Greichhardt's turn to be dissatisfied: 'And how d'you expect us to work on empty stomachs?'

'That's enough of your lip, Greichhardt. You'll get your rations when you've earned them.'

When Greichhardt led his motley band outside, always under the eyes of the guards, Zorn saw that the rest of the inmates were being marched off somewhere, with four guards in attendance. Greichhardt and another man had also been marched off under escort in search of tools, while Zorn's group started carrying planks into the shed. On empty stomachs, they made heavy weather of it. Zorn found it possible to talk with impunity.

They worked in pairs. His own partner was a dark, curly-haired man.

'You'd think the Wehrmacht would be better prepared,' Zorn muttered, testing the air.

'Prepared?' the man replied. 'Why should they be, for the likes of us?'

'But isn't this place something to do with the Wehrmacht? We've all been called up, so you'd think they'd have food and beds ready.'

The man stopped to look Zorn up and down. 'Look, mate,' the man said with what Zorn took to be contempt. 'Are you some sort of plant?'

'What d'you mean? I've been called up, to join the Wehrmacht.'

'How old are you, son?'

'Nearly nineteen. I was medically examined yesterday, and two men brought me here by train.'

The dark man scratched his head, but still stood, trying to weigh up this youth who claimed to have been called up to the colours.

'Not yet nineteen? Bless my soul!' he said. Then, *sotto voce*, to himself: 'Barely out of nappies – and they send him here . . .' Still not satisfied. 'Called up, you say? To the Wehrmacht? What are you? What's your name?'

Clearly, the man was fascinated by Zorn's whiteness. He kept looking up at the barleycorn hair, the fair eyebrows, the faint white bristle already showing on the chin, for washing and shaving had not been on the agenda so far.

'Zorn. Dieter Zorn. From Welckmar.'

'Come on. Get a move on, you louts!' a guard shouted, and Zorn moved with his interlocutor at either end of a plank. Otherwise, the guards showed no concern about the general languor.

'The sooner you get the job done, the sooner you'll have somewhere to sleep,' the guard mumbled on, plainly as bored as his charges. Then he leaned against a wall alongside his companions. The sergeant was not in sight. He reappeared around midday. Greichhardt was back with his tools too, and the guards generally bustled among the workers now that the sergeant was present.

Then there was another muster, four lines, two guards to each. They were marched off to another, smaller building. Tables, benches, an all-pervading smell of cabbage. As a canteen, it had all the signs of haste in preparation. They queued at a long table. A bowl of cabbage soup and a hunk of rye bread was served to each in a tin plate. There

81

were only spoons, a sign that this was to be the entire meal.

Zorn, with the rest of them, wolfed it in his hunger and felt the stuff coursing through his bowels. The dark man kept close to him.

'You say you're joining the Wehrmacht, so what are you doing here?'

'Just what I said. I got my papers a week ago.'

The man obviously found this difficult to take in. 'D'you know what we are?' he asked, signing with his eyes at his comrades round the room.

'No. Unless you've been called up too.'

'Well, you could say that.'

The man's evident caution, his cageyness, began to irritate Zorn, whose tolerance was wearing thin by now.

'What I want to know,' he said, and audibly enough for the guards to hear, 'is why the Wehrmacht brings us to a dump like this and treats us like this – no toilet facilities, no food, no beds even!'

'If you want to piss,' a guard shouted at him, 'go outside and do it against a wall!'

'Don't let that bastard go without an escort,' called the sergeant, banging his rifle butt on the floor for emphasis. The guard slouched after Zorn.

The guard was no trouble, in no hurry. So Zorn took his time, suppressing his guilt at urinating against the canteen wall.

'Suppose I decide not to join the Wehrmacht,' he said to his escort, 'and jump the fence and go home.'

The guard merely shrugged his shoulders with the pathetic tolerance of a dog that is used to being kicked.

Zorn looked at the man closely. Then froze. It was not tolerance so much as apology that he read in the tired middle-aged countenance. This was an ordinary German, a railwayman, a roadsweeper or labourer, probably below par medically. Otherwise, why was he guarding this motley gang? It was the patient, silent apology in the guard's face that brought

Zorn up short. Quickly, he recalled one or two utterances, hints – and it dawned.

'This isn't the Wehrmacht, is it?' Zorn asked. 'This is some sort of camp – for – *what*?'

'Dunno. All I know is that I don't like it any more than you do. Come on, you'd better join the rest.'

'But tell me. What is this?'

But the guard was not having any more, brought his rifle to the horizontal by way of persuasion, and motioned Zorn towards the canteen door. Back inside, Zorn sat down by his dark companion.

'Now I know what you're talking about,' he said. 'This is not the Wehrmacht. It's some sort of camp. What did one man say? That it's a collecting point for undesirables of the Third Reich.'

'Yes,' the man replied. 'That puts it just right. So I ask again. What are you?'

'I told you already. Who are you? What?'

'Me? Everybody calls me Philo. I'm a Romany. Satisfied?'

Zorn looked up sharply. 'And you are undesirable?' he dared to ask, for there was a latent belligerence in the man's expression.

'I am. So are all the rest. And you?'

Was it a statement, or a question?

Philo's general inscrutability worried Zorn. He was worn out, sleepless, hungry – above all, bereft of all that eighteen years of life had brought his way. Before Philo's questioning look, he felt unsure of himself.

'Undesirable?' He weighed the word and its implications. 'Why should I be?'

'Indeed. Why should any of us be? But we're all marked in some way or another. Mine's the mark of Romany. But yours? I can't work out what you're doing here. You don't look . . . marked to me.'

Zorn blenched at the thought. His mother? Was it a sin, or a blemish, to wear the mark of your mother? The Nuremburg

Laws? They had seemed so remote from Welckmar . . . Yes, his mother would be 'marked'. And he came out in cold sweat at the memory of the medical, of how a circumcision now aroused sufficient interest to initiate a bureaucratic search into antecedents. So, in answer to Philo's question, what was he and what was he doing here, building bunks with a bunch of undesirables? Was circumcision, was your birth enough to render you an undesirable of the Third Reich?

That moment of chill would remain with him always. It was a fulcrum to his life. Hitherto he had lived peaceably enough in Welckmar, worried only by his parents, but finding his own life with Stentewik, Nelli and the community in general. He had been accepted. Now he was undesirable. His Jewishness bore in on him, the birth, innuendo, slurs he had occasionally heard and comfortably ignored, all now reared before him like a great prison wall – *and he on the inside*. He saw now why Philo was cautious. In such a crowd, where an 'undesirable' might be anything from a politically innocent gypsy to a sophisticated political dissident, a plant would be an understandable ploy by the authorities.

'Marked?' he mused aloud. 'Marked?' He looked Philo in the eye. He told him all the previous day's events, including, with horror, every detail of the medical. For there lay the crux.

Then the sergeant shouted: 'Back to work!'

Greichhardt was consulting with his joiner colleagues on the best tactics for constructing bunks. Greichhardt assumed command easily. If they had to construct their own bunks, then it was best done his way.

He gestured, marked out, generally brought order to what could have developed into chaos. Doing what had to be done had nothing to do with the guards. His quarrel with the guards was a quite separate matter, and he had a way of keeping them at a distance. He gave the air of a man who would deal with them as and when he required.

Greichhardt divided his sixteen men into four teams, a

professed joiner in charge of each. Each team was given a section from corner to middle of a long wall. The respective lengths of timber were divided accordingly, tools were distributed and work began. That was the way Greichhardt tackled problems – a born leader, however 'undesirable'.

Within each team, the joiner called for timber and a hammer or saw from the others, who mostly stood about and watched balefully. It was obvious many had never hammered a nail in their lives.

Zorn's team did not cohere at all. It emerged that their leader was no joiner, and in fact had no experience with tools at all. Apologetically, he confessed he had worked in a bakery, and in volunteering as a joiner had thought it might bring him nearer food.

Zorn took the saw from him, measured a few lengths, marked them off, sawed a few, then asked the next man to carry on likewise while he began to construct a frame to take the first three bunks. The baker handed hammer and nails to those with any competence and dreamt of pretzels running with butter.

So they worked, hungry, driven only by the will to get off the cold concrete floor, and by the supervision of Greichhardt, whose general assumption of foremanship at least kept the guards out of sight. Zorn was even glad of the work. It occupied his mind, removed him for an hour or two from the unthinkable.

As darkness fell, the sergeant came in with two privates, carrying a cardboard box each. They dumped them in the middle of the floor, and retreated sharply.

They all gathered round.

'Here!' Greichhardt called. 'Sink your teeth into these if you can, then see if you've got any teeth left when you've finished.'

It was iron rations, the hardest, drabbest biscuit.

'You could fire this out of a bloody howitzer!' Greichhardt declared. But to a man, they struggled, trying to soften the biscuits in a mug of water.

'Carry on, boys,' Greichhardt ordered them. 'Eat what you can manage. We don't know where the next meal's coming from. It's fatal to leave anything. The bastards'll only cut our rations further if we leave any.'

So the day ended, a new life for Zorn. Already he felt the claustrophobia of the prisoner closing in on him with the dark as the rest of their group were marched in.

He felt the magnetic pull of the north from the moment the guard had dumped him among all those bodies. He wanted to flee, but knew he was caught like a fly in a spider's web, where the more he struggled the more he became enmeshed. He felt the dull ache of suppressed flight, a constant nagging, like a carious tooth, that never left him. It was not only the unfamiliarity of the imposed social conditions of living cheek to jowl, the foetid proximity of unwashed bodies, but the prevailing ugliness and poverty of spirit. It did not take him long to see that his companions had begun to live without hope. He saw it in their eyes, in the slope of their shoulders as they mustered and shuffled about in the yard. The only man anywhere near his own age was Philo the gypsy, and oddly enough he was the only one whose head was still relatively high, eyes still alert for any passing crumbs of hope – a door left ajar, a slackness in the barbed wire, or a faintly sympathetic guard.

Home, past, future – all was closed off in the sudden preoccupation with his plight. This was life, the struggle with hunger, with trying to find sleep on the concrete floor a second night, and with living with his newly stirred consciousness.

It emerged that the returning group had fared even worse. Zorn did not realize that this was their second day and that he was the last of the group to be 'mobilized' and collected at this makeshift location. He gathered from their conversation that they had been marched to a factory halfway towards the town and put to work assembling the machinery of a new aircraft components unit.

The factory apparently had been assembled as hastily as their sleeping quarters and the canteen arrangements were just as extempore. But the work had been harder, manhandling heavy machines into place under the fractious supervision of experts.

The men slumped on the floor. Zorn spent another hungry and restless night.

It took three days to complete the bunks, and on the fourth day Zorn's group was merged with the rest and marched off to the factory. It seemed odd to him that 'undesirables' should be put to work on aircraft components, but he soon learned that the components were aircraft seats to different specifications: pilot, navigator, engineer, various gunner positions, all for Dornier bombers. They were not a commodity that could be easily sabotaged.

Canteen facilities had recovered from the initial chaos. Breakfast and a midday meal were provided, and rations had been extended from cabbage soup to a thin stew of meat and vegetables, with the latter predominating.

His spoon (the only article of cutlery issued) became a precious possession. Its loss would mean eating more slowly, the meagre solids with his fingers, the more liquid by tipping the plate to his mouth. To eat slowly meant missing the little extra that was sometimes handed out when the cook cleaned his bowl.

The food was appalling, yet Zorn and his companions wolfed it – it was more fuel. Before each meal, and especially the midday one, Zorn felt empty to the point of fainting. He had learnt to hang on through the attack of cold sweat. He might have fainted had he not seen what happened to an older man called Stern who did faint. Stern had been among a group putting the last touches to fixing one of the machines, a heavy metal-folder, to the floor. There was much standing around as the expert fastened bolts and made various adjustments. Suddenly, old Stern fell to the floor. There was a temporary panic, which startled a corporal guard nearby.

The guard looked down at Stern, shouted: 'Get up, you stinking Yid! Come on!' He held his rifle butt over the unconscious man, then struck Stern hard on the shoulder blade.

Greichhardt saw what was happening, brushed aside his own guard and rushed over.

'Leave him alone, Vogel!' he shouted at the corporal. 'Can't you see the man's fainted?'

Vogel retreated before Prisoner Greichhardt. Zorn knew in his heart that they were all prisoners. Hunger and the effort to work had the effect of deadening his mind. He could not think, unless of a larger hunk of bread. He felt like a prisoner, felt confinement keenly – the loss of freedom of movement, the sea, trees. But, above all, the loss of simple unrestricted movement. He moved like an overburdened domestic animal, in mindless response to the orders of its masters.

His adjustment to the humiliation of the medical and then to the dull, boring and hungry life of forced labour was not keeping time with the facts. The facts came in only slowly. His body was adjusting as best it could to the food, and in consequence, the first days were totally mindless. His body would have to be thinner before it got used to the meagre diet.

His initial 72 kilograms demanded its normal daily ration, even in the rigours of wartime. He had been lean but fit, perhaps all the fitter for the civilian wartime diet. But his prison food was such a drastic reduction that his first days were akin to illness, almost delirious. His body longed for the oblivion of Stern's faint, but he held on, because he had reserves of strength that Stern lacked. For it was only afterwards in the shed, and settling down in their new wooden bunks on straw, that he learned about Stern.

Philo was in the bunk below Zorn.

'Poor old bugger,' he said, 'he's been inside the wire longer than any of us.'

This was one more fact that Zorn had to take in. 'Why? Were we not all mobilized at the same time?' he asked.

Philo smiled at the persistent allusion to 'mobilization', but he recognized the first dazed days of the prisoner.

'No, only a few of us. I've been inside for nine months. This is a new camp, for what it's worth. We've been dragged from all over the place. We make the bloody aircraft seats, and it releases others for the Russian Front. Maybe we should count ourselves lucky . . . They brought you off the streets, but old Stern has been inside, one way or another, since 1940. He's a Jew, you see. They seem to catch it worst for some reason. They hauled him all the way from France, where he thought he was safe. He'd escaped from Austria when Adolf marched in. Have you heard him whimper at night? Poor old sod . . .'

Philo, who was quite a chatterbox, mumbled on and on. But Zorn heard no more. The fact had come home, and in his physical weakness, waves of sweat broke out over his body. *He* was a Jew, son of a Gentile father but a Jewish mother – and so, a Jew.

What had been humiliation at the medical turned to terror, not only for himself, but for his mother. The anti-Jewish laws had not been applied so rigorously in peripheral areas like Welckmar, where more often than not the nastier implications were cloaked in general propaganda statements or even ignored, though not always. Josef Tadziewicz, Zorn recalled, had not been heard of in a long time. Was he, too, a prisoner, bullied like old Stern, too weak to work for the German 'war effort'?

The general attempt to incline people's minds in a certain malevolent direction was blunted by the problems of daily living, the meagreness of the rations, the absence of firm news from the Russian front.

Now, as Zorn tried to achieve the oblivion of sleep, the full meaning hit him as never before: his whiteness, the barleycorn hair, the 'Swedish' look had disguised his Jewish heritage – and the *laissez-faire* torpor of Welckmar did the rest. The whiteness was superfluous there, he had had no need of it. He was so like thousands of other very blond *Ostseevolk* round the Baltic that he had merged with a general white subconscious not calling for thought.

89

This was his new consciousness, his Jewishness. He was as white as ever, if a little grubby for want of a wash – so white as to stand apart from the rest. He was aware of his physical isolation here, the reason for the original suspicion that he was a plant: his whiteness among so many darker types.

But like the dark Philo, he was now conscious of his new status. It was not that he was different here; it was the stigma of being one of them, of being *unerwünscht* – undesirable – because he was a Jew? – an outcast.

And his mother? He recalled Pastor Stentewik's warning. Why had he not conveyed the message? Because he was afraid? No – but certainly because they always excluded him, shut him out from their conversation. They only quarrelled in front of him. But now he knew he should have spoken out, and persisted.

The world was suddenly divided into two distinct parts. A week before, there had been many worlds, and if you were free you chose one of them, or accepted one if you were not. Now there were only two: one of choice and freedom, the other of bondage. There was inside, here – and outside, beyond the wire. Inside, as the weeks went by, it became more and more difficult to imagine the 'outside' world from which one came. That was it: 'outside' had acquired quotation marks. And which world did his mother occupy? Why had he failed to speak when there was still time? Guilt assailed him.

As they marched to work, manned the machines, gulped their rations in the canteen and slept in their barracks, Zorn watched Philo and Greichhardt. How did they take their *unerwünscht* status?

Philo would make something out of nothing, even out of hostile circumstances. He would volunteer where it suited his purpose, for instance to clean the swill bins in the canteen and so add a mouthful of extra food to his diet. He could be invisible to the guards, and when visible would ingratiate himself with them, yet keep his dignity. That was it: Philo

90

retained his gypsy dignity in this most undignified status of prisoner. He worked the system, not by crawling but by simply being Philo.

Greichhardt, on the other hand, defied the guards, challenged them whenever possible. From the status of non-person, he nevertheless managed to make the guards fear and respect him. He too worked the system, but by taking the guards to the edge of irritation and then forcing them to retreat.

Prisoner Zorn adapted as an animal takes to protective coloration. He watched others, principally Philo and Greichhardt, and learned the ropes that way. He learned to keep out of the way of the guards, who were a bored and sullen lot, but who, at Sergeant Quaeck's instigation, could be violent at times and vindictive.

The guards would not go for Greichhardt, but for figures like old Stern. Corporal Vogel had not forgotten Greichhardt's intervention at Stern's fainting. He kept clear of Greichhardt, but tailed Stern at every opportunity.

So the confinement, the constant shadow of the guards, the slow adjustment of the body to the low level of food and of the mind to the new status, reduced Zorn to virtual automatism. It was not that he did not think; he could not.

After three months, he had reached a state of leanness that would have alarmed his mother. When he stripped, his ribcage showed clearly and his hips bit so hard into the straw at night that he learned to sleep on his back. In that position, when sleep would not come, he began to remember – and to think.

If he was a Jew, and therefore *unerwünscht*, how much more so his mother? Had his father perhaps seen the danger and carried her off to the safety of Sweden? If it had not been for the damnable curiosity shown by the doctor at the medical, would she have been any safer? Surely not, since what had rendered him 'undesirable' would have implicated her no less – as that doctor had put it, unfit 'to perpetuate the pure blood of the German race'.

'Is there any way of getting in touch with one's family?' he asked Philo.

Philo said he would consult Greichhardt, but in his usual offhand manner, while polishing away at some knick-knack. Philo always kept busy as he chatted.

A definite pecking order had settled among them. Without any procedure such as a democratic vote (for such a formal association would have been dispersed by the guards at once), Greichhardt had become the acknowledged leader, and without any established rules, there were certain routes to his wisdom through those immediately below him. This hierarchy was governed by the respective capacity of prisoners to work the system, which meant suborning the guards or, in Greichhardt's case, even intimidating them. The guards could not be described as the cream of German manhood.

Zorn was part of an amorphous middle order who felt they could approach Greichhardt only indirectly – in Zorn's case, through Philo, whose capacity to work the system was next only to Greichhardt's. Zorn, on the other hand, would feel responsible for a pathetic, helpless victim like Stern.

Next evening in their bunks, Philo mumbled on as usual. Having been a traveller all his life, his present constricted movement might have sent him mad. But Philo had a way of talking his way through the day, and even the night. That kept him sane. His leanness was natural, his mind as keen as ever, and his appraisal of the guards as alert as any. He too knew how to suborn a guard and was the only prisoner who still enjoyed the occasional cigarette.

Zorn would lie back wearily on his straw and listen to Philo's Black Forest accent droning away below: tales of horses, women, dogs, poaching, even cockfights. Tonight Philo went on and on. And then, just before it was time to sleep, he startled Zorn, who was dozing off, by suddenly appearing with his head over the edge of the bunk.

'You asked me to see Greichhardt,' Philo whispered. 'Well, I've seen him. He says to write your letter home and to put on the top this address.'

He handed over an envelope and a stub of pencil. Zorn actually did not need the pencil, but tucked both envelope and stub into a pocket.

'But we're not allowed mail,' he said. 'How can they reply?'

'Don't worry about that. Just tell them not to put your name on the envelope. Only this name and address, he says. Understand?'

'May I write freely?'

'Don't be daft. Just say you're well and all that, and ask for news. No more. Nothing about this hole, in case it's picked up. And don't forget to write the address in capitals.'

'Capitals?'

'Yah. Tell them to write the address in capitals. Then it won't be opened. That's the arrangement. See?'

Zorn heard Philo's easy breathing as he dropped off to sleep, as if he hadn't a care in the world.

Next evening after work, Zorn took out the envelope. It was blank. Inside was a single sheet of paper. On top it bore the name and address of one of the guards, one Glebel, probably a supernumerary who lived at home in a nearby town.

Painfully, he composed his note.

He was well, he wrote, but missing home very much. How was Mama, Father, Berthe and *Donner*? Shouldn't they think of a Swedish holiday? He longed to expand, but resisted the temptation. In closing, he stressed they were to write not to his own name, but Glebel's, with the address all in capitals, adding, 'for the sake of clarity and security'. He handed Philo the letter before the early muster.

At the midday meal, he found an opportunity to talk to Philo.

'All right?' he asked, sick with anxiety.

'On its way already. Glebel's off this afternoon, it'll be in the post by now.'

Zorn was curious to know how Glebel had been persuaded.

'Easy,' replied Philo. 'He's got four daughters, probably all as ugly as he. They like *Schmuckstücke*.' He pulled a necklace

93

out of his pocket and, under the table, showed it to Zorn. 'All day long I'm stamping bloody holes out of metal seat bases. To take the wiring, or air conditioning, or whatever it is – how am I to know? Result? Piles of these small aluminium discs, size of a *Pfennig*. I punch two holes in with this.' And he proudly showed his companion a tiny punch made of stainless steel, needle sharp at one end. 'Then I nick the old belts the polisher's finished with and buff the little discs till they're like silver, wire them together with strands I untwist from bits of electric cable I pick up. Piece of cake! They love 'em, probably flog them for food. Glebel'll take as many as I can make.'

'So that's where you get your cigarettes.'

To that, the voluble Philo gave no reply. Carefully, he replaced the necklace and punch in his pocket.

So that was what Philo was polishing as he gossiped of an evening! Zorn wondered where Philo got the strength, for when work was finished, all he could do was flop on his straw and try to recover from the day's efforts, for which the food was less than adequate. And all the time, Philo was making a necklace, *eine kleine Schmuckstück*, a trinket for Glebel's daughters. Typical Romany, Zorn thought, to make something precious out of leftovers. The result was beautiful in its simplicity; Nelli would have been delighted to receive one.

Now that his body had adjusted to its appropriate leanness, Zorn remembered. And although he did not whimper like poor old Stern, his mind went over the past without daring to think about the future.

Until one day all hell was let loose. The guards were in a frenzy. One of them was being dragged along the fence by a large dog on a choke-collar. The beast was sniffing at the base of the perimeter wire. The sheer malevolence of its movements struck terror into the assembled prisoners, whom the guards were counting and recounting, with more rifle-butt play than usual.

Greichhardt had disappeared. They were not informed by

the guards, but they knew it. While the shock-waves of apprehension went through them, they also felt the agony of hope, that one of them, their leader, had been able to penetrate the wire. But their whisperings were soon silenced by the guards' rifle butts.

From the morning muster, through the working day, till night when they were locked in the shed, they were constantly under surveillance. Any further prospect of escape was sealed off. This constant shadow was one of the most oppressive aspects of their imprisonment.

The guards might be lazy, indifferent and bored, but they were always there. All day, as they worked under the tightest supervision, the prisoners speculated in their minds, not even whispering to one another. The guards' presence was so persistent that even those prisoners near the top of the hier-archy never discussed breaking out. Glebel, Vogel, Sergeant Quaeck and the other guards were never far away, and when they were off duty, others fell in behind. Escape was impossible therefore. Until Greichhardt proved otherwise.

'Do you think he got away?' Zorn asked Philo that evening.

'He's been in prison before, proper prison, not just a knocked-out dump like this. He's been behind bars and got out. He's a member of the Party . . . a Red, you know. The Gestapo would shoot him out of hand, but the Wehrmacht always intervenes.'

'Why should they protect him?'

'Two reasons. First, the Wehrmacht hate the Gestapo. Bunch of upstarts they are. So whenever the Wehrmacht have power to interfere, they do so regardless. And there may be a second reason. Greichhardt's the sort of chap who can hold a bunch like us together. Look how he organized the bunks. He might make the system work for his own ends, but he makes it work for the guards too. Where would we lot be without Greichhardt? Just you watch. We'll be a right awkward squad now he's gone.'

'And you think he'll get away?'

'I reckon he's had it worked out from the start. His one

95

problem was Vogel. That bastard's had it in for Greichhardt since the time Stern fainted. Never took his eyes off Greichhardt after that. But Friday's Vogel's day off, and Greichhardt slipped the net.'

'Any idea how he did it?'

'I have a fair idea. He didn't discuss it with any of us. But this morning, Greichhardt managed to break his pliers. He's been putting springs in the seats. How the hell you break a pair of pliers, I don't know. Glebel tells him to shove off and get a new pair quick. Sergeant Quaeck must've been asleep or something and forgot to call for an escort. Greichhardt's good at being invisible when he wants to. Out he goes, innocent as a babe, and that's the last they'll see of him, mark my words . . .'

Zorn felt a lift of the heart, but also alarm. Glebel was involved. But Zorn reckoned without the ways of the Wehrmacht. Glebel was overlooked, and it was Sergeant Quaeck who caught it: he lost his stripes. Corporal Vogel was promoted in his place.

Even so, Zorn wondered how Glebel would react. There was no doubt how the upper echelons reacted. Four additional guards were drafted in and extra security measures were taken. Barbed-wire festooned the compound like a malevolent plant growth.

The prisoners, when they had finished work and the box of hardtack had been distributed, were used to a comparatively free couple of hours when they were permitted to stroll around the yard outside their shed. Now that two-hour privilege was withdrawn. They were locked in, and their claustrophobia intensified.

Zorn had only one thought on his mind. Would Glebel deliver the letter from home? His anxiety increased when the new Sergeant Vogel came to him. Zorn's job was to shape and fit the plywood panel to the seats. He was a meticulous craftsman, as ever. He could not help himself. The seats had to be perfect. He simply was incapable of making a botched job in the cause of speed. As a result, he was creating a bottleneck, and seat-frames piled up at his sanding machine while he shaped his plywood to perfection.

'Zorn!' cried Vogel, as though he was the length of the room away. 'What's this bloody pile? You're so fucking slow, we might as well close for a week while you catch up. Unless you sharpen up, Zorn, you'll feel this!'

He gave Zorn a whack over the hip with his rifle butt. Zorn felt the pain on the raw bone and winced, but stood his ground as best he could and carried on sanding a panel, willing Vogel to go away. But Vogel stood his ground too.

'I've been through your papers, Zorn,' Vogel said slyly, standing over him. 'Welckmar folk know how to work. It's fucking parasites like you Jews who've been dragging us down, like this pile here!' He kicked at the pile of waiting seat-frames. 'If this lot isn't moved by tonight, I'm going to recommend that you be moved – further east . . .'

Zorn raced through the seats until only a few were left by nightfall when the bell summoned them to muster for the march back to the barracks.

Vogel came over, could be construed as vaguely satisfied, but glared at Zorn to reinforce the threat. And it was with added dread that Zorn realized that Vogel, for one, knew his status – that he was 'undesirable' because he was a Jew. The signs were ominous – what was behind that sudden mention of Welckmar? Had Glebel talked? If so, the reply would be intercepted by Vogel. What would his parents write? Anything that might further implicate his mother was unthinkable.

Distractedly, he rubbed his sore hip and eventually fell into a fitful sleep. But he had reckoned without Philo, who after Greichhardt's disappearance had assumed leadership.

It was not an easy mantle for Philo. He had rivals where Greichhardt had had none, and he was a gypsy. Some prisoners did not relish dependence on a gypsy, having their own shades of *unerwünscht* and not being loath to express them. *Unerwünscht* was a status Philó was well used to, and he had his own personal difficulties in assuming the role of a leader.

He was quite accustomed to being kept waiting outside doors. He and his kindred were perpetually doubted, that was their lot. Selling *Schmuckstücke*, begging and poaching, even stealing when times were hard, the gypsies were bound not to be trusted. It was their way of life.

Philo was much happier exercising his native guile under a leader like Greichhardt. But no other sub-leader showed eagerness to take Greichhardt's place, and anyway, in the general mood of pessimism, they expected Greichhardt to be recaptured any day. In the meantime, despite their reservations, people began to come to Philo with their problems and representations to the guards.

Philo took it on therefore, and if his physical and mental presence lacked the qualities and stature of Greichhardt, he worked the system in his own way and was effective. For one thing, not only was he supplying Glebel with his knickknacks, but two other guards as well. And he had another weapon in his armoury: blackmail.

For two days, Sergeant Vogel stood over Zorn, to make sure that each evening the pile of seat-frames was fully processed with their plywood panels. After the shift was finished, when they were locked up for the night, Zorn decided he must talk things over with Philo.

'Oh, I wouldn't take too much notice of a bastard like Vogel,' Philo comforted him. 'About as much brains as a strained fart.'

'What if he's been on to Glebel and intercepted my letter with the address?'

'I wouldn't worry about that either if I were you. Glebel knows me well enough by now to understand that I'd shop him if he lets me down.'

'How's that?'

'Well, if he splits, I'll tell Vogel that he's getting scrap material out of the factory – my *Schmuckstücke*.'

'Won't it get you into trouble?'

Philo grinned at that. 'Of course. But Glebel's too dumb to work that out. It's his own skin that worries him. Anyway, his women have him under tight control. I know by the way he thanks me. It's me who's doing the favour, not him. Just take a look at this!' Philo revealed a flat tin full of cigarettes. 'And here – have a chunk of this . . .' Philo broke off a piece of cooking chocolate, sheer gold in any stratum, much less a prisoner's.

Zorn settled down satisfied, but still fretted over the Welckmar connection. Vogel . . . Corporal Vogel – from Welckmar? Not unlikely, although in colouring much darker than himself. Not much of the *Ostseevolk* about Vogel! And yet, the name now stirred up a forgotten chord of trauma, too distant to recall. Why was he so obsessed with Vogel? Unable to focus on more than a mere shadow, a hallucination perhaps in his present weakened state in prison camp, Zorn sought reassurance in Philo's description of their new sergeant: 'About as much brains as a strained fart . . .' But the acute sense of being threatened would not lift.

A week later, Philo came to him in the canteen as they were shuffling back to work after the midday meal.

'Got it. I told you, didn't I?' Philo gave the air of a man who had successfully completed a mission. 'Later, not now!'

The afternoon was painfully slow for Zorn. He ripped through his quota of panels, so much so that Sergeant Vogel showed less interest and went to stand over Stern, who by now was relegated to sweeping scrap metal and shavings from the floor.

The march back seemed endless, and the Griechhardt incident having passed apparently into oblivion, they were once again granted open door, two hours' recreation in the yard before lock-up. This meant extra surveillance, and Zorn spent a further two hours in an agony of suspense. Eventually, they were herded inside, door bolted and barred, windows closed and shuttered. They settled down in their bunks in the darkness, some talking, some seeking the oblivion of sleep.

After a wakeful hour or so, Philo's head came up over the bunk rail. 'Got any biscuits left?' he asked. 'I'm hungry.'

'Just a half,' Zorn replied and handed it over. As he did so, he felt the envelope in his hand in exchange.

The problem now was when and where to read it. The letter burned in his pocket as he tried to sleep. And even after breakfast, there was never a safe moment. There was only one possibility. When he asked permission to visit the 'long drop' (as they called the latrine outside), the guard directed and escorted him in the opposite direction. It was unwise to argue. They stumped to the far end of the factory floor. Zorn was filled with dread.

'In there,' said the guard.

Zorn opened the door indicated. This was a new situation. He presumed he was meant to close the door behind him.

Inside was a lavatory with a wooden seat. Wonder of wonders! This, for the prisoners? Was it merely a fit of absent-mindedness on the guard's part? 'Pull twice!' a notice warned. The chain was broken in two places and repaired with string. Feverishly, Zorn took out the envelope and tore it open.

My dear Dieter, Your letter came as a great relief. You are alive and well, and thank God not in the East. It is the best news I have received since you left home. You will understand only too well when I tell you that an official visited us the day after your departure and informed us you were not eligible for the Reich Forces on account of certain decrees. He then told Mother to pack for a journey next day. She was only allowed change of underwear and toilet requisites. I have not heard from her since she left. It is a great sadness to me. In view of your own position, I debated whether or not to tell you and decided you should know. I am taking all steps possible to have the decree reversed and would not wish you to be under any illusion should you be allowed home (perhaps furlough?) as a result of my efforts. I will say no more. I can only hope and pray that things are better for both of you than I fear. Try to keep your spirits up and always remember that personal cleanliness will help in the present circumstances, whatever

100

your station. I hope this reaches you. I have obeyed your instructions. Your loving Father, Thorvald Zorn.

'Whatever your station' . . . Had his father guessed that he had no station? He was a non-person, miserably housed and fed, fit only for cheap labour. And where was his mother? In the dreaded East . . .? Why hadn't he heeded Pastor Stentewik's words?

There were tears in his eyes as he pulled the chain. Nothing happened. There was a sharp rap at the door. Zorn rammed the letter in his pocket and opened the door to let himself out, to come face to face with Vogel.

'Hi, you there!' snapped Vogel. 'When you use the toilet, pull the chain twice! Can't you read, you filthy little Yid?'

He did not dare to turn suddenly. Vogel was in the habit of reacting violently to suddenness. Slowly, slowly, Zorn turned and pulled the chain. There was a suppressed sigh, like an asthmatic microphone. It came from the depths. Then, as he pulled hard a second time, and as the pan nicely prophesied in exquisitely engraved letters – N-I-A-G-A-R-A – Woosh!

The prisoners did not altogether take to this new dispensation. The lavatory had fallen from better times into desuetude and had been repaired at the behest of the guards, who loathed the 'long drop' even more than the prisoners. Yet many prisoners preferred the openness of the 'long drop', having developed a phobia about being behind closed doors. From then on, Zorn insisted with his escort that it was the 'long drop' he would rather visit, to which the guard responded with a disconsolate shrug. In the 'long drop', for three long days, pleading a touch of *Durchfall*, Zorn read and reread the letter, and despaired. For it did not answer questions so much as pose them.

When he confided his worries to Philo and suggested that it was urgent that, like Greichhardt, he should find a way to escape, Philo proved totally uncooperative.

101

'Greichhardt was a pike among minnows,' Philo retorted sharply. 'Even the guards were minnows to him. You are a minnow, boy, and don't forget it . . . They locked us in after Greichhardt slipped away,' he went on musingly, 'they raised the fence, they put on more guards. But they knew Greichhardt was a one-off job, so they let us out again. They know the rest of us are minnows. Greichhardt was their mistake, and they know it – too late. They know his type can only be held by maximum security. Maybe they believed he was the only one who would make a load of creeps like us work. There's something in that, so maybe they took a gamble. He shouldn't have been here. Too hot to hold!'

'Why shouldn't minnows try to escape?' Zorn asked very quietly.

'Because that'll prove the system so loose, they'll make this into a real camp. One minnow out, the rest of us locked in good and proper, and bloody well punished for one man's offence. So don't come to me, boy. You'll get no help from me. Anyway, there's no way out now Vogel's in charge.'

But as he trimmed his plywood panels, marched back and padded disconsolately round the yard for the two hours' 'exercise', then flopped on his bunk, Zorn now had only one thing on his mind. Philo's collective argument carried weight, but like Greichhardt, the need was great. He had to get out, so Philo's warnings were soon forgotten. The questions raised by his father's letter could not be laid aside. He must get out, to Welckmar.

One thing was in his favour: the prisoners had not been deprived of their own clothes. If this was prison (and only the prisoners saw it as such), there was no prison uniform. In the view of the *Regierung*, they were workers for the cause of the Third Reich, contributing to its destiny. The aircraft seats were just as vital to the war effort as howitzers or Spandaus. They were only paid a pittance, but this made them workers, not prisoners. So no identifying uniforms were issued.

If he could break out, there would be no problem on that score, and he recalled that all sorts of shabby workers were constantly on the move, by road, rail, on foot or bicycle. The question was: *how*? Remembering Greichhardt, he realized that he needed a combination of organizing (the broken pliers) and chance (Vogel's day off). When the chance came, Greichhardt was ready.

Although the hardtack was practically inedible, Zorn knew he could survive on it for a few days or even longer, sufficient to get him to the Baltic, to Welckmar, should the chance occur. So he began to hoard his hardtack and what money he could save. He was thin, already undernourished after nine months, but he had youth on his side. Compared with old Stern, he was a Titan. All he needed was a chance, for there were too many questions tormenting him to heed Philo's warnings.

But Philo was acute. Zorn now had an extra guard. He realized he had failed to learn one lesson from Greichhardt, who had confided in no one, asked no questions or advice from anybody. The big man had led his motley workforce, satisfied the guards while keeping them in their place. He had worked the system, had kept his plans to himself and had finally broken out without reference to anybody, guards or prisoners.

Zorn's first mistake had been to mention escape to Philo. It was one thing getting a letter out and in. Philo had enjoyed that little conspiracy. But another break-out – no. Philo was apprehensive, for he knew the consequences, or so he gave Zorn to understand. And it occurred to Zorn that Philo himself might have plans and was saying nothing, still less allowing competition.

The miserable weeks passed without the slightest opportunity. Zorn even doubted if he would recognize a chance should it come his way. Philo's zealous surveillance as leader made it even worse. By now, he and Zorn hardly had a word for each other. It was as though Philo could read his mind.

Zorn made a habit of surreptitiously changing the hardtack

in his straw, replacing the stale with the less stale. Sometimes he carried two or three biscuits to work in his pocket, which was a risk since they were frisked from time to time. But even this business of transferring was difficult, for Philo was watching his every move.

One night Zorn got a fright. With the obsessive secrecy of a solitary conspirator, he was about to change his hardtack. But his searching fingers found nothing. He had hidden eight biscuits. He could not find one. Rats? The guards kept a couple of terriers for that purpose, and in any case, food was so scarce that the rats would find little to encourage them. The terriers, then? From a top bunk? Surely not. A guard? The guards tended to shun the shed, content merely to lock the prisoners in and leave them to their own devices.

It could only be Philo. Now he watched every move of Philo's, just as Philo watched him. In a silent, undeclared way, they became two gladiators circling each other, waiting for the first jump. On top of the driving necessity to break out, Zorn had this additional battle on his hands, to keep Philo guessing, not even to mention the disappearance of his hardtack. From then on, Zorn kept a few biscuits in his pocket, for as long as production at the factory was on target, the guards, even Vogel, seemed content to let things run themselves.

By September 1944, a general lethargy had settled among both guards and prisoners. For months now, almost every night, the bombers roared overhead and the thump of anti-aircraft guns could be heard in the vicinity. The district was on a flight path, but was not a target. The night's roar of bombers was merely part of life's present pattern.

Was this Zorn's chance? He would have liked to discuss it with Philo, to learn about their possible location, about roads, railways, routes north. But the silent gladiatorial circling continued unabated, till the two men had tacitly agreed not to be on speaking terms.

Then one night, the nearby town appeared to be the target, for the bombs were scattered indiscriminately over their

104

district, and one or two screamed alarmingly near the barracks. Prisoners heard the guards running about and shouting. No one could sleep. They were locked in, helpless should a bomb, perhaps an incendiary bomb, fall on the shed. One or two of the more fearful, like Stern, hid themselves under bottom bunks, as much from the racket as from actual danger, for nothing could protect them from a direct hit.

Zorn tossed restlessly on his bunk. He noticed that Philo was wandering about, as though on the alert for any emergency. At about three in the morning, the raid was over, with only the pulsating drone of a returning night-fighter overhead.

Next morning, providentially, the guards were slow to rouse them and to unlock the door. The prisoners knew the guards had news, for the raid had been heavy and prolonged, but were unlikely to pass it on. As they were mustered, they saw a pall of smoke rising a mile or two away. The guards, equally short of sleep, were morose and fractious, and rifle butts were more in evidence than usual. On the march to the factory, they could see the occasional bomb crater, and the hope rose in their minds that the factory had been hit. But it was unscathed, and work proceeded as usual.

The camp food, and the night's uproar, had upset Zorn's bowels. The prisoners were always either hopelessly constipated, or running, so much so that it was the most obsessive topic of conversation among them. At around eleven, Zorn asked a guard for permission to visit the 'long drop'.

'Go, then!' was all the guard had to say, too short of sleep to bother further.

In the 'long drop', Zorn found Philo, also unattended, sitting on the bench but with his trousers still up. He was puffing at the end of a cigarette.

'Caught short, eh?' Philo asked, amiably enough.

'Three days!' Zorn replied as he quickly dropped his trousers.

'What? Three days' rapid fire, or nothing doing till now?'

Which was the normal conversational gambit among the prisoners.

'Three days, nothing – now, this . . .' replied Zorn as he painfully voided.

'But you feel all right?' Philo went on.

'As well as can be expected.'

Zorn wondered about the sudden concern in the hitherto silent Philo.

'Got your hardtack?' Philo persisted.

So that was it. Philo was going to have it out with him at this moment of weakness. He was going to check on his plans.

'As a matter of fact, I have.' Zorn pulled up his trousers. 'What's that to you?'

Philo stubbed out his cigarette on the bench. 'Come!' he hissed, pointing towards the closed end of the 'long drop'.

The urgency startled Zorn. Was Philo to settle things between them here, in the 'long drop'?

'Come!' Philo repeated, very low.

Philo pulled at a board in the end wall. It came off easily and quietly. Philo had obviously been at work on it already, over days, even weeks perhaps, with his home-made tools, drawing a nail here, another there. Zorn was mesmerized. A second board came away, and a small panel beside it.

'Come!' Philo hissed again.

Philo was through the aperture. Zorn followed. Philo replaced the board, keeping it in place with a stone. Behind the 'long drop', there was a gap of about five yards to the wire fence. Now Zorn understood why Philo had chosen action today. A bomb had fallen just outside the perimeter, and the bottom strands of the wire were damaged.

There was nobody about in this noisome quarter of the compound. Philo led the way, quick, like a fox on his belly, through the damaged fence, with Zorn following. They were both outside, and it had taken less than half a minute from Philo's first bidding. They held tight to the ground, Philo

106

glancing left, right and above. The guards were indeed half asleep, for there was no one in sight.

The factory was quite isolated, and there appeared to be no cover to run to. Philo moved, crawling frantically on his stomach, Zorn copying every movement. It seemed an eternity before they reached a shallow ditch. Zorn felt as though he had been stripped of his clothes and the air round him impinged dangerously on his naked skin. He had been like a caged bird that had forgotten flight. Now, without warning, he must learn to fly again.

There they lay, panting, already exhausted beyond words. They were too weakened for any strenuous effort and could only lie helplessly, gasping for air. But there was no move from the compound where everybody, not least the guards, was half asleep after the night's bombing.

They both knew that it was only a matter of minutes before they were missed. Still without a word, Philo rose, with Zorn at his heels as they ran towards a hedge surrounding a field. They ran through a gap, desperate to distance themselves from the factory compound.

Philo nodded towards the now thinning smoke over the town, not more than a couple of miles away. Zorn followed. He was committed. As they trotted painfully along the headland of a ploughed field, he thought Philo was mad to be running into a town. But Philo kept to the field, always heading towards the smoke. Zorn pulled at his arm.

'You're crazy, Philo. We're bound to be picked up in the town.'

'For Christ's sake, man, either follow me or piss off! I know what I'm doing.' And Philo kept going. Zorn could only follow, more in desperation than in hope. To return now was unthinkable, and he had no idea of going it alone. It had all been so quick. Now here they were, outside the wire, and away.

After about a quarter of a mile, in this huge open field, they climbed over a gate. There was a road, apparently leading towards the smoke and the town ahead.

'All right,' Philo said. 'Now just act natural. We'll walk into town. We've either been bombed out, or we're workers shifting the rubble. It'll all be a shambles anyway. The best chance is in the town, get among the poor sods in there, act like one of them. See?'

They walked quickly, putting as much distance between them and the factory as possible. Suddenly Philo's eye caught something in the ditch by the roadside. He did not miss a thing. He looked up and down the road, was satisfied, and picked up a spade. Its owner, probably a ditcher, no doubt had abandoned it, and either fled or gone to help in the town.

'Carry this over your shoulder, kid. It'll look like you're ready to help.'

Zorn got the point. It was a prop that helped him play the part. The nearer they got to the town, the more secure they felt. The bomb craters got bigger. Nobody bothered the two walkers as they began to meet people, most of them as dazed and lost as the two fugitives. Then they saw the first real damage as they approached the town proper. Buildings were gutted. The fire tenders were still pumping water into some of them. A few had obviously been written off, leaving only a great pile of smoking rubble. Men and women were pulling aside masonry, clearing bricks from what had been town houses. But Philo walked on, as though to some specific destination.

They came to a factory area, which the bombing had devastated. Here whole armies of men, some with shovels, others with their bare hands, were frantically removing rubble. A chain was passing bricks to a waiting lorry.

'This is it,' muttered Philo. 'Just do as I do.'

They joined the chain near the lorry. One man, apparently exhausted, was grateful to make way for them as he dropped out. Everybody worked with a will. The factory had to be cleared, everything possible had to be salvaged. No one talked. It was just a matter of handing bricks to your neighbour, till you were exhausted. The lorry filled up. The driver got into his cab and started the engine.

'Right, up you get!' Philo called. As he clambered up over the tailboard of the lorry, he held out a hand to Zorn, and in no time the pair were enjoying free transport across the town.

'If he turns left, jump for it!' Philo shouted above the lorry's roar, for that way led to their factory compound. The lorry turned right and away, out of town.

Zorn looked for the sun, half-hidden behind the still-rising smoke. But he knew it was behind them. They might not be going far, but they were on the north exit out of town.

Only a mile beyond the outskirts, the lorry turned off the road, to pull into a municipal dump. Other lorries were tipping rubble too, in a separate area from the midden. Zorn looked to see which birds were scavenging, but they were not seagulls. They must be well inland.

They helped the driver clear the lorry, then simply walked off, like regular workers at the dump. Nobody took any notice. The bombing and its ensuing chaos had numbed senses, curiosity. They walked back to the road. Here, terrifyingly for Zorn, he and Philo parted company. But not before they had their first opportunity to talk since the frantic break-out.

'Why didn't you say anything?' Zorn asked. 'I would've been better prepared had this been planned.'

'You don't plan, son, you grab your luck. D'you think I planned the bombing?'

'No, of course not. But you must've known all the time you were going to run for it – those loosened boards in the "long drop" . . . yet you never said a word.' The relief of once again talking to Philo was more than he would care to admit, yet his first feeling was resentment.

'No more will I say anything now,' Philo replied, quite unperturbed as he looked up and down the road. 'I've got no plans, have you? All I want is to be out of that place, away from that bastard Vogel.'

'I'm going to travel north if I can,' Zorn confessed, then regretted it. Better to say nothing, in case Philo were caught and interrogated; he might be forced to divulge Zorn's general drift north. But he knew that Vogel would not have forgotten the Welckmar connection, whether or not Philo was recaptured.

'Right then,' Philo said with the air of a man with a special mission. 'I'm off. Best of luck. Just act natural and you'll get there.' And was gone, not along the road but away from it, on the far side and towards a dense wood that looked like the beginning of a forest. No handshake, no turning round to wave – a gypsy on a desperate bid for freedom, a freedom that meant detachment from the rest of humanity. Philo would lie low, live off the land and just sit it out until things turned for the better.

Zorn marvelled at the generosity of that first bidding – 'Come!' – in the 'long drop' after the weeks of silent hostility. Philo, so to speak, knocked on Zorn's door, as a gypsy will – then departed from whence he had come, to his tribe. For, without doubt, if anybody was surviving in the forest, it would be the gypsies, since they alone knew how to live off the forest if they had to. And they had to, if they were free, for the Third Reich had pronounced them *unerwünscht*. As he waited and watched from a hidden spot in the trees, Zorn reflected that gypsies did not give a damn. Having closed him out for weeks, then actually engineered this terrifying escape, Philo now had just abandoned him.

He had left his hideout and was standing, like a dummy, at the junction of the main road north and the spur into the town's tip, when a motorcycle-sidecar drew up.

'Jump in!' the driver shouted.

'Act natural . . .' another voice spoke to Zorn as he jumped as bidden into the sidecar and pulled the cover over his legs. The machine was off with a roar.

'From the town?' shouted the driver.

'Yes . . . factory bombed out . . . lost everything . . .' Zorn shouted back, learning the new art of lying.

'Far to go?'

This needed thought. 'Got to get north . . . my parents . . .'

'Only natural. Bound to be worried.'

Zorn was grateful that conversation had to be shouted at the top of their voices. It made it easier to 'act natural'. He longed to ask where they were, where heading. This was freedom indeed, the wind whistling past his face at fifty miles per hour, every mile a further distance between himself and the accursed Vogel.

'You exempt?' the driver asked.

This too needed care. 'Yes. Aircraft worker.'

'Me too. I'm on subs. Been on leave for the weekend.'

The man would be quite a gossip but for the racket of the engine. The wind in their ears only just carried away their shouted words. It heartened Zorn that his general shabbiness had not been so noticeable as to attract undue attention. In between the snatched gossip about last night's raid, about the bombing in general and about the rigours of reserved occupations, Zorn found that he could guess where they were heading, and his heart lifted. He learned the game as they went along: you discussed things only in general terms. The man worked in submarine construction, but where and precisely what he did not disclose. Zorn, likewise, worked on aircraft, but would not expand further. It was not done. The driver wanted company, that was all, and a sidecar machine was better balanced and easier to handle with a passenger. Zorn made things up as the occasion required: about his wrecked factory, though not specifying what sector of work it was concerned with. He guessed that they were travelling in the direction of Hamburg, or Bremen, or Bremerhaven. Any of these would help.

'Poor old Osnabrück got a pasting as well last night, I hear,' the driver shouted.

That was indiscreet, defeatist talk. Zorn took care. 'Really?' he said. 'I didn't know.'

So they travelled, eating up the miles, crossing flat country where farmers carried on their dismal round. They passed through villages and small towns where the war might never have been heard of, until they came to the outskirts of a city.

Zorn could see the distant haze and the chimneys of factories. The driver pulled up at the verge.

'Things are bad in the middle of town,' he said. 'Which way are you heading?'

Zorn decided he was quite safe with this man. 'Welckmar,' he answered.

'Right. I'll drop you here. That way heads east. I'm off north.'

So Bremerhaven would probably be his destination. 'Thank you, it's very obliging of you.'

'Please. I've enjoyed your company. The machine rides better too. Your parents will be pleased to see you. Glad to help a fellow-worker. Best of luck.'

And he too was gone, leaving Zorn once again to his own devices on the eastern edge of what he presumed was Hamburg. He was starving and dreamt of the midday swill at the compound. Even that could be missed! Traffic was very thin on this route, mostly military. Each time an army vehicle passed, he made a show of doing something. 'Act natural . . .' By nightfall, he was still there, and knew it was time to move from the spot. Gossiping motorcyclists did not turn up twice in a day.

He walked on, and on, past the endless dank, flat fields of the north. After painfully masticating two hardtack biscuits, he lay down behind a haystack. 'Act natural' was all very well, but how did you 'act natural' in the open at night on the outskirts of a strange city?

As he dropped off to sleep, he saw the searchlights stabbing the sky over the city. Then came the rumble of bombs and anti-aircraft fire.

He woke shivering. He had never felt so cold. Even in the depths of winter, with no stove in the shed, the foetid warmth of so many bodies built up sufficiently to provide comfort of a sort under the one issue blanket. When he stood, the blood drained from his head, a horrible blankness and nausea assailed him, and he clung to the stack to ward off fainting.

His instinct told him not to risk another lift. The motor-cyclist had been sheer luck. What if he had been an SS man?

112

So he plodded on, yet remembering Philo's dictum – 'act natural' – when he encountered humanity. Public transport was denied him, even had he saved enough Marks, for he was devoid of papers. Outside the camp, he did not exist officially.

Day after day, he lumbered on. Somehow he crossed Lüneburg Heath, most favoured stamping ground of the tank squadrons, and was not picked up. He could smell the Baltic, and as he inched nearer, the wilier he became. He learned to be invisible, for he knew that a shabbily dressed man without luggage, vaguely waiting for lifts at the roadside, would arouse not only curiosity, but suspicion and even downright hostility. People did break out of detention: prisoners-of-war, various detainees, criminals, even the *Unerwünscht*.

He negotiated the woods. On either side of the road, set back sometimes by a field's length, the trees stood silently, immured by their density from anything the cold nor'-westers could do in winter. There was a dense blackness under the canopy of greenery, mostly conifers, that invited a man so dangerously exposed. He used the forests only in pursuit of his goal, however. He would not exploit forest resources like Philo. He was too anxious to get on.

He learned the value of haystacks. They not only provided warmth and comfort during the hours of darkness, but errant fowls often laid their eggs there. He could only stomach their raw mucus by mixing the eggs with crumbs of hardtack held in his cheek.

By the time he staggered to Welckmar, he was at the end of his tether. He was dragging his feet and holding off bouts of fainting. He was intent first on reaching the harbour. What had Stentewik said about getting his mother to Sweden . . .?

He must see *Donner*.

IV

'Alone, alone, all, all alone,
Alone on a wide, wide sea . . .'

S. T. Coleridge

The harbour had hardly changed. It had been almost two years since Zorn had last seen it. *Donner* was still riding at her moorings, but looking distinctly the worse for wear. A film of algae was creeping up the topsides from the water-line, a sign that below she would bear a foul growth of barnacles. She had not been out of the water all winter for defouling and painting. Normally, his father would not have countenanced such neglect, for he was as meticulous over *Donner*'s structure and finish as he was about personal hygiene. But of her general soundness Dieter had no doubt, for he saw that *Donner* still rode the water well.

He had been intent on this visit, as far as he could now be intent on anything. In his present state, he was unable to think properly. He could not remember when the last food had passed his lips, and he was conscious of just hanging on. But he was determined first to see *Donner*. He had plans concerning *Donner*, but at this stage could not remember quite what plans.

He must then see his father, out of duty – and filial love – or was it, rather, filial piety? He would never know how he stood with his father. Perhaps it was even fear.

That done, questions answered, problems (if possible) solved, he would seek out Nelli. Then *Donner* might just figure in some plan he thought he had. For thinking was difficult. What about his mother? Perhaps he could help there. There were things he understood now.

He shuffled along like an old man, weaker than he had ever been. He could not remember how he had arrived in Welckmar beyond the night before, when he had slept under the lee of a barn on the outskirts, unable to muster the strength to walk the last mile or so.

He suffered a horrible confusion of mind. Welckmar seemed different, eerie, quiet, as though it too was waiting and enduring. There had always been an urgency, a busyness in the streets, imports and exports, production, loading and unloading. Now there was hardly any traffic. He had assumed Welckmar would help, would connive at his concealment and might indicate some sort of future, some point of departure. But time had stopped and he felt exposed.

He was so weak, it took him an hour to cross the town to the east side where their house stood. He noticed people, and every so often he simply stood and rested. But people did not seem to notice him. They too had reached that state of lassitude he knew so well. The war was at a stalemate and rations were low on the home front. Zorn was very weak, but no more so than a soldier invalided from the Eastern Front, from Stalingrad or Moscow perhaps, where casualties were now an acknowledged fact. He was far from alone in his weakness. He saw more than one man on crutches. At such shops as were open, queues waited patiently.

He now had one more goal, to reach home. But he was finding it more and more difficult to put one foot in front of the other. He had only fifty yards to go. He leaned against a wall to muster strength to face his father in his present lean state, to find the answer at last to so many questions. Then the cold sweat once again swept over his brow and he slid down in a faint.

When his eyes opened, a woman was bending over him.

115

Over her shoulder he saw a policeman. As consciousness came and went, he realized the worst, that Vogel or his minions had known all along he would arrive at Welckmar. The thought sickened him. The tentacles of the State penetrated the remotest recesses, extricating its victims from any nook or corner. There was no hope, nowhere to hide, no escape.

The policeman dismissed the woman and half-lifted Zorn into the back of a van. It was all a pale copy of something that had happened before. Zorn was a package to be delivered. He had been expected albeit for several days and without a specific date – but expected. Now, in accordance with orders, he was to be delivered. At the railway station, the policeman even handed him out of the rear of the van and coaxed his steps towards a room where he was handed over to two plain-clothes men. Zorn looked closely. They could be the same, they too had been expecting him. They bore the same faceless aspect. They even got him a meal from the buffet, a bowl of thin stew with a dumpling in it and a hunk of black bread. Things seemed almost humane after living on his wits for days on end. Zorn wolfed the food. He was then given a mug of ersatz coffee.

They all three were simply waiting for a train, and when it finally chugged in, the two men took an arm each and walked him into a reserved compartment. It had all happened before. The men had their flask of coffee, which they shared after three hours' travelling, but not with him. Seven hours later still, the men ordered him to get ready. For what? The train pulled in and Zorn recognized the station.

Unlike the first time, both men travelled with him in the van. After his meal at Welckmar station, it occurred to Zorn that this system of recapture was well organized – it *was* a system. However long he took and whenever he turned up they were ready, organized, efficient. A system like that was more important than the individual. It produced nothing, except a recaptured prisoner, and it involved a chain of personnel to achieve this meagre result. Even if systems are wasteful in manpower, they have their own momentum, appetite, objectives, so must be kept going.

Zorn, beneath his dazed condition, was thankful these men were less brutal than his first guards. Had German manpower been drained to such an extent that they had to recruit these grey elderly men for the job of rounding up the *Unerwünscht*?

Zorn, who at least produced plywood panels for the Luftwaffe, reflected that he, a recaptured worker, kept this particular system going. He was its raw material. Had that woman been part of it, or was she purely incidental? Was she a neighbour, warned to tip off the police? Zorn could not recall her face.

As the van trundled over the cobbled road, Zorn was sure he was bound for the same destination. If so, this time Vogel, not Quaeck, was in charge. He hoped neither Greichhardt nor Philo would be there. And another difference – he would not have to climb over bodies on the floor when he arrived at the barracks. They had their bunks now, always assuming they were delivering him to the same camp.

When the van drew to a halt and the door opened for him to climb down, he knew, even in the blackout dark, that it was the same shed.

Again, the two men handed him over to security, who once again unlocked the door and pushed him in – another package delivered. But immediately, he felt a difference. He was stumbling and groping his way among bodies sprawled on the floor. The smell was overpowering, foetid. He staggered towards his own bunk. It was occupied. He had no strength to argue. He subsided to the floor, sobbed weakly and miserably to sleep.

Next morning, had it not been for the pandemonium among the new bodies on the floor, it would have been the same as ever. In the growing daylight, Zorn recognized his former comrades getting stiffly down from their bunks and being mustered in the yard. All instinct told him he must not be identified with the newcomers, who were ordered to remain on the floor of the shed until the workers were

117

marched out to the factory. Extra guards milled about in the confusion of bodies. But Zorn, weak with starvation, was determined not to be left behind. One of the old inmates, recognizing him, pushed a hardtack biscuit into his fist. Zorn bit at it hungrily as they staggered out. The guards at the door checked that none of the new arrivals was trying to join them. The guards knew their birds and sent one or two back with a show of rifle butts. Zorn was relieved to pass muster. Was he not to be singled out and punished? A guard recognized him.

'Ah, *Arbeiter* Zorn, yes? You're for the chopper, boy. You report to Sergeant Vogel at the factory the minute you get there. Understand?'

He trailed along with the others in a state of dull despair, beyond resistance, for was he not marching, or rather shuffling, to the factory? He noticed too the total indifference of his comrades. No particular welcome, no apparent curiosity about the outside world. But then, had Philo not preached about the anti-social effects of would-be and successful escapers, how the punishment had to be shared by his fellow-prisoners after a break-out?

'I'm to report to Sergeant Vogel,' he told a guard.

'Oh, yes. He's expecting you.' Said with a hint of venom, for an escape was a reproach to the guards, a denial of their vocation.

The guard pushed him inside the door of Vogel's office. Sergeant Vogel sat magisterially at his table, which he treated as a desk, with its three filing trays – one IN, one OUT, one TOO HARD. He scribbled as though Zorn were not present. Zorn stood and waited. For five minutes, Vogel wrote with painful slowness, while Zorn waited for the wrath to come. Vogel signed the document in hand, raised his mean eyes, stood up laboriously, pushed back his chair, sauntered slowly round the table to face Zorn. He struck hard with his fist at Zorn's mouth. Zorn flinched, so that the blow was partially parried. His lips burst as they cracked against his teeth. But he felt with his tongue to find his teeth intact while Vogel stood back, content with the show of blood. He returned round his table, riffled through some file till he found what he wanted.

'So you got to Welckmar, Zorn,' he murmured. 'A bit late for our convenience. What kept you?' Zorn had expected a shouting match. 'No bombing, eh?' Vogel droned on. Was Zorn expected to answer? 'Well, *was* there?' Vogel asked again, raising his voice menacingly.

'Not that I saw, Sergeant.'

'I see, I see . . .' Then, in a patronizing tone of Vogel the production manager rather than the martinet: 'We all missed you, Worker Zorn. I put that idiot Schnehohr on your machine. He's quick – quicker than you, Zorn. But the bloody state of them – they were diabolical. They've rejected half his production, damn it. We're glad to have you back, Zorn!'

He came round the table again, could not resist a half-playful, half-vicious dig in the ribs as he looked Zorn in the eye. 'Don't try it again, Zorn. Not worth it, is it?' Another hard prod, just short of a punch. 'I'll have your guts for garters if you do. See?'

Then once again, full circle, he returned round his table to an official position, as he saw it. 'Now, what do we do with you, Zorn?'

Zorn almost prayed for corporal punishment, anything short of garrotting. He would be willing to accept anything. But not further incarceration . . . Let it be a whipping, since he must be punished, let it be a punch, so long as they did not damage his face, let it be anything that would be over and done with in the day, today. Let the blood flow, but let not the brain be paralysed under the constraint of four near walls. But it was neither. Sergeant Vogel's need, it seemed, was greater than Zorn's.

'Are you fit to go back on the machine, Zorn? Can you start today?' Vogel was actually pleading. 'Say, a gentle start, today. I'll arrange a bit extra for you at the canteen. You look a bit starved. Didn't they feed you outside? Not worth it, you see. Is it? We'll build you up, Zorn, get you back to

119

where you were, eh? Get the panels back up to standard. You look to me as if you've learnt your lesson. It was that bloody gypsy, wasn't it? We're best off without him, that sort always brings trouble. Anyway, you won't try again. Not worth the trouble . . .'

And coming round the table yet again, he even took Zorn by the shoulder, turned him, and walked him out of his office towards the machine, where Schnehohr was battling away with the panels.

'All right, Schnehohr, back to the fucking floor where you belong!' The vicious flick of the jackboot at Schnehohr's knee was expected routine. Schnehohr gratefully limped towards his old friend Stern and was only too glad to take up his floorbrush again.

'Right, Zorn. Break yourself in gently. No rejects. Take your time to begin with, and step it up as you go. We're all for the high jump if there's any more rejects. They're raving mad about it up at HQ, I can tell you. So mind how you go!'

And that was it. Vogel's need was too great, so the whip was withheld, an extra hunk of bread was prescribed, while his own comrades glowered at Zorn. They had taken the heat as soon as Philo and he had broken out. Now that he was back, he was accorded a welcome by Vogel, while poor Schnehohr was kicked back to the floor. Zorn's escape had confined them to barracks for two weeks, and his welcome by Vogel rendered him *persona non grata* among his peers in forced labour.

Vogel stood over him, cajoling, wheedling, threatening, blackmailing – anything to relieve this particular bottleneck in quantity and quality – even flicking a vernacular cane of office he had recently taken up, quite irregularly and against all military practice, since he did not hold a commission. He monitored Zorn's production, even secured his extra bread from the obstreperous cook, whose great sagging belly under his filthy apron would account for quite a proportion of the workers' rations.

Zorn was cornered as no corporal punishment or additional

120

restriction could have done. He ate, he worked, he patronized *Niagara* (by tacit agreement he was forbidden the 'long drop'), and he endured the cold shoulder of his fellow-workers. Furthermore, he was none the wiser about his mother's fate, for which he felt responsible, since he was certain it was his medical that had set the bureaucratic wheels in motion.

It was agreed, ordained and implemented, no appeal was allowed. There was no Greichhardt to listen or rule over their heads, no Philo whose brief friendship had been deep enough to hear him out and help him.

The bitterest pill to swallow was not succeeding in seeing Nelli. If only he had thought, put her first on the list, let her help him think things out. Nelli was resourceful. She might have acted as courier to his father while he himself kept under cover. Nelli would have thought of something. Yet his first duty had been to see his father, to find out what had befallen his mother. Perhaps his father would have refused to see Nelli . . . It was too late now. But the thought of Nelli, whom he had kept in reserve till last for some vague plan he had already forgotten, was the hardest of all to bear.

True to Philo's prophecy, the departure of Greichhardt, and now his own, had left a tank of minnows squabbling among themselves, without a natural leader or spokesman, united only in one thing, that Zorn was to be left out in the cold.

Listening to them, he learned that the new intake who had sprawled over the floor on the night of his return had been merely in transit for a camp further east. The prisoners speculated miserably over their probable destination, and Zorn picked up the infection of worry and despair. But he could only go on working, eat his extra food (for his system craved for every scrap he was given), try to lay aside his sense of guilt and endure the ostracism of his colleagues. At least he had his bunk again, his only refuge in a cold world.

At work, *Unterscharführer* Vogel stood over him, as always monitoring the relief of the bottleneck in plywood production. Dornier bombers could once again reach for the sky, he seemed to say as he playfully poked Zorn in the ribs and promised a permanent extra ration if this went on.

The winter of 1944/5 was well through. Spring was on the way. Day followed day and no opportunity presented itself for slowing production or lowering quality. Until one day Vogel came up to him. 'You've got used to this machine, Zorn,' he said casually. 'Suppose I asked you to wreck it – sabotage it, you know . . .'

Zorn could not believe his ears. Had Vogel read his thoughts?

'Think it over, Zorn. I might ask you to do just that one day.' And sauntered off importantly.

Back at the barracks, Zorn listened to the talk and began to understand Vogel's query. Apparently, the Allies had established a Second Front and were making such progress that there was constant German movement backward. How near the Americans were (the British and French were never mentioned, having been defeated in 1940) nobody knew. One rumour had it that they had breached the Rhine defences, though that was hard to believe. Some prisoners were worried that their status as forced labourers might not be understood by the Americans when they arrived.

Vogel was restless, jumping from one guard to another and oddly loath to touch the prisoners. He had dispensed with his cane, as though casting out temptation. He was constantly in and out of his office, where the telephone was more importunate than usual.

Obersturmbannführer Wechter, the co-ordinating officer with other camps, rushed in one day and was closeted for an hour with Vogel in the office, leaving only two in charge. Work audibly slackened as the two guards muttered to one another. The urgency and foreboding of Vogel's comings and goings infected the workers, but there was no firm news to explain the change of atmosphere.

That night the town suffered its worst bombing. The barracks, however, were untouched, though nobody slept.

Still, they were mustered and marched to the factory in the morning. Breakfast at the canteen was sparser than ever, and the mood that overlaid every action now was heralded by the ultimate doom that threatened the collapse of the sewage system.

The cloacal deficiency literally undermined everything. It was not the end, but it marked the end, and the prisoners were quick to catch on. The problem for everyone, whatever your status, was where you stood when you were finally caught with your pants down. Some prisoners claimed they could hear the guns. Zorn strained his ears, but heard nothing. Above all, if you were caught, liberated, rescheduled, redesignated, filed, dispatched and resettled by whatever means, let it not be the Russians, all agreed. The Americans, even the British – anyone would do, so long as it was not those barbarians from the hated East. Both prisoners and guards, without communication, conveyed this in an atmosphere of exultant dread as the system gradually fouled up.

The day after the raid, *Niagara* ceased to function altogether. Not one, or two, or a dozen pulls on the chain had any effect, beyond a dry throaty cough. Old insomniac Stern would be the first to announce it to the factory floor. If the thin soup of late had left him with a sizeable jet to discharge, he knew that to sit and strain in a solid way would not only be useless, but would further drain what little strength he had left. So he directed his jet with one of the few satisfactions left to the senescent, pulled the chain once, twice, to no effect, and when he guiltily pulled a third and fourth time (what was the regular punishment for drying up *Niagara*?), he trembled and made to shuffle away as discreetly as possible. Guilt rather than possible retribution mortified his ever-doubting flesh. Ah! Unclean as they all were by now, polluted, beyond the Holy Law, all would be as nothing should *Niagara* now fail them. Uncleanness – the ultimate uncleanness! Stern shrank, but bent over his floorbrush and swept a few crumbs of collapsing production.

But at once his crime was uncovered, for he saw with

downcast eyes the unmistakable suitcase-clad feet of Kremft describing the straightest possible line towards *Niagara*. By the speed of Kremft's shuffle, Stern sensed the brotherly urgency of the suppressed incontinent.

Stern clutched at Kremft's sleeve. 'No good – *kaputt* . . .' he cried, his eyes glazed by the vision of uncleanness compounded. 'No good . . .' he hissed with added urgency as Kremft, in an agony of need, sought to detach himself. He was gone, already searching for buttons, as Stern continued to mutter: 'No good, *kaputt*, the toilet is *kaputt* . . .'

'Well, you forgot to pull it twice, that's all,' Kremft called back, and as Stern gave way weakly, no strength left to argue, Kremft was already inside, trousers down and sitting on the throne of civilization. While Stern watched fearfully from the floor, Kremft, apparently eased, rose and adjusted his trousers, pulled the chain twice, and thrice – four times and five – then howled down the floor: 'Ach! Stern! You've broken *Niagara*!' He emerged with his hands held away from him, as though to shed this ultimate uncleanness.

The guards were by now so nervous and irritated with the commands and countercommands from above, whether production or scorched earth, that this quarrel between prisoners brought two of them up quickly. Rifle butts flailed Stern and Kremft apart. Stern, weaker than ever, fell to the ground.

Sergeant Vogel rushed up. 'What's all this?'

'They've broken the damned toilet between them,' a guard answered, pointing towards *Niagara*.

'Right! That's it!' Vogel screamed hysterically. Between HQ and the prisoners, he had had enough. His Mauser came out of its holster in one frenetic movement. He aimed for Stern's face and the bullet splattered into the concrete floor. Frustrated, Vogel raised the Mauser and shot again, at Kremft's chest, so near he could not miss. Kremft doubled forward with a cough, then crumpled over the trembling Stern.

'You pig, you!' shouted Schnehohr, Kremft's friend, and

124

rushed towards the prone figure. 'You've no right, you've killed . . .' But again, the frenzied Vogel shot, this time straight at Schnehohr's head. Schnehohr collapsed over the other two on the floor. It had all taken only a few seconds from Kremft's cry of despair.

Guards and prisoners stood around in horror. Vogel's hand shook so badly that he had difficulty returning the Mauser to its holster. His face had gone a pasty grey. He marched down the room towards the refuge of his office, then turned and shouted: 'Outside with them, NOW! And bury them . . . anywhere . . . d'you hear? NOW!!' And fled into his office, banging the door behind him. Trembling violently, old Stern struggled from under the bodies of his two friends.

The prisoners had endured the curses, the insults and the blows in the name of production. But they had survived. It was all part of their condition, their status. Now, as they clung ineffectually to their machines, not knowing if they were meant to slow down or speed up, they fumed and wept inwardly over the callous murder of two of their comrades. Blows and curses were one thing, but this murder over the breakdown of a lavatory was altogether a new dimension of horror. Vogel was a killer, a vicious murderer, and they were helpless, forced as they were to live with his constant menace. Murder! A new uncleanness polluted the air. . . .

Vogel had new orders, then yet newer orders countermanding the first. For days now he had not touched one of his forty charges and seemed unusually subdued. Worst of all, he now clung closer to Zorn than ever, as though anxious to establish a relationship that transcended that of jailer and prisoner.

The prisoners had been paraded outside the factory, then allowed to wander around the compound. The guards watched every move, but beyond that nobody, neither guards nor prisoners, knew what to do, or what was coming next.

Zorn stood alone, gazing beyond the wire at the still-unfilled bomb crater, where Philo and he had crawled under the wire. He noticed the wire had been replaced and re-inforced.

Vogel, awaiting further orders and with his own system collapsing round him, might have been reading Zorn's thoughts as he sauntered up to the wire with the air of a convert and conspirator in a new cause.

'Looking to the future, Zorn?' he said, reasonably enough for Zorn to wish to strike him down with the nearest brick. 'We'd best stick together, Zorn, you and I. Anything could happen in the next few days. We may have to move.'

Zorn could say nothing to that. He would rather not have it from Vogel. If his own comrades would not speak to him, the last communication he wanted was with the infamous sergeant-in-command, a murderer. He turned his back to the wire, dared look Vogel in the eye, felt almost he might spit into it in this oddly liberating limbo of collapse and waiting for news and orders from on high. But Vogel was not one to be put off.

'You been left comfortable?' he asked.

'Comfortable?' Zorn queried warily, for Vogel was not yet to be provoked with interrogative sarcasm. Perpetually, you had to watch every word, every expression on your face, so as not to provoke. The Mauser was still there in its holster.

'Your mum and dad – still alive?' Vogel persisted.

'Ah. I see. I don't know. You see, when . . .'

'Like as not, resettled as well, eh? And not having the advantages of youth, like . . .' Vogel went on, hardly needing a response, for he could be quite talkative and liked to speculate. How was one supposed to respond to such a question? But Vogel, on his day, could be left safely to rabbit on. 'Then everything would be settled on you, I suppose,' he added.

'"Then everything would be settled . . ."?' Zorn ran his tongue over his gold fillings. Was Vogel hedging his bets, keeping his cane in the office on the chance that one day the wire might come down and Zorn be worth cultivating?

'You the eldest son?' the little man probed yet further.

'Oh – yes, yes. The only son. Yes.'

126

'Ah well, now. See what I mean?' Vogel continued, pluck-ing at the wire with his left hand, as though this were his God-appointed instrument of expression. 'You won't forget your old friend, Vogel, then? When the time comes, eh? I've fed you, haven't I, when I had the right to skin you alive? So don't forget, when the time comes. We're all in the same boat. The *Bruderschaft* of the barbed-wire, you might say . . .' And he deliberately pricked his finger lightly, drawing the tiniest drop of blood, then made to touch Zorn's arm with it – or, for a moment, that was what Zorn thought he was going to do.

Zorn found himself watching Vogel's right hand, like a rabbit a stoat. How nervous the sergeant was. The hand that had been playfully, or provocatively, pricked on the barbed-wire was shaking. The next move might be anything. Does a murderer carry the mark of Cain throughout life? If so, is the burden any heavier if it happens again? Were these Vogel's first murders?

Then, just as jumpily, Vogel darted off to his office, to wait at the end of the telephone for the latest instructions. For even the prisoners could feel that things were on the move, though in what direction became a matter of heated debate. New orders arrived. *Obersturmbannführer* Wechter himself arrived and rushed into Vogel's office. Guards and prisoners were suddenly joined in a conspiracy of fear – who would do what, commit what atrocity, tell what lies, or recall what kindness (if any)?

The prisoners were again mustered on the factory floor. Vogel came over to Zorn: 'Right, *Arbeiter* Zorn,' he shouted for all to hear. 'You remember about your machine? The best way to bust it, sabotage it? You didn't answer. But don't tell me you don't know the answer. So now just get on with it. Show the rest how to do it!'

Zorn was nonplussed. Sabotage? He did not move. There was no point in getting shot at this stage.

'Well, come on!' Vogel yelled hysterically. 'Get a bloody move on! Smash it up. You're finished with it. You're leaving.

This plant's done its bit. We're moving on, d'you hear? So smash the bloody thing. Make a right good job of it, and the sooner the better, then we can move on to new pastures.'

But Zorn stood his ground. Vogel made to strike, but forbore at the last moment. The eyes of the prisoners were riveted to the scene which, like *Niagara*, marked a change of some sort, cataclysmic in some way they dared not face yet.

'Right, Zorn, come on. I'll give you a hand. Come on, smash it up!' He took Zorn forcibly by the arm, bent over the machine. There was no electricity, so no chance of shearing a spindle by shoving grit in. 'Come on. What first?' Vogel screamed, beside himself with frustration.

Zorn straightened up, looked Vogel boldly in the eye on equal terms and said:

'If you have no explosives, then a sledge-hammer might do it. These things are made of cast-iron, you know – or didn't you realize?'

'All right.' Vogel turned to two guards standing nearby: 'Go and get some sledge-hammers,' he shouted frantically to guards and prisoners alike, 'and the rest of you, smash up everything you can lay your hands on. Do anything you can think of, but not one of these machines is to be left in working order. So get on with it. Understand?'

But neither guards nor prisoners understood, not knowing how to take the outburst. It was such a complete reversal after constant harassment over production. Then the two guards returned with four sledge-hammers.

'Cast-iron you say, Zorn?' Vogel screamed. 'Right. Smash it with this.' And he handed Zorn a hammer.

There was no choice – why should there be? It was not Zorn's machine. He took up the hammer and set about the weakest section of the cast-iron frame, the legs. He was surprised at the ease with which the iron cracked, and the machine table soon collapsed over the crumpled legs.

'Splendid!' Vogel cried, as though he was enjoying this Valhalla of the machine. He distributed the other three

128

hammers to the prisoners. 'Now, set about it like Zorn here, and when you're tired, hand the hammer to somebody else. Don't leave a thing in working order . . .'

A storm of destruction followed as the prisoners set about the hated machines with a will. After an hour, the floor was a mess of cracked and collapsed metal. When the last machine had been laid low, there was an eerie silence. After such a scene, what might follow? Vogel rushed in and out of his office.

'Why didn't he just burn the place down?' Zorn heard one prisoner mutter.

Vogel called four prisoners into his office, filled their arms with boxes and files, and ordered them to burn them outside. That done, he got his guards together into the office.

Then out they came after ten minutes to muster the workers (as they were now scrupulously delineated by all guards). They were filed into the canteen, issued with half a loaf each (such scruples the 'workers' could not credit) and walked, rather than marched, back to the barracks, though not without a certain urgency. The guards instructed them to gather their belongings, to be ready for a train journey in half an hour.

The demolition job had healed the rift between Zorn and his comrades. On the train, a group of Poles surrounded him. He could have done without it, for he was concerned more about Stern at this moment. The Poles had got it wrong. As they saw it, the war was nearly over; they were on their way home to defend their country against the Russians, and Zorn was a good fellow, because he had shown them all, including Vogel, how best to demolish the machinery of their bondage. Those sledge-hammers had done something for the Poles – they were men again!

Zorn longed to interrupt their fun. The smashing of the machines and this train journey, albeit in cattle-trucks, had released the most unlikely laughter in the Poles. But Zorn was aware of Stern, fretting away in the corner of the wagon.

For Stern, a cattle-truck journey was no laughing matter. Zorn wished the Poles would shut up, but they kept roistering him in broken German which he barely understood.

At a halt, they were allowed out for some reason that appeared to confuse the guards. They came along the track, unlocking doors and shouting contrary orders: 'Out, out!' and 'Stay where you are!' The prisoners simply charged. It was a chance to ease themselves. They jumped down into the daylight and freedom, wandered in the woods, but always under the watchful eyes of the guards, still armed and anything but happy with the general air of release in the prisoners since the demolition of the machines.

Zorn, remembering Philo's stealth, plunged almost at once into a rough area of gorse, and lay doggo in an agony of small pin-pricks. When the prisoners were herded on to the wagons again and the train pulled away, Zorn knew he was free. Nothing is so complete as that silence left by a departing train out in the country. From being cabined and confined, Zorn stood up out of the gorse and suddenly possessed the whole round earth again. It had been so easy, just as Philo had told him – watch for your chance, then grab it. He wondered if he was alone. For one thing, there would be no guards. He was free and uncluttered to start his journey north and east again, in the same direction as the line.

He set off into the woods first, away from the line. He had one fear – he had no food. Everything he possessed, and that was little enough, was on the train. He had been through all that before, the light-headedness, the weakness, the black-outs. A fighter plane rent the air as it roared barely above the tree-tops for a second or two before it passed out of hearing.

He found the going quite easy between the trees. It was like walking in some mine of semi-darkness, with a carpet of conifer needles underfoot. Those needles, though comfortable to his feet, denoted a certain lifelessness. Nothing lived with those needles. They lived only unto themselves, allowing no other life, bestowing life only on their parent tree above. Hunger gripped him, inevitably. He began to hate the needle floor and quickened his step, intent on reaching a clearing where he could think – or even an end to the forest, where a farm might offer some hope of food.

After half an hour, and by now very hungry after the heightened activity of a sharp walk, he saw light through the tree boles and knew it was more than a clearing.

He sat with his back against a tree and tried to think out what course of action to take. If he came to a farm, should he knock at the door and trust to their mercy? Or should he, like Philo, trust nobody and go in for plain thieving? He was so hungry, he felt no scruples about the latter. He needed to get to Welckmar, that was all, and urgently too, for if the rumours were anything near true, the Russians would be on the warpath in the east, and nobody knew what to hope or fear from that. Mostly it was fear, a fear among the *Unerwünscht* almost as great as of the Reich.

He looked up through the tree-tops. How blue the sky was, April at its best, with not a cloud on the horizon. Only an ascending lark broke the silence. As he rose to reconnoitre the open ground ahead, he heard another noise, but the rustle of his own movements confused him. He stood stock still, listened carefully – then ran.

'My God!' he wailed. 'Will it never . . .' It was a dog, loping straight at him out of the trees, a loathsome creature with tongue lolling as it scented the ground, coming straight towards its prey.

Quietly does it, he thought soberly while panic gripped him. He turned to walk slowly rather than run, in an attempt not to provoke the beast. But it caught up with him as he broke inevitably into a run. It had him by the ankle, and he fell. Zorn struggled, but the dog only held more tightly. It did not seem particularly vicious, more simply persistent. When Zorn relaxed, so did the dog, but if he tried to shake it off, it merely tightened the grip.

Two guards appeared, with Vogel out of breath behind them. Roughly, the guards manhandled the dog away; while one put it back on the choke-collar, the other dragged Zorn

131

to his feet. Vogel intervened, brushed aside the guard, and took Zorn's arm. Zorn watched him put the revolver back in its holster.

'Come on, Zorn,' he said quietly. 'That was foolish. Lucky for you you didn't get far. We need you, so come on, and don't try any more silly games . . .'

Was he never to be free of Vogel and his shadow? Hate welled up in Zorn as the sergeant put a hand on his shoulder and directed him back towards the track.

Vogel's too demonstrative benevolence had to be borne. There seemed no particular hurry. If anything, prisoner and guards, not to mention the hound, might be seen as enjoying the exercise. The train was surprisingly near. It had not gone far. Zorn guessed he must have travelled in a circle. He was pushed back into the truck and locked in. The Poles welcomed him warmly. They told him the engine was damaged and the footplate crew were repairing it. Hence the delay which had prompted Vogel to call a muster. Otherwise, Zorn might not have been missed.

They were not the only ones locked up on this cursed train. The Poles answered Zorn's question about the hound. Where did Vogel get it, he wanted to know. Vogel, they replied, had borrowed a guard-dog from another, more professional party further up the train. And what was wrong with the engine? Zorn demanded all the answers. But here the Poles began to argue among themselves – was it good, or bad, that the engine was damaged? Both. Good, because anything that damaged the Reich was welcome – and bad, because it meant more delay before they could reach their beloved fatherland and defend it against the Russians. Anyway, the Germans were hardly the enemy now – that fighter plane, a Mustang, was the mark of it. It had seen the smoke plume of their engine and strafed it without a shot in the air against it. The Germans were *kaputt*, the Poles declared, delighted at the punishment the Reich was now taking, yet impatient at its inability to deliver them back to Poland. They speculated, volubly and incomprehensibly, while Zorn recalled the air of

132

freedom in the woods. Most of all he had been free of Vogel's presence.

After an hour, the train shattered the general silence with a burst of steam and shuddered into motion. It was very slow, but it kept up a remorseless progress towards some unknown destination, and even the Poles began to have doubts. Their mood changed from the exultation of the machine-smashing to a dull despair.

Still the train battled on, steam escaping and hissing along the track. Everybody hoped the plume would not attract further Allied attention, in case another strafing should see them totally annihilated. Then the engine drew to a halt with a dramatic burst of steam and a screech of brakes. Guards came along the tracks, unlocking the doors.

As the prisoners jumped down, they saw in the moonlight that this was no friendly neutral location of trees and fields that welcomed them, but barbed-wire again. They felt cheated. The journey, the rumours, the changing attitude of their guards had all promised so much, and here they were, still behind the wire. They were in a huge compound with its own rail sidings.

But the overriding impression on Zorn was that if the breakdown of *Niagara* had been an augury, then this place marked the final cloacal collapse of the Third Reich. The smell was nauseating, overpowering. There was absolute chaos.

Vogel was screaming more at guards than at prisoners, who were now almost irrelevant. It transpired that a few guards had deserted. With his beloved papers in his hands, his orders, Vogel rushed about among guards and prisoners alike. Was this the *Bruderschaft* of the barbed-wire? Were all men, suddenly, equal again? Vogel tried desperately to explain to anyone who would listen that they were to report to *Obersturmbannführer* Doenerbisch or his office, but apparently had no idea how to achieve this.

The Poles again speculated. It hardly seemed the right thing to disturb a lieutenant-colonel at this time of night, they thought. But Vogel was mad anyway, and they did not hesitate to let him hear it.

The dysenteric fog and the chaos were all-pervading. Whatever this camp was, its dismal mark was its appalling foetid smell and its sheer confusion. Prisoners could only look up forlornly at the high fence. It was a good moment to walk away. But where to with barbed-wire all round?

Then the prisoners were herded rather than marched, with Vogel still fussing over his papers. The camp, whatever it was, appeared endless, with rows of huts either side of the road they were shuffling along. Vogel had linked up with a local guard, and for a moment there seemed almost a logic to his movements as he led the straggle to a hut in its own compound. Still, there were doubts and hesitations. After hope, a despair settled on the prisoners. The smell was enough to depress even the most sanguine. They began to wander off among the huts, having lost all confidence in the guards. But the guards scurried after them, and in the mutual irritation there was a little too much rifle-butt play. Even Vogel had to intervene.

Then, in a frenzy of irritation and frustration, Vogel, not having found his *Obersturmbannführer* or his office, or his minions, had hold of a local guard by the collar and extracted a promise of some sort. They were led to an empty hut in the long row, recently evacuated. It was theirs for the night. In the morning, Sergeant Vogel could report to the *Obersturmbannführer*'s office. The prisoners filed in reluctantly, while outside Vogel continued to harangue the guards about his own quarters for the night.

The prisoners were mad with hunger – but this hut was too revolting. Some gagged as they entered. The stench was unbearable. Rows of benches, hardly bunks, on either side and down the centre offered plenty of room. There were only a hundred of them, including the Poles, and the hut had once held two hundred or more. Overused straw was strewn everywhere, some discarded filthy rags, and yes – everything was practically moving towards them – yes, lice. To a man, they regretted their old camp. The guards withdrew hastily and left them to it. When the prisons and the cloacae collapse, that is the end of civilization.

Some managed to doze off, after clearing the straw off the benches. Zorn was among them, dozing, waking, aware that daylight would bring anything but the joy of liberation.

As day dawned early in a cloudless sky, most of them were awake and restless. Automatically, they waited and waited for the sound of the door being unlocked and for the morning muster. Would there be new work here? A more rigorous regime? As the light filled the sky and yet another day of this brilliant spring began, the mutter of speculation increased.

Zorn, unable to sleep, got down from his filthy plank-bed and went to the door. He tried the latch. It turned. Light flooded over the dirt-ridden floor. They were not locked in. His fellow-prisoners rushed to join him.

'We're free!' Zorn shouted. 'Free! They've gone and left. The Americans will be coming . . . That's what it is. We've lost the war!'

Still afraid to step out of the door, they talked excitedly.

'How d'you know?' one sceptic asked him.

'The guards,' Zorn replied. 'They've gone. No locks on the door.'

And he dared to step outside, to prepare to welcome the Americans. The sight that assailed him at once was like the descent of a bad dream to an appalling nightmare. Already in the crisp light of morning, hundreds of spectral figures were shuffling along the road between the huts. Skeletal and hollow-eyed, they were clad in striped jackets and baggy trousers, denoting a depth of *unerwünscht* that Zorn could never have imagined. Only a few wore anything resembling shoes, and their heads were shorn to a man – or was that small shrunken figure a woman?

Zorn retreated, guilty and horrified, back into his own crowd which stood at the door, equally bewildered.

The sight of those ghosts of humanity shuffling in front of their eyes was too much. There was even a collective sense

135

of guilt in the movement back to their hut, that however badly off they had believed themselves to be, they were in good condition compared with the spectres outside. Because they had had no recognized leader since Greichhardt and Philo, they now turned to Zorn.

But Zorn had withdrawn into a private world of his own. There were women among those ghosts, women with shorn heads, shorn to reduce infestation, women whose dugs and smaller frame might be the only indication of their gender – but WOMEN! Zorn's brows knitted and his eyes closed with the pain and horror of it, for yet again it was coming to him. Should he search among them? Was she here, perhaps unrecognizable but still alive? In an agony of despair and guilt, he ran over to one group. Yet as he neared them, he found them strangely unapproachable, as though they, but not he, had passed beyond a precious bourn.

They had plumbed depths beyond humanity. Their eyes stared out of the dark sockets of their bare, bony skulls.

But he must ask. He took a last few steps, plucked at the filthy sleeve of one he took for a woman. 'Please, is Frau Zorn here? Frau Etta Zorn from Welckmar?'

They only looked as blank as ever, clinging to the last remnants of life and for the present void of intelligence. They shuffled on compulsively towards some, as yet unknown, liberation to life – or to death.

From group to group, Zorn plied frantically, but where he did receive a reply, none knew a Frau Zorn. As he returned to his own comrades, he knew in his heart that here, or perhaps somewhere farther off, in 'the East', his mother might still be half-alive. If this had been her life, then there was nothing he might have done to help, for here the barbed-wire was higher and thicker, and the watch-towers more frequent. Nor indeed could he help now, for she might be anywhere – or perhaps already dead. This was a ghastliness beyond contemplation. It was important to get to his father at the earliest moment.

'The bastards!' a Pole shouted. 'The Prussian bastards have

flitted and left this lot without a bite to eat!' But it was, surely, more than that. 'This lot', thought Zorn, was a matter of policy and design rather than a mere accident of war.

'They must have been gone some time,' he said. 'No wonder Vogel couldn't find anybody to report to. So he's gone too, most likely.'

They gathered round him, anxious for any kind of direction now that their guards had left.

'We'd better know where we stand,' Zorn went on, assuming leadership. 'This camp shows weeks and months of neglect. If those poor wretches are the walking, God knows what they've left back in the huts! There's no food, that's all too obvious. And judging by their present condition, my guess is they've been without for weeks.'

The situation was so ominous that every man was listening, waiting for a lead.

'So what *is* this?' asked Zorn. 'A prison of some sort? Are they criminals or what? They're in prison clothes.'

'I know what this is,' Stern mumbled in the silence. 'This is no labour camp. This is a concentration camp. Now you know, now you can see for yourself. Nobody would believe, would they?' From whimpering in his characteristic way, old Stern began to weep, his body swaying back and forth, in a litany of muttered prayer for the dead and dying – the *Kadish*: *Yitgadal ve-Yitkadash Shme Rabba* . . .

For there was no doubt in any of their minds that the figures outside were the doubtful survivors of a camp regime that, at best, had abandoned them to a slow death, cynically leaving them to the encroaching enemy to rehabilitate where it was not too late. But Zorn and his companions knew from that one glance outside that it must be too late for too many. What else had the decomposing regime been guilty of, apart from neglect? Remembering his mother, Zorn did not dare pursue the speculation any further.

'Unless we move, we'll join them,' was all he could say. Then, looking at Stern swaying in the corner, he added: 'There's nothing we can do to help here, and there's no point in adding to their numbers. While we've got some strength, we'd best help ourselves.'

There was a general move outside. Then they saw why the half-moribund skeletons were moving with such agitation. Two tanks had burst through the gates and were cautiously rattling up the road. The slow pace and the great nodding gun suggested the same disbelief that Zorn's party had felt. This was a collision of the military and the dying. No cheers, no flowers for the victorious tank crew, but a mute gathering of the half-dead, the *Unerwünscht* of one society round the machinery of victory of another. Neither side was able to understand.

The tank crew stayed in their iron-clad vehicle, the spectres stood round it, neither able to communicate with the other. The tank came to a halt against the press of humanity.

Then the hatch-cover lifted and an officer popped his head out. He surveyed the scene before him – the pathetic figures crowding round the tank, then row after row of huts stretching indefinitely either side of the road. His nostrils twitched visibly with nausea at the all-pervading stench. He rose till he was waist-high out of the hatch.

'Anybody in charge here?' he called to the throng.

But it only provoked a suspiration of hoarse whispering from the crowd. He tried again in halting German:

'*Er verantwortlich sein für hier?*'

Zorn pushed forward, recognizing the attempt at German.

'Nobody in charge here,' he shouted back in his school English. 'The . . .' (he was lost for the word) 'they . . . go . . .' Zorn pointed vaguely towards the end of the camp.

'Who are you?' the officer asked him.

'I am Dieter Zorn, from Welckmar.'

But the officer dismissed this as irrelevant. He would not climb out farther. He was in enemy territory and seemed more intent on the huts.

'Who are these people?' he asked, pointing to the spectres below.

138

'The prisoners,' Zorn replied. 'All hungry, very hungry. No food – no food for many days.'

The officer glared at him, all suspicion.

'I can see that,' he said grimly. 'And you? Are you one of the guards here?'

Zorn was horrified. *That* was the word – 'guards'.

'No. We are all prisoners. All here . . .' Indicating his own small crowd in the large throng. 'All guards gone.' And again, he pointed northwards.

'My God!' was the only reply, and the officer disappeared inside the hatch again.

The crowd shuffled forward, began touching the warm steel of the tank. They could hear the officer shouting inside over his radio transmitter. And then there was silence. For a quarter of an hour nothing happened. Everybody waited, and whispered or wept in silence. Some collapsed and sat on the ground. Zorn saw more figures crawling from the huts, many of them filthy and utterly emaciated with the effects of dysentery. He banged his fist against the metal.

'We are all prisoners!' he cried in desperation. 'Help us!'

But there was no response. And Zorn too wept. Then he saw why the officer had waited. A column of vehicles rolled through the gates. Infantry dismounted, and the officer ordered them to fan out, break in and search the huts nearby, but above all find and deliver any German Army personnel.

The picture the troops brought back was even more dismal than the crowd round the tank. People were lying dead or dying on their bunks, the huts were running with lice, rats – and death. None of the soldiers had any stomach for it; one or two retched involuntarily.

The officer was by now down off his perch on the tank. He was satisfied militarily of the safety of their position, and could now examine in person the burden of Zorn's statement. He came over to Zorn.

'Who did you say you were?' the officer asked.

'Dieter Zorn, from Welckmar.'

'Why are you here? Are you a prisoner?' He seemed to note

again the contrast between Zorn's party and the pyjama-clad ghosts.

'We,' Zorn replied, indicating his own party, 'are from forced labour camp. We come here – yesterday. We also are prisoners.'

The officer held out the hand of the liberator. 'I'm Captain Buckminster,' he said. 'I'm glad we're here in time to save at least some of you.' Clearly, he was appalled. He walked through the crowd, cautiously edging his way towards the nearest hut. He could do no more than peer in briefly. 'My God . . .' he murmured – and was forced to turn away.

It was Zorn's one experience of what Stern called a 'real camp'. For three days, he watched the beginning of an operation to sort out the quick from the dead. There was quite as much work for the engineers with their bulldozers and quicklime as there was for the medical personnel, and the military was now merely a support. Civilization had retreated to its nadir. The tide would return with the engineers and the medics. Zorn saw the bulldozers ripping up the earth to make mass graves, then, as he reflected that his own mother might be one of the victims, he could bear no more. The bulldozers had reached the stage of pushing the corpses into a pit. Zorn turned away. He did not deserve to be alive. The British had fed him. He wandered towards the gate, knowing that to ask for permission from the British authorities would meet with a flat refusal. He was now just strong enough again to take off on his own.

Traffic of all sorts, but mainly medical and Red Cross, flowed freely in and out. Prisoners, British soldiers and nursing staff kept coming and going through the gates. When finally a film camera crew breezed in to photograph the horror of it all, Zorn walked out and took to the road again, north and east. The only traffic in that direction was military. Nobody took the slightest notice of him. There was just the grey, anxious, one-way flow of army traffic. Any German troops had simply disappeared, as though into the ground.

Zorn sensed the total collapse of his country. He was not sure whether he was glad or sorry, for the implications either way were too horrible to contemplate. Welckmar could just as well be a Russian target as anybody's, and that was too awful a prospect. So he walked by the side of the road, and on to the north and the east. He walked doggedly on for the whole day, then dropped wearily into the straw of a barn.

Next morning, with the weather still bright, he set out again. The heaviest of the military traffic had passed – now lighter vehicles sped along, in full control of the countryside. He had been walking for an hour when a small army truck pulled up beside him.

'Where're you going, mate?' the driver called out. 'Want a lift?'

It startled Zorn to be addressed thus, on equal terms.

'Please, I go to Welckmar – on the Baltic,' he retorted. He could not believe his luck.

'Jump in!' the driver said cheerily. 'We're all going somewhere in that direction.'

Like his former motorcyclist lift, the truck driver was bored, only too glad to have someone to talk to. He told his army life story to Zorn: Western Desert, Italy, Normandy – and now this drive across a dying Germany. He plied Zorn with cigarettes (which he refused) and with chocolate (which he devoured gratefully).

Judging by the villages they passed through, there might never have been a war. Life and work continued as normal. Cattle were being herded for milking, though nobody was out in the fields thinning the beet and turnips. That would have been too exposed. Some shops were shuttered, but people went about their business. As always, whatever might go on in the western and southern areas of Germany was irrelevant here in the north. They passed British Army posts, and nobody questioned the driver further when he declared that his passenger was a refugee concentration camp victim being returned to his home on the Baltic. From the tone of conversation, Zorn guessed that the Allies had reached the

141

Baltic. Like a good German, his chief concern now was how far the Russians had come along the coast from the east.

But still, they drove on. The driver chain-smoked, lighting one cigarette from another. He asked Zorn his life story, and offered bits of his own. He was Service Corps, he said, with the air of a man who knew all there was to know about life. He drove his truck full of supplies, and his load this time was powdered milk, penicillin, denim fatigue clothes and boots. Nothing was secret with this man, who kept his Sten gun loose between them on the seat, where Zorn could have picked it up had he felt like it. This carefree attitude raised Zorn's spirits more than anything. He had not seen such easy-going freedom and trust for years.

After two hours' drive, they rattled across a Bailey bridge over the Elbe, and another hour brought them into thicker concentrations of British troops. They were stopped at a check-point, where the driver was ordered to drop Zorn. Zorn climbed down. Once again, he could smell the Baltic. The driver was asking the whereabouts of Third Battalion. Three soldiers bent over a map spread over the bonnet of the truck.

'They're at Welckmar, here . . .' one of them declared, pointing to the Baltic location, then tracing a route for the driver's benefit.

'Welckmar?' The driver turned to Zorn, who stood aside, awaiting instructions. 'Isn't that where you want to be?'

'Please,' Zorn replied. 'My father is living there.'

'Might as well take the poor bugger the rest of the way,' said the Service Corps driver. 'He's had three years in one of them bleedin' camps.'

Nobody argued. But they were warned that the Russians were just over the way. Zorn was all eagerness to be off, anxious to get to Welckmar before a confrontation with the Russians. He jumped quickly into his seat again. He was not slow to note that the Russians, rather than the Germans, concerned the British.

142

'It's all over bar the shouting!' one soldier called over the noise of the engine as he beat the side of the truck as a signal to be off.

Welckmar swarmed with British troops. They were much more in evidence than the local citizenry.

'Here!' the driver muttered to Zorn as he dropped him on the outskirts. 'Take this. Your own rags are fallin' off your back . . .' He flung a denim suit and a pair of boots at Zorn. 'Hope you find your dad OK. Best o'British luck!' And was off, leaving Zorn to face Welckmar at last.

With his new clothes rolled tightly under his arm, he set off to walk the last stretch to his home. His heart pounded. The East was constantly in his mind as he allowed himself to think about his mother. She could never have survived what he had witnessed so recently. But first, he must see his father, to get the whole truth if possible. He steeled himself. He saw how the people had drawn the blinds or curtains, or closed shutters, in all the houses, hiding from the truth of defeat.

Then he arrived. The shutters were closed. He tried the front door. It was locked. He pulled the bell. No answer. And again. Still not a sound inside. He went round to the rear, where the French window gave on to the garden. Here too, the heavy curtains were drawn, and he could see nothing of the interior. He tried the door. It was locked. He knocked hard – once – twice – thrice. But not a thing stirred in the house.

Quickly, he went to the garage where the Adler was housed. The Adler was not there – probably commandeered, he thought. He felt for the loose brick in the wall. The spare key was still in its place.

When the world finally fell round your ears, you could not move. You lay on your back. You stared vacantly at the ceiling. There was no more to be done – except, perhaps, to die. The silence, the perceptible layer of dust on everything,

143

spoke of months of emptiness, stillness, lifelessness. There were no answers here.

Whatever animus or anxiety had driven Zorn at last to Welckmar finally dissolved in the sullen emptiness of the house. He could not lie on a bed, not even in his own room. It would be sacrilege, though violating which faith was difficult to know unless it were simply, in Paterfamilias's terms, *domus*, and that certainly figured in Zorn's mind as he crept into his own home for the first time in three years. He was not only thoroughly institutionalized, he had been brutalized, and he knew it. He was used to straw and all that lived in it. What lived in it you carried with you, desecrating all that was private and dear.

He crept in the half-light, afraid to pull back the curtains and let in the light and the truth, and as the fact, if not the whole truth, of the emptiness finally weighed down his spirit, he lay down in the hall, not ready to inhabit a room in his own house. He had not been prepared for this. At best, he might find his mother released from . . . from what, he did not, dared not, contemplate. At worst, his father alone and frightened perhaps. But to find not even Berthe, this utter desolation – this he had never imagined.

He lay on his back on the floor, his new denim clothes still held tightly by him. He had not for one minute released them from his grasp, for they were the badge, sign-manual, uniform of his liberation. Liberation from what he was not quite clear, apart from the ubiquitous Vogel – but liberation *to* what? He knew, from that unbroken membrane of dust, that his father had not been gone for the day, he had been gone for many months, and so had Berthe, who would never countenance dust.

With this emptiness he could not cope. He lay still, tried to empty himself of all thought, memory, will. He might not even wish to live, but that was a choice beyond him, for he was like an engine geared for survival. It had been switched off, but its fly-wheel still ran on, ready to take up again. He lay like this for fully an hour, then rose, still grasping his bundle of denim, and crept as furtively out of the house as he had entered. He locked carefully, replaced the key in the garage, and walked into town. He could not be sure if there was a curfew, but was aware of figures moving westwards out of town. They could be none other than German, the new refugees.

British troops occupied intersections and strategic build-ings, he noted. Although there was no traffic but their own military vehicles, they had road-blocks at various points.

He vaguely remembered where Berthe lived. She would understand his present state. Although Nelli was at the fore-front of his mind, he was not ready for her. He must be clean. Berthe would understand: she always did, was always the first and the last refuge. He would not see Nelli while he was still in the rags of the *Unerwünscht*.

Everybody was battening down the hatches against the Russians, or fleeing from them, as though the British could not be taken seriously as conquering enemies. Compared with the Russians, the British only played at war and were not to be trusted therefore. They might politely give way should the Russians insist that this was their sector, as well they might. As he moved on, more and more people were leaving their homes, with bundles on their backs, or pushing laden carts. Fear infected the town like a plague.

Zorn alone was heading east. Everybody was fleeing west-wards. The rumour had burst – the Russians were coming, and the British would not stand in their way, despite their firm presence in Welckmar. They were no longer moving forward: that was too apparent, but neither were they moving back. So the Russians were just over the river, or moving up in accordance with some prior arrangement.

Zorn found the street, not far from the harbour, and uncomfortably near Nelli's. By now the entire population appeared to be moving out. He asked a man about Berthe, but was brushed aside impatiently. He asked everybody, but was ignored. They were worried about themselves. The Russians . . . one woman pointed back . . . didn't he under-

145

stand? He looked like some sort of idiot, going the wrong way. Then another woman pointed out Berthe. 'There she is . . .' and rushed on.

Berthe, a great deal older than he had expected, was there, just locking her door. She was alone. She had a large basket on her arm, covered with peerless white linen, as though she were about to sell fresh bread.

'Berthe! Berthe!' he called, for it was she, he knew it. But she too tried to brush him aside in the headlong flight to the west.

'Berthe! I'm Dieter, Dieter Zorn!' he shouted after her as she fell in with the stream of people leaving the street. She did not know him, but the name arrested her. She paused, looked back, and he caught up with her, held her back by the arm and cried: 'It's Dieter. Don't you recognize me, Berthe? Dieter – Dieter Zorn!'

Her mouth opened with a stupid gape. She could not connect, frowned, looked forward again towards the people hurrying off, fleeing from the Russian Bear. But he persisted with his hand on her arm.

'Dieter?' she murmured, unbelievingly. 'Dieter? My Dieter?'

She peered into his face, up at the white hair, which, however unkempt and dusty from his recent travels, was still as she had known and loved it. 'You? *You* are Dieter . . .?'

He smiled at her incredulity. Then she knew it was he, and put a hand to the wall for support. He held on to her, concerned, not knowing what next to do, for she had gone pale.

'Are you all right, Berthe?'

But, once again searching with her eyes the end of the street and her departing neighbours, she summoned up all her latent strength and hugged him to her ample bosom, crying and keening with a blend of love and deep concern.

'Come,' she beseeched him. 'There's no time now. We must hurry. The Russians . . .' Her eyes looked eastward with such apprehension. She grasped his hand and tried to

146

drag him with her. But he was not to be moved. They might all be going westward, but not he.

As ever, where the name Zorn was concerned, Berthe was all obedience. Resignedly, she directed him back to her house in the street, opened the door with two keys, pushed him inside, locked and bolted the doors securely, and directed him in the gloom, for every window was firmly shuttered. She guided him towards a chair, lit a candle, for all power had been cut off, stirred the embers in the little stove and put a few sticks on it, trying to generate enough heat to boil a kettle.

'What have they done to you?' she keened away, occasionally stroking the white head. He sat silently, patiently, knowing he must wait till she had prepared whatever she had in mind, for that was her sacred duty and she would not be gainsaid. Finally, she had a kettle boiling. 'But you're so thin . . .' she mumbled sadly.

She brewed coffee in a pot. 'No sugar,' she complained, 'and only ersatz.' She lifted the cover of her basket and extricated a pack of carefully prepared rolls. Despite their lack of butter, they tasted delicious, though he was unable to identify the contents. Probably some kind of fish. 'Oh, Dieterchen . . .' he heard her lament.

He braced himself. 'So, Berthe. You must tell me everything. Why is the house empty? It's been empty for so long, I know . . . Where is Father?'

'Ah, Dieter. They wouldn't let me go there to keep it clean. I wanted to. I have a key. D'you want it? But the police warned me not to go near it. It was forbidden, you understand? So what could I do?'

She was so wrapped up in her apologies about the state of the house that she was not answering his questions.

'But where is Father? And what news of Mama?'

She turned away, a handkerchief to her eyes. He must wait, for she was suddenly prostrate with weeping. He went to her, put his arm round her shoulder and repeated his question.

147

'Ah, Dieterchen . . .' she started again. 'It's too sad, too sad . . .' She had difficulty bringing it out. He shook her gently, trying to draw the answer from her, yet careful not to upset her.

'They've gone, Dieter, gone . . .' she whispered, so that he had difficulty in catching it.

'Gone, do you say? Gone where, Berthe? Come, you must tell me everything. I must know. Gone – where?'

Finally, she blew her nose, wiped her tears and looked him in the eye. 'Your mama died.' She struggled with herself. 'They all died . . . over there . . .' She pointed vaguely towards the turbulent East. 'Your mama died. They all died, all her family. Nobody knows the details. They just tell you, that's all. And you know it's true. Such dreadful times, Dieter. When will it end?'

Inwardly, he saw those spectral figures in their thin prison outfits like pyjamas, the skeletons in the huts. Somehow, he had to match the nightmare with his last memory of his mother trying, like Berthe now, to press sandwiches on him, and there was only a hollow dryness in him. He could not weep with Berthe, yet.

'And Papa?'

Berthe had to be given time. She dabbed her eyes, summoned up the strength to face him again. 'I don't know,' she answered. 'I don't know why . . .'

'Don't know what, Berthe?'

'Ah, poor soul,' she continued at her own pace. 'As soon as the news was brought – I'll never forget the day – he never looked up from that day forward . . .'

And was there no message, he asked, but knew from her tears that he had been excluded, even at the end, and felt a desperate loneliness.

Berthe was all compassion for this bereaved child before her – 'child', as she would always see him, now so thin and undernourished as to be barely recognizable. Dieter had to dig out every word. She was also keeping an eye on the door and the shuttered window, as though a Russian would burst in at any moment. But now he knew. Both his mother and father had gone – and his greatest distress was for his mother, for of that he would never know the whole truth. Although he could guess; he had seen too much for comfort.

Berthe, against her utter devotion to the Zorn family, and to Dieter in particular, was restive. Not all the memories, or the anxiety to help, could deflect her eyes and ears from the outside world. She must flee, with the rest.

'Now we must go,' she whispered. 'The Russians . . .'

He was never to know what the Russians were supposed to do, or even if they would ever enter Welckmar, where the British were all too obviously in possession. As far as he could gather, the British were too busy among themselves to bother much about the local population. People might be streaming out of town in their stuttering carts and prams, but the British took not the slightest notice, so long as they could occupy certain key points without interference. And so the procession west continued, by car, by bicycle, on foot – with bundles carried in any way possible. It had happened before, but not to Germans. The message of the camps had got through, but the attitude of the British appeared to be a calculated coldness rather than revenge.

After his own liberation, Dieter could only think that his own people should be grateful to be under British protection, however cold it might be. And he could think of no reason why the British should relinquish Welckmar to the Russians. But he recognized the depth of Berthe's agitation. Nothing would persuade her. Gently, she insinuated him towards the door. Outside, having locked securely, she presumed he would flee with her, anywhere, so long as it was away from the Russians. There was further agitation when he declared his intention to stay, and amid more tears she finally kissed him goodbye, and was off – probably to seek shelter in some barn overnight and then to struggle on. Zorn knew all about that and tried to warn her, but Berthe was adamant. 'Better to be dead . . .' She was gone.

149

'I'll see you when it's all over!' she called from the end of the street.

'But it is all over!' he called back, standing aside to make way for a family struggling by with bedding and cooking vessels piled high on an old cart.

He knew he could not go home again. Automatically, he wandered towards the harbour, to see if *Donner* was still there, either at her moorings or laid up in the yard. There he could think, also get cleaned up, get rid of the years of camp that clung to his flesh like a fungus. Only then would he look for Nelli, always assuming she had not fled with the rest. If there was anything left of life, then Nelli was his only hope, and he prayed that she had not yet fled. He thought of his parents, united at last after the years of tension and perpetual conflict. How often had he himself been the bone of contention. What would they think, he a man of nearly twenty-two and still without his *Abitur*? There was so much to feel guilty about, if only because he had survived and they hadn't. He was dry-eyed, yet a deep mourning gripped him, tinged with ghastly speculations about his mother's sufferings in the accursed East. What right had he to be alive?

His feet carried him along the quay. The only troops there seemed to be off-duty. It was a mark of the German defeat that they should feel so confident. A dozen or so privates were stripped to the waist, resting and sunning themselves on the wharf, and quite unconcerned about his presence. Three more were rowing a dinghy across the harbour, where the indifferent gulls glided over them, screaming among themselves at their own never-ending private war. *Donner* was still there, motionless at her moorings. Zorn sat down wearily, his feet over the edge of the quay. One or two fishermen were still about, indifferent to either the British or the supposed threat of the Russians. There were more important affairs, nets to be mended, decks to be caulked.

'Can you row me over to the *Donner*, please?' he asked one of them.

'Why? You're not the owner,' the man retorted, not happy to leave his nets.

'My father was,' Dieter replied.

'Ah, Herr Zorn. So you're the boy.' The man stood up, put a hand on Zorn's shoulder. 'These are hard times, Herr Zorn. Sure, I'll row you over. But she's been in the water these last couple of years, so I expect she won't be ship-shape.'

The man sculled single-oared at the stern with that skill Zorn had never been able to master.

'Give us a shout when you want to come back,' the man said as Zorn stepped aboard *Donner*. He was alone again, as he wished to be after all that Berthe had told him. This must be his home for the present. He could never enter his house again. Here he would prepare for the next and only possible step – Nelli.

As he stood in the cockpit, feeling the boat under his feet, his spirits revived at the realization that *Donner*, despite the long neglect, was very much alive. His father must have left her, knowing she was to stay in the water for some time. There was no way of knowing what was in his mind as he left, but with both wife and son sequestered in unknown camps as prisoners, *Donner* must have been low in his thoughts. Nevertheless, everything was well battened down, and the main sliding-hatch was firmly locked. The little pram dinghy was shipped and tied upside-down on the cabin-top, so Zorn knew he could row ashore and back on his own, without relying on the fishermen, a small indulgence that gave him immediate satisfaction, and his first self-appointed task was to unstow the dinghy and launch it, tying it up at the stern.

He had lost all except *Donner*, and that small, immediate independence at this moment of flux between war and peace became his only anchor. He would still depend on others for a while – he would need help to release the sliding-hatch before he could take full possession of the boat – but the less he needed people, the better he felt. He had been locked

151

away from the world for too long, he had depended on guards, authorities, comrades, just to stay alive, and all he wanted now was to take charge of his own world, of what the outer world allowed him or might allow him in the future.

For a beginning, he stripped off his prison clothes, the last of his civilian wear now nearly in shreds, washed himself briskly in several buckets of water drawn up from the harbour, and donned his British denims and new boots. The latter were a bit loose until he could acquire socks somehow. But he felt like a new man as he ritually cast his old infested rags into the water.

Of the loss of his parents he tried not to think. His mother's end was unbearable even to contemplate, but he knew he must hang on somehow if he was to get through. And his father? His world had collapsed and he had succumbed at last – his 'strength', his 'steel', even his 'hygiene' had proved futile in the face of his personal loss. Maybe his father had suffered from a belated sense of guilt, wondering if he might have prevented the ills that had befallen his wife and child. This Dieter would never know.

As to himself, undernourished and buffeted by the flailings and thrashings of the dying Third Reich, he had youth on his side. He would survive – he had to. And he would do it independently.

First, he must borrow a screwdriver from one of the fishermen, to force the lock on the hatch.

But as he rowed the pram ashore, shipped the oars and tied her up, he was suddenly aware that his every move was being watched. At the top of the sea-washed steps a figure awaited him with more than interest. While he had rowed with his back to the shore he had been unsighted.

'It's you! I knew it was!' A woman's voice. His heart leapt as he saw, first the bobby-sox, then the small figure he had dreamed about, forgotten in the drab routine of labour and survival, then dreamt about again – for how long now? He was not yet ready to look into faces. It was too early, too much of a shock. He had cleaned up, stripped his body, but not his mind, of three years of filth and deprivation. He had forgotten why he had rowed ashore in the dinghy and showed an odd reluctance to climb the steps. He lumbered painfully, not from any physical ache, but from some horrible dearth of the spirit, unable to think, but worse still, unable to respond to the beckoning of love.

'It *is* you, isn't it?' she cried again.

She too had doubt in her words, in her voice. As Zorn climbed the steps, he still forbore to look up, he had got so used to not looking guards and prisoners in the face.

She knelt down on the wooden baulks of the quay, ignoring the hurt, to be that little bit nearer. So long as *Donner* was there, she had always clung to the hope that he would return. *Donner* would reunite them. And here he was. She was sure it was he. She grabbed him by the arm, stood with him as he set foot on the wharf, looked him in the eyes. Then the note of disappointment: 'Is it possible you don't remember me, Dieter?'

He turned his head slowly, to stare in turn into her eyes. They were no longer the laughing eyes he had remembered, but large orbs in a pinched, frightened face.

He could not take it all in – the fact of her, her living presence, for had he not gazed too recently into the face of so many transmuted into half-life and death? With Berthe's news of his mother and father, he had felt an inclination towards sinking away, to join those ghosts in their endless procession of despair. Even at their end, he had been excluded, no message even, though what that might have been was more than he dared contemplate, yet he felt the lack keenly. The past had been rudely cut, their past with him. Gently, Nelli detached herself, the better to see him, for it was unbelievable that he was here.

For a moment they stood slightly apart. Whatever doubt there had been was dispelled by his pottering about on *Donner*. Yet he was also a stranger. Nervously she put out a hand to touch his cheek. 'You haven't shaved' – and sensed at once

153

the irrelevance of it. As she felt him flinch under her fingers and recognized the shame, the sheer want of soap they had all suffered, she slid her arm fondly around his waist. 'What does it matter? You're here. That's all that matters. And *Donner*. We can go, can't we, just us, somewhere, anywhere – away from all this?'

Still he hesitated, finding it difficult to adjust. Suddenly here was a future, Nelli, undeniable as ever, coaxing him away from his willing descent into a void. The shock of confronting this little wisp of life and love after all that hate and dying was too much, too much of a turn. 'Ah, Nelli!' he sighed as he folded his arms round her, at last, after three years of non-life in the fight for survival.

'So you do remember me,' she murmured, drawing away from him to look him up and down. Then she kissed him ardently, as though to expunge whatever shame she could read of the years since their parting. At first she had been bewildered by his silence. He had simply disappeared. He had promised to write, but no word came. She had not cared to ask anybody about him, had desisted from approaching the Zorn yard where a discreet inquiry might have elicited some news, but might compromise Dieter. The Zorn home was beyond even thinking. She knew vaguely of Berthe, but distrusting servants' gossip, avoided her.

The bewilderment had turned to a deep hurt and disappointment, and, she would admit to herself at her lowest ebb, to a feeling of betrayal, for he of all men had promised nothing yet was to be trusted, or so she had felt. She lived in hope nevertheless, day by day, until like the rest of the town she reached the dull routine of endemic hunger as the war dragged towards the impending defeat that none dared admit. It became a matter of which way to turn. Westwards she saw the desperate flight of refugees, with what prospects? Eastwards the Russians. Her instinct was to frequent the harbour. Somebody was bound to think of that exit, surely. Then as evening approached, she thought she might have chosen the worst course, for nothing seemed to move in the harbour.

154

As she shuttled frantically between home and the quay, hope faded, until she saw the unbelievable, a figure moving about on *Donner*. Her heart pounded as she saw him rowing in with the dinghy. And now she was sure.

'Of course I remember you, Nelli,' he replied, striving to crack his solemn face into a smile. 'How could I ever forget?' Then, by way of apology for his slowness and solemnity, he added: 'These are times . . . times when . . .'

'I know,' Nelli readily took him up. 'That's why I'm so happy to have found you. I've been hiding, watching, waiting. I knew you would come back.' She nestled up to him, exercising her 'rights'. 'You see, the Russians are just over there. I've seen them, you know, in the distance of course.' And continued, now surer of herself: 'Can you imagine what it's been like here these past few days, wondering who would get here first? Can you imagine what the Russians would do if they got here?'

'But the British are here. The Russians won't come into Welckmar, the British won't allow that.'

But she remained unconvinced. 'I don't trust any of them,' she said scornfully. 'Please, take me away, Dieter . . .'

'But I'm not leaving, Nelli. I've been away for so long. The war is over, there's no need to leave . . . I . . . I'm not fit to see you, Nelli . . .' His vague wave of the arm might have indicated anything.

'Oh, yes, you are! You're fit to see me, Dieter. We belong together. And you *are* leaving, or why are you messing about on the boat? Why didn't you stay at home, or go away with the rest of them, away from the Russians?' Her logic was not to be denied, the words implied.

Slowly, with her arm secure under his, he led her away from the wharf. They were too conspicuous here. And he wondered why, on the contrary, the British were so inconspicuous in the harbour area. Was it possible that the Army was leaving maritime areas for the Navy to take over? And until their Navy arrived in the Baltic and got firmly established, Welckmar might be anybody's. The fishermen attended

155

to their tackle as though a war had never been fought and lost. The only evidence of the British presence was the sprinkling of private soldiers larking about at the upper end of the harbour and the three in the dinghy. The latter seemed to have taken possession of somebody's yacht, which made him even more determined to establish ownership of *Donner*.

'I can't live at home,' he said miserably.

He could feel her breast against his, secure in possession of him.

'They'd kill me, but not before they'd had their way with me. You know what the Russians are . . .'

'As a matter of fact, I don't,' he retorted mulishly. Was it possible that Nelli's only interest in him was as her protector against the Russian hordes?

'Oh, come, everybody knows them. You should hear the stories from those who fled from the East: rape, looting, murder – the lot. And they're so dirty, they say, running with lice, not to mention the . . .' She decided against specifying the worst, sensing his mute suspicions. She looked him up and down. 'Well, *you* don't look in too good shape yourself. Where've you been? You need looking after, Dieter. I'll look after you, I promise. Oh, how glad I am I waited and saw you!' She went on and on, marking out her territory with every word and the rub of her arm against his. 'Take me with you,' she pleaded, her eyes searching his. 'Then we'll be safe, all of us . . .'

'All of us' – did she mean Stentewik by any chance? Weak and by now hungry, Zorn passed a hand over his brow.

'I really don't think of moving,' was all he said.

There was silence. 'I just planned to stay aboard, till the troubles were over,' he added wearily, 'then think it all out. My parents . . .'

'Are they going too? Why not? There's room for all of us, isn't there?' she said eagerly. Then she looked into the worn face, and knew. She sensed his grief at once. 'Oh, I'm sorry. You've lost your father, haven't you? And your mother too? I'm so sorry.' But showed no inclination to detach herself.

'I can't leave,' he persisted. 'I've no food, nothing.'

'As bad as that. You've had a bad time, haven't you? Well, don't worry. I have enough for all of us.'

So how many? He wondered where she had got her provisions, but remembered that goods, food in particular, had been a more reliable currency of late than Marks. She was well stocked, had been 'entertaining', no doubt.

'I can bring lots of food,' she said, 'tins and things, you know – and a liver sausage, a whole one. Think of that!'

She was laying out her wares in front of the hungry. She was leading him away, firmly in possession, he compliant, if only because there was no choice. But his mind was turning. Even the smell of this country was repellent. Over to the east, the grumble of guns persisted still. He had had enough. Nelli was right. It was time to get out, to somewhere clean, like Sweden, clean of war and all that it brings. To get out, to sail *Donner* across the Baltic was not only possible, it was quite easy, especially if, as Nelli claimed, they would have provisions, for sailing needed strength, and that meant food.

They passed Nummer Neunzehn, to which neither gave a thought, then back to her street and the house. Nelli pushed him indoors. It was so cosy, so colourful, he wondered how she could think of abandoning it. The divan invited, as ever. On one wall hung a new enlarged photograph of a tall youth, blond, naked except for very brief shorts, bronzed and showing a comely rather than muscular figure. There were photographs too of Conrad Veidt and . . . No! Were they also patrons, he wondered. But then he recalled that Welckmar was rarely visited by the famous or the powerful. Perhaps the anonymous photograph was her latest swain. There were souvenirs of every kind, from an Iron Cross (a replica, surely) dangling on the wall to a tobacco pipe carved suggestively with tiny intertwined figures round the bowl.

He watched Nelli disappearing into the little room beyond. Did she propose leaving all this behind, this home that he knew so well? But she called him.

'Come, Dieter. Come and see him.'

Who was she hiding there? Must she be so persistent about having a crowd with her always? He followed sullenly. Even Nelli asked too much of him.

Nelli was bending over a cot. 'Here he is . . . . What d'you think?'

The child was fast asleep. Dark lashes on heavy lids, white hair spread over the pillow, the exposed cheek flushed with deep sleep.

'Isn't he beautiful?' Nelli asked, turning towards Zorn.

Weary beyond words, barely conscious, he knew.

'No doubt, is there?' she murmured, gazing at him for approbation.

'But how . . . when?'

She smiled. 'You can't play about as we did without . . .'

'Ah, Nelli . . .' and he collapsed on the floor in a fit of uncontrollable weeping.

'September 'forty-two,' she said, trying to comfort him, to turn him towards her, to share the unalloyed joy she so obviously felt at the little white figure in the cot. 'He's two and a half, and as good as gold, bless him. I called him Dieter, because I thought you were never coming back.' She purred on, delighted, yet frightened. And busy all the time.

'Oh, I could give you coffee,' she went on. 'But we haven't got time, have we? We'd better be off. We'll get the stuff together before they come in with their big boots.'

While she pottered about in the back, he gazed at the child. From time to time, she would reappear, asking would they need this (a jar of pickled herring) or that (a jar of *Sauerkraut*), to which he said yes, provided they could carry it all. She might have been packing a picnic, like Berthe in the old days. All kinds of things went into an enormous market basket, and now she was hurling things into a sack.

'Let's hope nobody stops us with this stuff,' she cried gleefully. 'It's hot black market, most of it. I've saved it up for just this sort of emergency. Anyway, the cops have all disappeared into the wall!'

He gazed at her. That beautiful roundness had gone. She

158

was thinner, even pinched – but then, who was not at this stage of the war? He had not looked in the mirror himself since leaving home, and would not, out of some irrational fear that the image would speak back at him with words he would not wish to hear.

'You don't say much,' Nelli chided him. 'You don't seem at all worried about the Russkis, are you?' She rammed a packet of *Knäckerbrot* into the basket. 'Come on, help me, or they'll be here!'

He saw clearly that beneath the general badinage she was genuinely fearful. He was quite willing to fall in with the game. Side by side, with the old physical intimacy, they sorted over her hastily tipped pile of provisions, and repacked according to a certain logic. There was something slightly wicked about the sheer quantity.

'If we're going to Sweden,' Zorn said speculatively, 'we'd be there long before we'd got through even a quarter of this.'

'Ah, well, you never know. And we don't want to leave it to the Tartar, do we?'

'I don't even know if I can sail *Donner* yet. She needs sails, you know. But if not, you're welcome to stay aboard if you like. But surely, you know that?'

But the laughing eyes were not amused.

'It's no use staying on a boat unless it goes somewhere nice and safe. Don't you understand, Dieter?' She was on the edge of exasperation, pushed the sack towards him, then turned abruptly back towards the kitchen. 'I nearly forgot this!' It was a pristine bottle of Vodka, no doubt looted from the Eastern Front. 'It'll help keep us warm on cold nights.' Clearly, she was enjoying the prospective intimate intrigue of it all, flinging a blanket over his shoulder and another over her own. 'We're ready, I think.'

She returned to the cot, tried to wake the child, but he was deep in sleep and limp to her touch as she lifted him. Zorn saw that he was fully clothed. She had been ready. She stood the boy on his feet, and he woke, swaying, with reluctance. She pushed his arms into the sleeves of his little jacket,

159

fastened the buttons, all the time murmuring endearments and pecking him on the white down of his head.

Even at this most distressing of times, nothing would disturb the even tenor of her ways. She might be frightened of the Russians, she was certainly undernourished, she had the added burden of a two-year-old child to rear, yet she garnered her resources and coaxed Zorn with the old familiar blandishments.

Zorn's own difficulty over the encounter was in simply being alive to her. He was vastly unprepared for Nelli. She represented, as she had always done, a simple affirmation of life and love, without strings or qualifications, and even if that affirmation was readily shared with others, Zorn knew with all his heart that he was most favoured, that it was he she preferred and needed above all the rest. She had been waiting. The child reaffirmed it. In the face of it all, Zorn was acutely conscious of the inadequacy of his response. It was not his diminished body, not even Berthe's chilling news of his family, but rather the blight of the labour camp.

Watching him, Nelli was at a loss, yet with that instinct of hers she was aware of his sufferings, even though he had vouchsafed no details. He must be nursed back to life after the brutalization he had suffered, wherever he had been. Gently, she laid the child in his arms, as though to declare a beginning of the process.

As he felt the child's warmth against him, Zorn smiled into his eyes. The sudden confidence of the child in him, snuggling up against him to prolong his sleep, marked the first step into a new family life, a turning away from the past into some unpredictable future.

Nelli looked up, smiled in turn, and addressed herself to her packing with renewed energy. 'Can you walk, Dieterchen?' she addressed the sleeping child. 'You're a heavy boy, and we have to go now. Just a little walk, then we sail over the sea to a new land . . .' But the child was blissfully asleep, undisturbed by his mother's chatter.

She was done. She looked round the room once more, then

nodded towards the door. They were off, Zorn with the child on one arm, the sack over his shoulder. He dared not say it was almost more than he could manage. He watched Nelli lock and secure the door and shutters, just as Berthe had done. He knew none of it would be secure against any army should troops feel inclined to force their way in.

Like the last of the refugees – for the streets now seemed deserted of residents – they staggered towards the harbour again, laden down with Nelli's wealth. Zorn felt guilty under the eyes of the fishermen as the little pram settled deep in the water under their weight and their loot. Worse still, he remembered that he and his prospective crew would be confined to the cockpit unless they could release the sliding-hatch to the cabin. He even thought of the hard pipecots, the folding bunk shelves up in the bows where they might sleep, not side by side, alas, but within hand-holding distance across the gloom of the forecabin. For a panic-stricken second or two, he hesitated as he placed the oars in the rowlocks. Should he try the fishermen for a screwdriver? They were watching every move. Any man setting sail with Nelli was bound to attract attention. He dipped the oars and turned the pram in the direction of *Donner*. He rowed across the harbour and gave Nelli her first lesson in seamanship, as he thought, by telling her to board while he held on and handed her the provisions, and then to hold on to the dinghy while he in turn stepped aboard. Promptly she reminded him that she had been through all that before, and he remembered times that now seemed to be at the other side of a great black mountain.

With a sense of sacrilege, he forced the sliding-hatch by sheer brute strength. It took all he had. He was ashamed of his weakness in front of Nelli. He had expected the dim light below, but the smell was overpowering, a mixture of stale sea-smells and musty canvas. But if they were to try for Sweden, at least he had the satisfaction of knowing the sails were there and not stowed in the loft ashore, as was more usual. He surmised his father must have abandoned the ketch in mid-season. There was a desperation about that which chilled Zorn.

After drawing the bolt and opening the fore-hatch to let air circulate, he told Nelli where to store the provisions in the various lockers. He then went back on deck. Nelli had settled the child on a pipecot. Having barely woken, he was asleep again at once in the captured warmth of the cabin. Zorn inspected the tackle. The shrouds were in good order and still fairly taut in their weathering. Next he returned below, stepping carefully so as not to disturb the sleeping boy, and fumbled among the sails folded in the fore-locker. He fingered the cringles at the corner of each canvas and found them to be sound, so there was no immediate impediment to bending on the sails.

'When can we go?' Nelli asked, with such appeal in her eyes that he found her difficult to resist.

'Well, if we're going anywhere . . .'

'But we are, aren't we? We must . . .'

'I know. The Russians,' he said patiently. 'But sailing at sea is not as easy as you think.'

'But why? We're ready, aren't we? We've got enough food. I can't wait. Oh, do come on!'

He recalled with a smile her earlier impatience at his slowness to rise to an occasion.

'In any case' – he considered the problems as he spoke – 'do we have to go anywhere? The war is over. Surely, we're safe where we are.'

'But . . .'

'The Russians. I know, I know . . .'

Nelli, in the close confines of the cabin, nestled closely up to him. 'If I meant as much to you as you do to me, we'd be off now and the Russians couldn't catch me,' she said. Her fingers insinuated themselves along his spine caressingly. But there were practicalities to consider.

'We haven't even got water,' he said. 'We wouldn't last a day at sea.'

'Well, how do we get water? Oh, do come on,' she said,

half-lovingly, half-chiding, with an eye always to shore, watching for any sign of her dreaded Russians. Zorn returned to the cockpit, unscrewed the cap of the water-tank and peered down. He saw it was quite empty.

'We'd have to take her to the wharf and fill her up at the tap. There's always a pipe there to carry it aboard – *if* there's water, of course.'

'Shall we do that then? Let's start now. You're so slow. I wish I'd gone with the others.' Clearly, he was a disappointment to her.

'Why didn't you?' he asked.

She took time to consider this. 'The devil and the deep blue sea,' she mused. 'One army is as bad as another for girls like me. And Dieter . . . He can't walk very fast, can he? And I couldn't carry him far.' Zorn at once felt the responsibility of that – *his* responsibility. 'Something told me,' Nelli went on, 'that you'd come back to *Donner*.' She had always been one for divinations. 'But there was nothing doing till you turned up. I watched you from that shed over there,' pointing ashore. Then she added, on a practical note, 'First we must eat, then let's get that water. I'll help you – with anything. Just you watch. I'm strong. I'll do anything you want.'

Of her willingness and strength he had no doubt. Of her capacities at sea he was less confident. 'All right. After dark, I'll ease her over to the wharf if I can.'

'I haven't slept for days,' Nelli said. 'None of us knew what would happen when the conquering armies got here. Not a sign of ours. We've been terrified, and nowhere to go. West the Americans – I mean, the English. East the Russians. It's been unbearable. Now it's all over. You can't imagine what it's like just waiting, and the guns getting nearer all the time. They say the hospital's a shambles, men dying for want of attention, no running water, toilets blocked . . .'

He had no need of this reminder of the collapse of the cloacae. 'Well, let's hope the water's still running on the wharf,' he said. 'Now we must wait for the dark,' intimating that she could catch some sleep till then.

163

Nelli settled down forward on the pipecot, pulling a blanket over her, more to be with the boy and to close out the world than for warmth, for it was a fine evening, with the sun taking its time to set out of a clear sky.

The silence and inactivity unsettled Zorn and he pottered about in the cabin, preferring not to go on deck till after dark. This detachment out in the middle of the harbour suited him. It was a measure of his own illusory safety – and Nelli's and the child's too. There was something he did not like about taking *Donner* to the wharf. But should they need to sail for any reason – supposing Nelli and the rest were proved correct in their fears of a Russian take-over from the complacent British – then they would need water.

When he peered into the fore-cabin, he saw that she was fast asleep, breathing evenly, her blond hair falling over the side of the cot. As the last gulls fell out of the sky and the light faded in the west, he knew the time had come to pluck up courage and move *Donner* over to the wharf. He pulled the dinghy in and boarded it, cast off the moorings, tied the dinghy to the bows and rowed hard till he knew *Donner* was moving. It was hard work, but it took ten minutes only before he had her bumping against the wharf. His heart was racing, as much from fear as from the effort, for he was not enjoying this approach to land. Too much was still going on in the town. But as he struggled to steer the ketch towards the side, then tied the dinghy and bundled himself back on deck, he was glad to see Nelli's tousled head appearing out of the hatch, eager to help. Using an oar, he manoeuvred the heavy ketch inshore towards the steps. But in the gloom, he could not find them, and there was no way he could tie up unless he found the steps. It was a fright, then a relief, when he saw there was a solitary fisherman still about on the wharf above.

'Catch!' Zorn shouted, throwing up a rope. The man obliged. 'Tie me up at the steps, please.' He felt the ketch moving slowly as the man hauled hard. Then Zorn heard him tying up. He moved to the bows and climbed the steps wearily. 'Thanks,' he said to the fisherman, who was waiting, as if for a tip. Then . . .

'That's all right, Zorn. Welckmar folk always oblige.' It was Vogel, in fisherman's kit. He had a briefcase at his feet on the quay, but in his hand was the familiar Mauser. 'What are you trying to do, Zorn?'

Vogel! Who else, at Welckmar? The Welckmar connection. He had always been there, was there all the time. He would always be about, as he was in the beginning. 'I thought you were going to hop it without me, and I see we have a woman aboard!' As the first shock of Vogel's black presence gave way to the old familiarity (as though life without Vogel would be asking too much of Providence), Zorn was ready to risk everything and fling himself at him, anything to be free of his malevolent shadow.

Vogel could read his thoughts. The Mauser pointed menacingly. The memory of Kremft and Schnehohr halted Zorn. 'I need water,' he answered sullenly.

'Well, get it then, and quick. Don't do anything stupid, or this thing might go off.' Vogel was always one for the dramatic gesture, an extra in the theatre of the Third Reich.

Weak though he was at this new confrontation, Zorn was not assailed by the old faintness. Anger gripped him, his fists clenched with violence at this murderer of Kremft and Schnehohr, and who knew of what others. *Of course* Vogel would home in on Welckmar, just as he himself had. Welckmar would not merely be a destination. It offered a point of embarkation, as Nelli had so eagerly affirmed, and a criminal like Vogel was bound to be looking for an avenue of flight from the Allies and possible retribution.

Zorn went through the whole drill, piped water into the tank, with Vogel trailing his every move up and down the steps. To have reached this Nemesis, the country in total collapse, chaos everywhere – and to have Vogel still at his back and a prospective passenger – it was beyond bearing. Zorn raged within as he screwed the cap back on the full tank. Vogel told him to cast off. They were adrift, the ketch moving inch by inch away from the quay. *Donner* rocked and drifted slowly in the idle river current, Zorn at the helm, Vogel watchful, while Nelli was forward in her cot with her arms round the boy. This irruption of a second man startled and horrified her, just as she and Dieter were reunited and they were about to sail off. Who was this man? Why did he flourish a gun? What was he to Dieter? She loathed him, whoever he was, for he had chosen his moment, had he not, when just the three of them, Zorn, the child and herself, should have been loving and alone, aboard *Donner*, ready to sail away from the armies to safety.

Donner drifted on in the gloom, out of the harbour, passive to an offshore breeze that carried them steadily out, with the two men keeping their distance from each other in silent hatred.

Zorn could see little of Vogel's face in the gloom. He felt command was essential at this early stage, for if this idle drifting were to continue, nothing but disaster would follow. He knew it would be useless to talk to Vogel about steerage way, bending on the sails and all that was necessary for a boat to be alive and in command of the sea and the wind, instead of a passive shell drifting helplessly out of the broad estuary.

Vogel was a murderer and Zorn knew that by now they were mere hostages, expendable as and when it suited the sergeant's purpose, whatever that might be.

Only Zorn could make anything of the ketch if they were to sail her. And of the three, he had the least ambition to sail anywhere. He would have been content to stay in the harbour, making his home aboard till things turned for the better, when he could think – always a need in him.

But then, in her way, Nelli was in command, since they couldn't survive long without food, and she had fulfilled that need – or would, if Vogel stopped waving his gun about. And since, in this last feeble flicker of the Reich, he had the gun, he could be said to be in control.

So the ketch drifted into the night. Zorn had left the tiller to itself and they were head on to such current as there was.

They might have been on a raft for all the steerage way they had.

'Can't you make this bloody thing go faster?' Vogel muttered. 'We're going backwards, aren't we?'

'This is a ketch – a sailing boat,' Zorn replied. 'I'd have to bend on the sails to point her in any direction you require. I don't even know where you plan to go.'

'We can try for Sweden.'

'Possibly, yes.'

'All right. Tie the sails on, or whatever you do. And move!'

'We can't do that in the dark. We'll have to wait for a bit of light. In the meantime, we're liable to ground or to hit something if we drift like this.'

'All right, go to the woman,' Vogel ordered Zorn, 'and bring me something to eat.'

Zorn disappeared through the hatch. In the pitch dark of the cabin, he bumped into Nelli. She reached out to him, clung to him in terror. 'Who is he?' she whispered. 'Why is he so nasty?'

'I'll tell you some other time, when we've got rid of him,' Zorn answered. 'But you'd better do as he says. He's a Party man. He wants food.'

'And what if I say no? There's no Party now.'

'Nelli, do it,' he said with all the patience of resignation. 'Do it, and we'll see later what we can do. Just now, it's what he might do that matters.'

Nelli groped in the locker and decided the liver sausage must be consumed first. Back in the cockpit, Zorn watched Vogel devour the sausage, then announced he must go forward to drop the anchor. Vogel suspected every move and followed him. There was little enough depth, as he had half-expected, so he veered as much rope again and tied up. Then, with a sense of foreboding he saw that somehow the dinghy had got loose in the gloom and was not in sight.

The night darkened briefly, and though Nelli, curled up in her pipecot with the boy, might have slept, the two men kept their distance in the cockpit. Out of the old familiarity of

167

jailer and prisoner, they half-trusted, half-feared one another as they dozed uneasily against the hard lines of the boat.

When the sun got up, both men jumped together away from the edge of deep sleep. It was bitterly cold. Vogel quickly asserted the power of the gun with one of his dramatic flourishes, telling Zorn to 'wake the woman and tell her to get me some breakfast'.

In the cabin, Zorn marvelled at Nelli's capacity for sleep. When finally he succeeded in rousing her, she had difficulty in understanding him. But when he reminded her about breakfast, her eyes opened wide, swivelling in the direction of the hatch. Zorn nodded.

'He says he wants to sail to Sweden,' he whispered. There was so much about Vogel that he could not share with her yet. The question for the moment was not what they were to do with Vogel, but what Vogel with his Mauser might decide to do with them.

Nelli searched among the rations for what was most easily accessible. She cut some bread and cheese and spread out three portions.

'What about Dieter?' Zorn asked. The child still slept under the blanket.

'I'll feed him when he wakes.'

She was a good mother, he noted, wondering how she had managed over the years. How would things have turned out had he not been in that camp? This was his family now, and Vogel's shadow was the more loathsome.

'Are we well away from Welckmar?' Nelli asked, for why else should she be here on a boat with a half-starved refugee and a lunatic Party man with a gun?

'Not a thing in sight,' he reassured her, spreading his arms, as though to declare the world was their oyster.

Outside, Vogel wolfed his food. Zorn handed him water from the canteen, but Vogel brushed it aside, preferring a flask he had in his pocket. 'Now, those sails you talked about,' he said. 'What do we have to do?'

By main force, Zorn dragged the folded sails out of the

168

locker and ran up the mainsail, then the mizzen, and finally the jib up the forestay, all the time shouting to Vogel what sheets to haul. At once, *Donner* shivered into life. The morning wind caught the sails and a tremor went through the hull as the boat leaned over and began to make steerage way. Urging Vogel into the cockpit and ordering him for his very life to hang on to the tiller, Zorn went forward and hauled in the anchor. Then, going aft again, he rudely snatched the tiller from Vogel and they were off. When it came to seamanship, Zorn made no bones about who was in command. He was no longer afraid of this man. Only the presence of the Mauser established precedence, but Vogel was pathetically dependent on Zorn to get the ketch under way. When ordered to haul in a sheet, he resembled more than anything a spaniel pup eager to learn the tricks from its master. Zorn demonstrated helm drill, then felt free to command the boat. But still, the gun bestowed precedence.

With the wind fresh on their starboard beam, *Donner* moved smartly through water bright with white horses. Astonishingly, they were out of sight of land and Zorn guessed that wind as much as current had carried them past the islands and had sent them miles offshore in the brief darkness. With no charts and only the vaguest memory of geography under the dubitable tutelage of Paterfamilias, Zorn could only speculate on a course. The last thing he wanted was to land in territory still occupied by Germans, for the war might not yet be over in all areas, in which case Vogel would be able to exploit his military advantage. As for Nelli, her need was to avoid all armies. So they must avoid Denmark and its Zealand and Laaland islands which straddled the Kattegat. Zorn's aim must be the toe of Sweden which stretched towards Germany, but whether it was to the north or to east of north he was baffled to remember. He wished Paterfamilias had been as meticulous over geographical locations as he was over etymology.

Calling to Vogel to haul in the sheets, he decided on a fairly close reach, vaguely east of north, though with no compass,

169

only the sun for direction and Vogel's watch for time, he could hardly be sure.

So over the sunlit sea they sped, as though the ketch was enjoying her release. Sensing that she was riding just a little heavy, Zorn worked the bilge pump and was hardly surprised at the amount released. After half an hour, he could feel *Donner* sailing that much lighter. He then returned to Nelli, who was puzzling over a tin. How was she to open it? Zorn set to with his knife. Greedily, they shared the contents, which even the child ate with relish. Zorn noticed how Nelli had him firmly in hand. His white hair tousled by this adventure at sea, he showed increasing confidence as Zorn moved about at various jobs. Only Vogel's malignant presence prevented them from enjoying this reunion and first intimation of a new family life. Zorn longed to touch and caress the child, but Vogel stood over his every move.

To kill this man was now uppermost in his mind; he must be got rid of, otherwise there would be no reunion, no enjoyment of his newly found family. Boldly, under Vogel's jaundiced eye, he lifted young Dieter and kissed him. The boy responded with wide-eyed wonder and a seraphic smile.

The wind kept well in the eastern quarter, and as far as sailing was concerned, Zorn was thoroughly in command. But as to destination, he had only the vaguest idea. He kept the ketch close-hauled all day, Vogel depending on his seamanship. Nelli kept to the cabin so long as Vogel was in the cockpit, and on the few occasions which brought her into close physical proximity, she made no secret of her loathing for the Party man.

The sun had got round to their port beam, and when Zorn thought he saw a dark line ahead over the scudding waves, he asked Vogel what time it was.

'Seven o'clock. Why?' Vogel queried every question. He was on edge, facing decisions one way or another – his own, but more ominously for him, those of others. Zorn could see he was anything but comfortable. Frequent eructations betrayed a slight sea-sickness, though there was no great turbulence to the swell. But it was affecting Vogel. He was afraid to go below. He clung to the cockpit, hunched at the helm, except when Zorn relieved him. He was reddening from the sun and the wind, and plainly suffering from immobility. But he would not move around. The cockpit offered the best vantage point should he need to exercise the authority of his gun.

Zorn took every advantage therefore, roaming forward, going below for a chat with Nelli, and generally feeling his freedom with each hour that passed. It fended off, too, the pain and guilt of never knowing where, when and how his mother had died. They had been sailing fourteen hours.

'Seven o'clock?' he mused in front of Vogel. 'If we've been doing, say, seven knots, that seems about a hundred miles, give or take.'

'So?' Vogel asked irritably.

'Well, then what I think is land over there must be a Danish island.'

Vogel rose sharply, hand to his gun, leaving the tiller to whip to port and the ketch in danger of gybing. The sails flapped uncertainly, Zorn ignored the gun, slapped the tiller back before the sails lost their wind altogether. He glared at Vogel.

'We're not landing in Denmark, Zorn!' Vogel snapped. 'I said Sweden, so get on with it.'

'I'm no more interested in Denmark than you are,' Zorn shouted back. 'You keep the tiller where it is, damn you, and we'll get past whatever it is that lies ahead, if that's what you want!'

Vogel complied, while Zorn checked sails, sheets, shrouds, doing anything that might be construed as seamanship. Then he returned to Nelli, ostensibly to inquire about food.

'I think there's land ahead,' he confided to her. 'It could be a Danish island, so we'd better avoid it if we can. Our troops could still be there.'

'So what about Sweden?' she asked.

171

'I'll do my best,' he replied. 'But with no charts or direction finders, I don't really know where we are. It'll mean another night at sea.'

'With *him*?' she whispered ruefully. 'Where does he want to go?'

'Certainly not to Denmark, he says. To Sweden, that's what he wants.' Zorn felt anything but comfort as he went out to Vogel with his rations. It was understandable that Vogel was all for neutral Sweden. But so long as Zorn was alive to denounce him, Vogel would not be free anywhere. It was a thought that froze Zorn, for he knew that Vogel would not hesitate to shoot them all once they were within reach of Sweden, then dump them overboard and throw himself on the mercy of the Swedish coastguards or some passing Swedish vessel.

He was so convinced of this argument by now that he knew there was no survival while Vogel was alive. Vogel's black presence clung to the boat like filth. All pretence of 'the *Bruderschaft* of the barbed-wire' was dropped in this battle of wits, of who would survive, who outwit the other in the appalling problems of the sea, of possible hunger, of which landfall would offer safe refuge to whom.

The dark line persisting ahead was definitely land, but falling away to port. It must be a Danish island. Zorn hauled the sheets just a little for a beat to starboard. He must steer with extra vigilance. Skerries littered Baltic shorelines, and although the day had been free of contact with other craft, who knew what was going on at night, who was fleeing from whom in this last paroxysm of the Third Reich? From now on, Zorn would have to pay strict attention to landfalls, and watch every move of Vogel's.

The sun dipped, and he envied Nelli her cot. He told Vogel they must anchor. Vogel was so weary hunched over the tiller that he did not protest.

'Right!' he declared. 'Tell the woman to join you out here. I sleep inside, and you two can do what you like, so long as neither of you touches the door.' He indicated the hatch. 'If

172

you do, I'll blow your heads off . . .' and, of course, he slapped the hilt of the Mauser for emphasis.

When Zorn told Nelli she must go aft to the cockpit, she refused. 'Not with *him*!' she protested. 'I can't bear the sight of him.'

Only when he informed her Vogel was to sleep in the cabin would she submit. She folded her blanket, snatched the second and followed him outside, the sleeping child on her arm.

The wind dropped to a light breeze as darkness fell. It was quite cold. With the boy between them and the blankets over them, they had the best night's sleep since leaving Welckmar.

The next day was much the same. The wind got up, they kept the same close reach with the sails taut to the wind. The distant line of land fell away to port and stern, and finally disappeared from view. It was only when Zorn spotted land to starboard that he guessed they must be in the Sound, with Sweden to starboard and a Danish island to port. When he confessed his lack of precise knowledge, Vogel snapped back:

'Bloody idiot! You never did know where you were, Zorn. This time you'd better get it right. Which is Sweden?' But Zorn spread his hands. Why should he tell Vogel anything, even if he knew?

It was apparent that Vogel had slept badly. His latent insecurity and a touch of mal de mer were enough to render him dangerous. Zorn tried to explain his navigating difficulties. Vogel always took bad news badly; he belonged to those who execute the messenger who brings it. Zorn watched the man's face closely. It was, surely, just a matter of time. In these conditions, the gun could not prevail indefinitely, and one thing Zorn never lacked: patience.

So he kept much the same course. It was a matter more of keeping Vogel quiet than of reaching any conclusion, since any announcement of land only made Vogel jumpy. Furthermore, should any landing be in prospect, Zorn feared that Vogel would collect his wits. Why else should Vogel take this voyage, except to land alone in safe, neutral Sweden as some sort of refugee without stain on his character? No doubt

173

he had false papers on him, in order to take up a new identity in Sweden, or ultimately further afield, well away from his crimes.

They had food and water for about a week, so the present indecisive course roughly north could go on until Vogel made up his mind. The weather continued fine and sunny, the wind still south of east, but the water smoother in the lee of land to the east, which Zorn saw from time to time. Any time now, Vogel would be working out how to dispose of his three companions. Had he lost his nerve? Zorn continued to watch closely. There was sea-traffic here too. The mercantile imperatives of all craft had little time to spare for a solitary ketch of unknown origin.

Still *Donner* sped on, not so much to a destination as away from a decision. At night the same drill took place: Vogel in the cabin, Nelli and the boy wrapped up with Zorn in the cockpit. At dawn, Zorn saw a tramp steamer crossing their bows. It sailed blithely on, ignoring their presence.

'What's that?' Vogel shouted, pointing to the boat ahead on their starboard bow.

'Just an old tramp, probably between Denmark and Sweden.'

Of one thing Zorn was now certain. Land was barely visible to starboard, and there was nothing to port, so it must have been the Sound they had negotiated, not an estuary, nor a strait between Danish islands. If so, they had now left the Sound well behind, and he knew then that the dark humps to starboard on the horizon were Sweden.

'To Sweden, or from it?' Vogel snapped back.

Zorn saw his mistake. Such a direction invited decision. Better to have professed complete ignorance than to offer Vogel a choice of direction. His heart pounded as he watched Vogel cogitating, possibly deciding that the time had come to deal with his fellow-passengers.

'Depends where we are,' Zorn dared to answer.

Vogel jumped at that, leaving the tiller to slap back to port. The boat careened violently, and as both men sought to keep

174

their feet, Zorn bumped into Vogel. Vogel snatched at his revolver, and in one movement flicked off the safety-catch and pulled the trigger. The shot thundered across the rigging against the sing and whip of the shrouds. Zorn lurched back. The ketch threatened to gybe. In this wind, a dismantling or a capsize . . . Instinctively, Zorn dived for the tiller.

Vogel panic-stricken, stood over by the hatch, covering Zorn with his gun. Nelli's frightened face appeared for a moment at the hatch, then retreated. The lurching of the deck frightened them all as the importunate white horses swept over them. But the ketch was soon righted under Zorn's hand, while Vogel slumped down on the deck. As they picked up way again, Zorn realized that no rational decision could be expected of this man. If this went on, they would all perish at sea.

There had now been no sight of land for two hours. The waves were turning into a long swell, a sign of more open water. Both he and Vogel jumped as yet another crack, almost an explosion, set the boat shuddering again.

'What's that?' Vogel cried, flourishing his Mauser.

'A shroud gone. Your work, curse you, Vogel!' Zorn flung at him, for he saw that Vogel's stray shot had indeed done some damage, fraying a shroud on the windward side. 'If we don't attend to it at once, the mast will go.'

'"We"?' Vogel asked viciously. 'You mean "you".'

'It'll take two of us.'

'Then take *her*.'

'No! Not strong enough. It'll take all our strength in this wind.'

'Then let her take this thing while we attend to it,' Vogel replied, pointing at the tiller.

It was with difficulty that Zorn persuaded Nelli of the danger and urgency of the situation. But he got her to the tiller, told her how to keep it well over while they worked. Then he and Vogel lurched towards the frayed shroud. The loose rope was swirling madly in the wind as Zorn struggled to catch it. He could feel the bend of the mast and hauled

175

hard while Vogel stood off uselessly, dramatically waving his gun.

'Help me, damn you! Can't you see?' Zorn shouted. 'Catch that rope and hold on while I bring up the other end!'

Vogel held back, unwilling to risk losing the supremacy of the Mauser.

'Come on,' Zorn screamed, 'the mast's going!'

But it was too late. Another shroud snapped with such force it lashed across Zorn's face. It might have been the blow of a cane on his flesh. As he flinched with pain, the torn shroud whipped out of his fist, and he watched helplessly as a crack slowly developed up the mast. The wind seemed to gather force as the mast began to topple. Sails flapped out of life. The whole structure, a sudden tangle of sails, mast, gaff and shrouds, fell before the wind and the boat yawed violently. Agonizingly, Zorn looked aft, where Nelli was trying to cope with the tiller. Vogel stood between them, his eyes dilated with fear at the rending of wood, sail and rope. The child, distraught with the mad movement and noise, was screaming in the cockpit.

'The tiller . . .' Zorn shouted. 'We've got to get her . . .'

As he made to push past Vogel, the Mauser came up at him. Zorn ducked in his rush and pushed with all his force. Vogel tipped madly over the rail, balanced for a moment. The gun cracked ineffectually into the air, Vogel spluttered hysterically, tried to regain his footing, when Zorn pushed madly at him again. With a splash far beyond his weight, Vogel fell backwards into the turbulence of the swell, the black hair falling like weed over the brow, the eyes dilated with panic. Then a hand appeared, reaching for aid. Did the mouth shape itself to shout 'Help'? Zorn, instinctively, half-reached for a rope, then fell back at the cabin door.

'Let him drown in hell . . .' he muttered passionately to himself. It was murder, yes, a man overboard on the high seas left to drown, an act unthinkable at sea. 'He's gone!' he cried in sheer exultation and looked in cold blood at the bubbles rising where Vogel had fallen.

His whole body shaking uncontrollably, he jumped up on to the cabin roof, arms held out wide, as though to rid his hands of some clinging mess. He wanted to shout – something, anything – but his lips would not respond to the mad whirlpool of his mind.

When Nelli's head, fearful and wide-eyed with questions, appeared above the hatch, trying to take in what had happened, and asked: 'Where is . . .?' Zorn's mouth spread in a wide grin and he shouted madly, all his strength returning: 'He's gone! *Mord! Mord!* Murder! I murdered him! He's gone – there.'

He pointed to the sea's turbulence, to the anonymous waves still washing over occasional rising bubbles of Vogel's last breath.

And as he leapt down beside her in the strange liberating silence following his shout, he laughed, hugged her ardently, then bent and lifted the boy and kissed his locks, exulting in their whiteness. Nelli, the boy and he were alone, at last. They could live – LIVE! Death was behind them, and it remained only for *Donner* to deliver them.

Nelli grinned at the innocence of it, that he could shout '*Mord!* Murder!' to the winds, and then come down and kiss them both. 'Murder' it might be, of a sort, if that was what he thought. But all that mattered, surely, was that a great load of grief and pain and maddening frustration had been dispatched overboard, and even *Donner* seemed lighter as she slopped about under the weight of her dismasting.

Zorn would never know if Vogel surfaced again. The ketch listed alarmingly to port with the weight of the wood, rigging and sails steadily settling in the water and getting heavier by the minute. Neither would speak of Vogel, nor even look in the direction of his fall. His black head might appear over the rail any second. As the waves beat against the passive hull, it might have been his skull battering away at the wood. The word 'murder' kept racing through Zorn's mind. But Vogel was gone.

That in the end it was the only solution, that it might have been Zorn himself in the water, was all that mattered, murder or no. His arms had pushed so violently at Vogel that he still trembled. But with a residual seamanship, he pushed the rudder hard over, in an attempt to turn the crippled boat head on to the swell. He instructed Nelli to keep it there with all her force, but the wind and the waves proved too much, and the craft floundered broadside on, threatening to capsize.

Zorn slashed through the sheets with his knife, and saw the sodden mainsail and jib go. He still had the mizzen. The list was now acceptable. Only the splintered mast weighed to port. Zorn went below to search for an axe, a vital piece of equipment for such an emergency, but to no avail. There was no way but to start hacking at the wood with the knife. He must have hacked for an hour till his right palm was bleeding. As he struggled, a formation of three heavy aircraft passed overhead in the blue sky. Their indifference accentuated the solitariness of their plight.

Meanwhile Nelli, whose hands had never been attuned to life's rougher edges, collected rope and bits and pieces, trying vainly to achieve order in what so lately had been Vogel's province in the cockpit, as though to expunge his clinging presence. It was her habit to hide from unpleasant facts by arranging things on shelves, on tables, on any available surface, where her eyes and hopefully her mind could be averted, small physical acts to keep large issues at bay. Her hands, still uncalloused by the sea's demands, riffled among the lengths of frayed rope, warding off the terror she sensed attended this crash of mast and sails. She had calmed the child, who clung passionately to her.

As for Vogel, he was just so much jetsam so far as she was concerned. But she had noticed Zorn's trembling, and when at last he returned to the cockpit, her hands sought his and she drew him towards her. If ever a man needed comfort, she thought, then asked: 'When . . .?' but broke off as she felt his uncertainty.

But he guessed. 'Sweden?' He had forgotten – Vogel's fall

and the dismasting had been as much as a man could take. 'It could be anywhere,' he murmured desperately. 'But it ought to be out there . . . or there . . .' Vaguely, he pointed upwind, so that even Nelli, who had never been strong on cause and effect, knew it would be unattainable unless the wind changed right round.

'But we shall get somewhere, shan't we?' She looked into his eyes for affirmation.

The ketch was rolling along, the waves slapping against her side in the strange silence now they had lost the perpetual whistle and whine of the sails and rigging. With this sudden transformation from lively ketch to almost passive hulk, Zorn knew they would get nowhere through his management, though you never knew where the sea might take you, one way or another. Their best hope now was any craft, whatever its nationality. Yet they could not have been more alone.

'Ah, yes,' he replied falsely. 'Somewhere, Nelli. I'm sure. Somewhere where there are no armies.' And smiled down at her. Then he took up the child and kissed him again. At long last, he could take them both in his arms, without Vogel's shadow over him. They were a family: Nelli, the boy, and he – alone on a waste of water, probably beyond help in a world that for the past six years had sunk below all civilized standards. At least, that had been his own experience. Others, like his mother, like those walking spectres in the camp, had fared worse, much worse, still.

The sea was now the only enemy, and that, he knew, could be formidable. Everything would depend now on *Donner's* soundness. And yet, with Vogel out of the way, surely there was hope of some sort, so long as he could keep *Donner* afloat. After all, the signs were that the war was coming to a close, with the probable defeat of the Fatherland, so all nations would now be in a mood, if not of reconciliation, at least of non-belligerence. Who would lift a hand against a helpless trio, a family like this, adrift in an open boat? It would not matter who picked them up. Zorn, disentangling himself from his newly found family, climbed up on the cabin roof

179

and clinging to what was left of the mast, scanned the horizon all round for any sign of a ship. But there was not even a trail of smoke. They might have been adrift in mid-Atlantic. As *Donner* rose to each crest of the swell, he gazed and gazed, but found nothing for comfort, just water, water, and for ever water.

He climbed down. 'It's only a matter of time,' he said. 'Somebody's bound to spot us and pick us up.'

He did not express that doubt he had at the back of his mind as to *Donner*'s soundness, her capacity to withstand the constant battering of the sea after years in Welckmar harbour.

'That's all right, then,' said Nelli, detaching herself with a reciprocal smile that would have comforted the dying. 'I'm going to get us something to eat. Something special that I kept from *him*.' And returned with a concoction, perhaps a pâté (he was so dull after all the effort), on the last of the bread that required a delicacy of handling, even a crooked finger, so evocative was it of high living.

'Truffles?' he guessed, as one still young to have lived so high.

'Officers are so generous,' she replied with glee, then regretted it in front of this half-starved innocent who, she recalled, needed better encouragement than that. But it was lost on him. He was thinking, and she detected no shadow on the harrowed face of a man who seemed to have got used to hunger and would relish every bite, whatever its source and however dry the bread.

'I'll need your help,' he said as they cleared the last crumbs.

'Anything. Just ask,' she affirmed with the air of one whose offers were always positive.

There was only the mizzen now to provide limited steerage way. What it would not do was provide power for the beat north and east that might bring them to that blessed land, possibly Sweden, or Norway, that he guessed now lay behind them. His only choice was to run before the wind. Nothing remotely like this emergency had ever happened to him before.

Since the wind, a still-benevolent north-easter, was now on their stern, steering was tricky and he had to keep the tiller firm under his hand to correct a tendency to yaw.

'At this rate, we're bound to get somewhere, Nelli,' he said cheerfully, because the blue of the sky and the smartness of the wind lifted his spirits to a belief that they must indeed 'get somewhere'.

Smiling assent, Nelli took the boy below. Zorn watched her, frowning. Even the Atlantic, he thought madly, has its limits. But then, listening to Nelli's movements, arranging, domesticating the cabin, he thought better of it, for the Atlantic was no joke. After all their efforts, it would surely be their end.

'It's all right, then,' she called back, with that absolute faith in him that she had shown from the beginning, fleeing from her armies. He felt the burden of it.

From anything they could see beyond the rolling swell, it might well be the Atlantic, he thought. But remembering Paterfamilias, he reckoned this could only be the famous German Ocean. On this present drift, and given this easterly weather, it was just conceivable they would find England, the enemy. They would neither question him about Vogel nor put him in a labour camp. And even if they did put him behind barbed-wire, at least he would have delivered Nelli and the child. Nelli would find her way. Perhaps some passing ship would see them. But with only the mizzen aloft, they presented such a low profile that they were unlikely to be seen on this wide waste.

And indeed, it surprised him how boundless the sea was, how little was to be seen on its wide expanse all round. They would see smoke on the horizon, but always it would either cross their drift and disappear, or become a cloud and disperse. There was almost always a plane in the sky, sometimes whole flights of them in tight formation, but it was increasingly obvious to Zorn that the ketch was either invisible to them or, more likely, meant nothing to them. He lost count of the days – seven – eight. . . ?

181

He took care not to transmit his worry to Nelli, who in any case was fully occupied with the boy, who had developed a cough. Besides, nothing was really a worry now that Vogel had gone where he could no longer pursue. Not that Zorn was fully convinced of that – when a shadow lifts it takes time to get used to the light. Nelli would smile and he would have no worries then. She lived day by day, hour by hour, minute by minute, one moment attending to young Dieter, the next humming contentedly over some self-appointed chore. The days and nights followed with a predictable sameness. The sun rose in a near cloudless sky, the wind kept its more or less easterly quarter, the sun sank, as though reluctantly, and *Donner* behaved, like any delinquent, as well as could be expected.

For the first three or four days after Vogel's sinking, it was the child who woke first and roused his mother by pulling her hair. He was still a little too shy of his father to try such liberties. The boy sensed the access of freedom from the horrid man with the gun. He was eager for life, inquisitive about the goings-on on the boat. A chip off the old block, thought his father, roused out of the deep dawn sleep that overtakes an anxious night-watch.

But then, as the days followed with the monotony of the featureless sea and sky, the boy grew more languid and would lie passive, devoid of energy, occasionally whining miserably.

In her better moments, Nelli had talked dreamily of silk stockings and exotic perfumes, whiling away the empty sea-girt hours. Recalling the generosity and comparative luxury of her hamper, he had thought it might be of food she would dream. But their now meagre diet of the last stale crusts and biscuits, obscure tinned pastes and the end of a cheese now hard as a lithographer's stone, had rendered all food merely a boring means of survival. They might see ships far off and planes overhead, but nobody noticed the stricken ketch. It was as though the world had come to a stop now the war was over. The oil in the Primus had run out, so the saving nourishment of coffee had gone. Nelli felt it more than

Zorn, who had long been used to living lean. Increasingly, she felt the cold when the sun dipped of an evening, when the wind would take on a keenness and a chill, and she would come to him for warmth, having sacrificed both blankets for the child.

Each night Zorn lashed the rudder, looking prayerfully at the eastward quarter of the sky for a change in the wind. He always woke early and made up his sleep in catnaps at the tiller. Nelli ranged restlessly over the boat, trying to keep busy. When she was not asleep and keeping the child warm, she eked out the diminishing rations, or swept the deck out of habit, or she talked. Zorn marvelled at this restlessness, for this new lapse into hunger was afflicting him with dreadful lassitude. She had reserves to call upon still, and something in her required this constant activity. Was it boredom, he wondered, boredom at the sheer confinement on a sailing craft? Yet when she came to the cockpit to join him, boredom was the last thing he read in her face. She would talk of 'old times'. It was when asking her about Stentewik that he suddenly realized his solitariness, in spite of her presence.

'Poor Gerhardt,' she mused, without evident grief. 'I heard he died at once on the Russian Front – that awful winter.'

But which awful winter was lost on him, for without news, all winters had been awful. Everything had fallen to the East – grandparents, parents, and now poor old Stentewik. No wonder people fled from any encroachment from the East. The East, one way or another, bore its own special malice. Old Stern had proclaimed it. Whether it was the Germans themselves, or the Russians, a particular malevolence was reserved for the dreaded East. The West, judging by his own impromptu liberation, seemed indifferent, even benevolent, though Nelli would not agree. All armies were to be avoided.

Now, reflecting on their present plight, adrift on the open sea, with only the mizzen for sail power, no charts, no knowing their position or even their direction beyond what could be read from the sun, he wished he had persuaded Nelli they would have been safer holed out in Welckmar harbour.

But Vogel had settled it for them. Yet, were it not for the lack of food and the quietness of young Dieter, Nelli might not have a care in the world. The sea, the sun and the wind had weathered her to a golden tan. Each morning, after attending to the child and bathing in sea-water hauled up in the bucket, she hummed to herself as she gathered her blond hair in two bangs over her ears. Nothing could dampen her spirits now that Vogel had gone.

'What shall we do when we land?' she asked, as though they were enjoying a trip round the bay, for she lived, as she had always lived, in hope.

'It depends where . . .'

But qualifications were not in her grammar. 'I hope they give us a good meal, yes – and coffee. What wouldn't I give for a large mug of steaming coffee!'

Zorn felt the all too familiar ache of hunger returning and wondered how the child and Nelli would stand up to it should they not find a landfall in the next day or two. They must have been at sea two weeks, he reckoned. Time was measured by the sun's arc over a sky barely disturbed by high cirrus clouds. Several evenings an incredible mackerel sky changing from scarlet to crimson to purple might have diverted them, but they were beyond aesthetic entertainment. However many days, weeks, Zorn found it impossible to reckon properly. He knew now he should have kept a log, for there was no way now of knowing where they were, where the nights had brought them, or the sharp breeze of day swept them on the sea's map. The very sameness of long sunlit days deceived them as they lay in the cockpit, not so much conserving energy as unable to raise any. Water was getting low. Zorn felt the responsibility. They were – simply adrift.

Then one evening, he was concerned about a long, low streak of cloud to the west. The mizzen flapped uncertainly. Seamanship might be necessary before nightfall. The swell was changing, the wind perhaps backing, but *Donner* rode well enough, and there was nothing to do but wait. He was very tired.

'Nothing wrong, is there?' Nelli asked as she read the care in his face.

'No. Just tired – and hungry.' He grinned.

She took him in her arms, her lips ruffling the now abundant beard that adorned his chin. 'Like lamb's wool,' she murmured, unaware of any dark clouds on any horizon. 'We'll soon get somewhere, just mark my words,' she went on, and he knew she believed it simply.

But feeling the incipient threat of the swell, he wondered. Was it cloud or land ahead, or both? And if land, how do you beach a deep-hulled ketch with a ton of cast-iron cemented into the keel for ballast? He needed sleep desperately, yet knew that if they were to approach land he must be alert. It was not that he reckoned to preserve *Donner*, much as he loved her. It was more a dread of being aboard if she grounded on inhospitable rocks. He was worried, if they had to swim for it, about Nelli's ineffectual dog-paddle. And with his own diminished strength, could he possibly support the child?

But *Donner* seemed to adjust of her own volition and rode as well as ever. There seemed no immediate danger, so he lashed the rudder and went below to stretch beside Nelli, for she demanded his warmth. He dropped off to sleep like a babe.

'Dieter,' Nelli whispered in his ear. He stirred in his sleep. 'Dieter!' He jumped. 'Sorry to wake you,' she continued drowsily, 'but why is there water here?'

Along the floor, a runnel of water slopped back and forth with the rise and fall of the swell. Zorn sat up at once and turned to the bilge pump. But he saw it was a losing battle. He rushed to the cockpit. The swell was quite high now. In the dark he groped for the dinghy, then remembered. Peering over the side he knew at once. The sea's turbulence was different, more mischievous as it smacked against *Donner*'s side.

Donner was sinking slowly. Zorn watched helplessly as the

hull settled deeper in the water with a sort of resignation. The years of neglect had taken their toll. A plank below had either been stove in by some submerged object, or the new agitation had discovered some flaw in the hull, from the years of neglect as *Donner* stood in the harbour waters over a winter, perhaps two or more. Panic-stricken, Zorn reached for the lifebelt and flung it towards Nelli and the boy. Her look might have been read more as disappointment than of despair as water reached her ankles.

It all happened very quickly. The deck settled in the water under their feet and slid away in an eerie turbulence, separating the three struggling figures as it sucked and pulled at their knees. Nelli was trying in vain to push the lifebelt round the boy. She screamed and thrashed the water frantically. Zorn, from more than five yards away, could just see the lifebelt slip away from her. He swam towards her, shouting, but the swell only washed her farther away into the darkness. He could see no sign of the child. Nelli, still just visible, was splashing with her weird dog-paddle, exhausting herself and crying, 'Dieter! Dieter!' Then, as another rise in the swell carried her on and over, he lost sight of her and she was gone.

'Nelli!' he screamed. 'Nelli!' He swam about in the half-light, calling, calling, then bumped into the empty lifebelt. He called and called, but knew they were gone.

He was exhausted beyond effort or rational thought, and more by instinct hauled himself into the lifebelt, to give in to the will of the swell in despair.

Somewhere, somehow, Vogel still cast his shadow. As Zorn half-swam, half-floated, he continued shouting for Nelli. But as he weakened, his one resolve was to flee that shadow. Nelli and Dieter would never be free to join him until Vogel was – (and as he floated on his back and rode the increased swell, and a darkness began to close over him, he dredged the word up) – 'resettled'.

V

'But grant me still a friend in my retreat
Whom I may whisper – solitude is sweet . . .'

W. Cowper

This, he thought in a sudden access of consciousness after the
delirious flight, swim, crawl, from the water, constant water,
is the classic position of the castaway. Lying face down at the
merging of land and sea, apparently nowhere in particular,
certainly without sign of humanity, he tried to take it all in.
Nothing. Just sand, a half-cliff – more a bank – then trees,
mean trees blown lean and hungry by the on-shore wind,
struggling to survive, like himself.

The sea, which had promised freedom, had proved yet
another persecutor and detained Nelli and the boy. Vogel had
corrupted the sea, as he corrupted all that he touched, recruited
its strength to his own purpose. Zorn's flat hand slapped the
wet sand in an agony of despair. If only he could move,
survive, he would wait for Nelli – and he cursed Vogel yet
again.

He belched noisily, all salt and saliva. Then, as his body
retched, he farted weakly like an old man. As the dryness of
the air just a hand's breadth above the wet sand revived him,
he turned his head sideways, searching for signs, remnants,
anything to accompany his own deliverance and just possibly
more. But there was not even a bit of rope or sail-cloth or

timber – nothing. Nothing but wet, clean sand and sea stretched between two low headlands. He was in a little bay, just more than a cove, less than half a kilometre across. Beyond the points there might be anything – *anything*.

Then, as he lifted his head once more, straining with the effort (his arms simply would not bear his weight), he realized with relief that the tide must be on the ebb, for only a few metres ahead he saw a line of sea-wrack marking the extent of the tide. Beyond that, dry sand, wind-blown. He knew then that, with an effort, he would be safe for perhaps eight or ten hours, when the tide would return.

He had ended with his head twisted awkwardly towards the sea, and he saw, with a dreadful leap of the heart, a dark head bobbing in the breakers out there where he had come from. Desperately, he tried to focus, but could make out no more than a black form, surely human, bobbing up and down in the rise and ease of the waves. His pulse raced. Only the head, but surely alive, rising and falling with a mad volition, watching his every move. As, briefly, he brought it into focus, he was even aware of baleful eyes. But then he flopped again, ready to die. And lay there, unconscious. The head was much too dark, alas, to be Nelli. Nelli had never really graduated in her swimming from that ineffectual dog-paddle.

When he came to, he saw that the sea had receded yet farther. Searching at once for the swimmer out in the breakers, he could see nothing but the white of the blown crests, and was relieved. For until he could reach the dry sand beyond the tide-line, he would be unable to cope with Vogel. But if Vogel could survive, was there not an even better chance of Nelli and Dieter getting ashore somewhere? He must gather his strength to deal with Vogel before he was able to interfere yet again.

Testing his arms and feeling the sun warm on his back, he felt stronger, and crawled crab-like over the line of sea-wrack and on to the warm dry sand. He turned with a last effort of will, so that he lay on his back and had to close his eyes against the sunlight. When, anxiety getting the better of him, he raised himself on his elbows to check if Vogel had gone, he saw with dreadful clarity that he was there, still bobbing up and down, too distant now on the ebbing tide to distinguish the eyes.

'Ah – ah . . .!' Zorn groaned, loud enough that his pursuer might hear him, a groan that might have been taken for a death croak. The head was too unmistakably black to offer any hope. He knew he must flee, yet again, wherever the strength might come from. By now, drying out in the sun, his denims and boots less sodden, he found he could move at will on all fours, turned over, crawled again in one bout of will, till he reached a rock at the foot of the bluff. He nestled behind it out of the sun and the sight of the swimmer, who neither came nor went, but just bobbed there, waiting, watching.

Although thinking, like seeing, was difficult, he knew he must stay concealed behind his boulder. While he was hidden from those distant eyes, he could simply lie and gather his strength, for what he could not yet think, except to wait for Nelli. He breathed more easily, huddled gratefully in a hollow of rough pebbles which began to press on his bad hip. I am that much alive, he thought, as he registered the old pain. He shifted. The sun was warm after the chill of the sea. His clothes gradually lifted off his skin, and he assisted the process of drying by turning on his back to receive the sun's full warmth. By now, he found every part of his body could be moved quite freely. He felt like a plant breaking the soil after the rigours of a long winter in the dark.

He now manoeuvred his head towards the edge of the boulder, to see if Vogel was still there. Inch by inch he moved, till with one eye he could see the sea. The head was there, riding the waves as easily as ever, deigning neither to land nor swim off – or drown. It was too far now to distinguish the eyes, and for that he was thankful.

But then, in despair, he withdrew his head. He was suddenly aware, in an agony of sweat, of two great black eyes, not twenty metres away in the seaweed, balefully watching his every move. An unflinching gaze, animal-like – Katya the cat, at her most maudlin, begging at your knee for some tasty scrap.

Zorn withdrew quickly, like a snail into its shell. But too late, for he knew that unblinking presence had watched his every move, heard every belch and fart as he struggled. Even now, it was waiting out there for his next move, probably in much the same state as himself, mustering the strength for a last *Putsch* – to his boulder?

The question was: which side was it on, this presence – his, or the swimmer's out there in the breakers? Was he the hunter or the hunted?

He lay back, his arms stretched out above his head, his legs parted, racked, not merely the classic castaway, which he had played many a time on the Baltic's silver edge, but now crucified, a suppliant to heaven, mumbling and muttering over the words, 'Why, oh why, hast thou . . .' but forbore, and lay silent in the sun.

Looking up across the scrub and exposed rock of the bluff that rose immediately above him, he knew he would only feel safe once he had reached the trees at the top. At least there the chances of hiding from the eyes were multiplied. The sun and increasing dryness strengthened his resolve.

The first problem was to establish the position and attitude of that creature out there in the sea-wrack. Perhaps this bay, like some god in constant need of propitiation, was habitually a landfall for castaways. Appetite might be involved, in which case even the bay would have to be watched, friend so far to him, but a potential enemy. Vogel out in the breakers was holding his distance and might be dealt with, as Berthe would say, 'in due course'.

Zorn peeped boldly out then, a rock in his fist. As his eyes confronted the other's, he was startled. The thing beseeched. Full black orbs, clouded with mystery, and suffering – and then the voice, plaintive, another cry in the wilderness, half hiss, half bark, but infinitely sad. As Zorn screwed up his eyes, he realized his friend the sun was enemy to this other, and felt sorry before the gaze, because he lacked the strength to help him back into his element, the sea. The rock dropped from his hand.

Mouth hanging open, Zorn could only whimper an animal apology, hands held apart in the despair of the physically spent. He could see even the dried lymph at the corner of the eyes, caked with sand crystals, and the white whiskers despondently spread in the wrack. The natural white of the creature's fur gave it the air here of a sheep rug cast up by the tide. Heartbreakingly, its colour was just that of Nelli's hair, white touched with a soft warmth.

Standing up bravely at last to appraise the Vogel situation, Zorn smiled, for he knew now that it was merely the mother out there calling to her babe. As his eyes swung back, he could now discern the pale pink of a wound low down on the babe's side. He staggered over to the young seal. The sad eyes swivelled to his every move. When he bent painfully to comfort it, it hissed furiously, exposing its vicious barbed teeth, ready to bite the hand that offered nothing but dryness. It frightened Zorn. Though he now felt no pity, he made to strew weed over it, to alleviate at least the effects of the sun's heat. For the young seal, in consequence of its wound, was more likely to die of dehydration. Back in its element, the sea would no doubt have healed the wound in no time. It would have to wait for the next tide, if it survived.

Zorn's own strength was limited. He too was now dry, and thirsty. He rubbed his tongue over cracked lips. Vogel, mother seal, was still out there. Well, he would do anything to help, but how could he? He also was bereft and stranded. One must survive, and wait. Wearily, he smiled. She out there would soon forget, very soon, and in a few hours would be off into the depths, snapping at fish with those barbed teeth. Looking down at the pup, Zorn saw how beautiful it was in its white furry innocence. Yet the tide was so far out by now, there was no way he could help the poor creature back to its mother. And he knew, if once those teeth fastened

191

on to his hand even as he sought to help, he could lose a finger or two. He must survive, in order to wait.

He returned to his boulder. 'You must go to bed early, have a nice sleep, gather your strength for tomorrow,' Berthe would say before some test, bringing him warmed milk, which he promptly poured on the window-box the minute her back was turned. He would stay at his boulder, gather his strength for the climb up to the trees and safety, and wait for Nelli and the boy.

Of that first momentous day he could remember little, but he must have climbed the bluff above the sands and found a hollow under the upturned root canopy of a tree that had fallen to the wind. Close by, mercifully, was a stream of fresh water. He must have slept in the hollow, then, with failing strength, spent the first two days improving his shelter. He was conscious of his empty stomach, so took his time.

With the moon riding high in an almost cloudless sky, he settled himself in his dugout under the great tree that had been master but now succumbed to age and the wind's depredations. He had lined the hollow under its uptorn roots with dead leaves, and overhead had draped two large pieces of canvas he had hauled up from the tideline after his first beachcombing expedition, when with growing confidence he had returned to the shore. Vogel's spectre still hung about. Zorn looked over his shoulder every now and then, became conscious of the habit, and made an effort to stop it.

He was surprised by the amount of rubbish the sea threw up. He surmised that there was a shipping lane somewhere out to sea, but in the first twenty-four hours he had seen no craft whatsoever. Shipping would not have worried him, for an isolated figure ashore would be of no concern to ships bent on far destinations. But small craft would have been different: inshore fishermen, lobster catchers, leisure sailors like himself once.

This bay seemed a haven free of mankind, given over to birds and the occasional seal. He noted the seal pup had succumbed to the sun's drying out. It was now just a tangle of white fur which the gulls were scavenging. The eyes had gone. Looking seaward, he could not discern the black head riding the waves.

Among the piles of seaweed, he saw how many lengths of prime timber there were. Then, with a shock, as he picked up an empty wooden crate, he read on its side: '48 × ½ kilo kannen milch – H. Winkelmann – Bremen'. He ran for cover. Had he journeyed thus far, had he struggled almightily for freedom, only to find himself back on his own benighted territory? As his heart thundered, he felt quite light-headed. But there was nothing to be done about it now. He must survive, must sustain his strength as best he could, so that he might wait. And though his plan did not extend beyond improving the shelter he had found under the fallen tree after his first climb, he knew that survival would entail improving that shelter. He must venture out again, for the beachwrack offered the only possible source of materials.

After gingerly handling Herr Winkelmann's crate once again, just by way of checking, he looked at others. He was eager for Norwegian, or Swedish (though how that could be he did not know), or even Dutch, where, if anybody native found him, he would have a chance of help. He noted with relief that Herr Winkelmann was alone. On a green bottle he read 'Gordon's Gin' in raised lettering, 'London and Aberdeen'. He took it up, wrapped it in the first piece of rumpled, sand-encrusted canvas about two metres square. There were more, all English. Germany was at war with England. So where did he stand now? Perhaps the war was over already.

If this were England, it was both startling and comforting. If he was seen, he would be taken prisoner, perhaps by some English Vogel. On the other hand, remembering his reading in English – *King Lear* (only a part), *Childe Harold* (most of it, because Paterfamilias favoured it above all other works), *Pride and Prejudice* (largely incomprehensible, even to Pater, but perhaps the most reassuring), William Wordsworth ('London Bridge' and 'Ode to Daffodils'), Shelley (not in

193

the least comprehensible, but again Pater's choice), and two that were of immediate import, *Swiss Family Robinson* and *Robinson Crusoe* – he felt that Vogel, far from being a jailer, would probably be put behind bars.

He decided that it must be all or nothing in this retreat, where there was no sign of humanity, either on land or sea. He would walk as he wished in the bay and up to his tree, which was already home, and if he was to be discovered, he would lay himself at the mercy of the English, for neither fight nor flight seemed feasible. He would live in hope that it was Sweden, even England, if discovery was inevitable. But otherwise he would keep himself to himself.

He walked the length of the bay, not yet venturing to climb the promontories at either end to see what lay beyond. In the wrack there was every sort of object, and though his immediate need was to improve his shelter, he also flung items of any conceivable use up above the highest tidemark: bottles, timber, one left shoe in fairly good order, and a glass float from a fishing-net. This last he saw no use for, but it was covetable, a green crystal ball, of potential comfort to his eyes and hands. And he could imagine young Dieter liking its firm green roundness.

So his first two days ashore were filled with diminishing apprehension and increasing activity, anything to keep memory at bay. Heaving the areas of canvas, heavy with damp and sand, exhausted him. But he feared inactivity as much as rain, so soldiered on. He lashed the canvas with odd lengths of rope and then returned to the beach to select a further load, this time of wood. Until, as the sun dipped towards the sea's horizon, he dropped into his tabernacle of tree roots, canvas and leaves, and was forced at last to think and to dwell on his hunger.

And fearing thought and memory more than hunger, he set off inland, keeping the North Star over his shoulder, noting each landmark, until after an hour of stumbling he came upon the wall. That was the first sign of humanity for Zorn, and from then on he moved with caution, till he arrived

194

at the settlement nestling silently in the moonlight. And so, in his hunger, took risks, and first encountered the 'enemy' – Frau Flood, who had not turned him in, but had said 'Call again', and given him two cans – 'on tick'.

Clutching his two cans to him, he went to sleep in his shelter, and woke only when the sun was already high in the sky.

From then on, there was never any question in his mind but that this was home. With Nelli and Dieter still to arrive, Vogel out of sight, and the wilderness enfolding him securely, he felt he had not chosen this, but rather it had chosen him. Nothing seemed hostile – least of all, that first sight of the 'enemy', Frau Flood, who had shown extraordinary benignity to an enemy alien who might be anything – spy, madman, rapist.

So, with even the sun at its best through the bursting leaves, he began at once to settle in. Water was no problem. The stream ran through the trees and spread its fingers across the beach, on its way to the sea. And with all this timber about, shelter was a matter of time and patience only.

Food was the difficulty, and he now addressed himself to the two tins Frau Flood had given him. One, named Spam, was easily opened, since it bore its own key. He devoured it greedily, decided that it contained real meat, maybe pork, and was not ersatz. He regretted having finished it in one feast. But two hours afterwards, hunger assailed him yet again, and the second tin needed an opener.

He would always remember the desperation of that moment. That was the beginning of his self-reliance. He went down to the bay and combed the wrack for a piece of timber bearing the right attachment of metal (it was amazing what ships threw overboard or lost on the way). He found what he wanted, prised the metal away, went back to his shelter, and using a stone he sharpened and honed the metal to his purpose. Despite his hunger, he took his time, produced as fine an object as he could in the circumstances, and in the end he could be said to have a sharp-bladed instrument with a point. It was his first real essay in wood and metal in his new-found land. From then on, he mastered both and provided for his needs in a variety of ways.

The walk, or, rather, scramble to the village had taken its toll of Zorn. He lay in his hollow as spent as he ever remembered. He found it difficult to think, so gave up trying.

His clothes, such as they were, had dried out thoroughly. He had a shirt, a British Army pullover, a pair of underpants, British denim trousers, and Army boots but no socks. If it rained, he would just have to hole up. Now that Vogel had, more or less, been relegated to natural history, he could accept his present anticyclone with due gratitude.

After the night's fruitful encounter with Frau Flood, he slept as he had not slept in many months, perhaps even years. Certainly, it was his longest unbroken sleep since those two men had picked him up at home and 'mobilized' him for labour for the Reich. He realized this with a start, because the sun was high in the sky when he woke. Castaways always wake with a start – they are alive when they should not be, alive when others, equally deserving of life, are dead. And they have their new-found land to cope with.

The day was already hot, so he took off his boots. Everything was a struggle, not only of body, but of will. He examined his boots. They were in good order. They had not suffered from the scramble through the wilderness he had inherited by landing. But his trousers, he saw with regret, had suffered, especially below the knee. If he was to visit Frau Flood again, he would need to measure up to some sort of decency, if not respectability. Frau Flood was not unlike those ladies he had known, sitting at their cottage doors in Welckmar, knitting in the sunshine for the winter, missing nothing, flaunting their own standards of frugality, industry and respectability, while exulting in the sun and gossiping the world to rights.

He was hungry – vacuous – yet again. Nothing was in him but a will to live, a will to survive and wait, a will that would

196

not evaporate. He whimpered at the memory of Nelli and his small son, not having the strength to weep. But even Zorn, low in body and spirit, bereft, cast away on an alien shore whose friendship or otherwise he was still to explore – even Zorn in his present state knew it was touch and go, and he must hang on if he was to wait for his own.

Water? Yes, he remembered that water was in abundance. Even in this dry weather, the stream inspired confidence, probably denoting a spring somewhere in the woods. He would call on Frau Flood again. It was she who had pointed the way to survival. Why else should she feed him as she had done, sending him away with his tins of meat? He would like to see Frau Flood in broad daylight. But not yet, not till he knew where he was and how he was regarded by the natives, and not with torn trousers!

Food? He must make the most of Frau Flood. Why had she come out the third time with those tins? He must make another night journey to ensure his survival. It was the first house, easy to find – in the villagers' terms, it would be the last house. If only it were easier to get there. But until he knew how he would be treated, he felt protected by that very distance. As far as he could tell, he was immured in a wilderness. It was gentle after barbed-wire. If he could contrive food and shelter, he would have time to work it all out.

Shelter? He would be all right while this weather lasted, in his temporary root-hideout. But fire? He must think about that.

For the moment however, he would conserve his strength for the long walk after nightfall. That was the one chance he must take. So he dozed all afternoon, resisting the temptation to explore the beach for anything useful it might throw up, and for any sign of . . .

As the sun fell towards the west, he donned his boots again and started off into the wilderness, noticing the sun's angle all the time. It was easy to get lost, even to go in circles. He was wary of further damage to his trousers, and brambles were the worst enemy. He knew it would take a couple of hours to get to that wall, but at least it was all visible now. He could negotiate by sight rather than feel his way, and he wondered how he had managed it the previous time.

Then – he fell to the ground. Suddenly, in the midst of the jungle, he saw what was unmistakably hard-edged, man-made: a building. He clung to the ground, determined not to be taken in yet. As he peered through the leaves of a rambling rhododendron, he saw it was – or had been – quite large. But it was a hulk.

No roof, just walls, crumbling and mostly overgrown with ivy. He crept closer. He saw it was old, empty and abandoned, so he fought his way towards it.

The final barrier was a line of box trees that had grown up to the height of what walls were left. He fought his way through hard-knobbed branches and found himself in front of a dank wall. He crept along it and arrived at what had been a window. It was a riot of ivy. But there were still signs of the frame, charred wood covered with a fungoid growth. He pulled at the frame, and it came away easily. He recognized the remains of a sound old hardwood, dark, almost black, probably one of the mahogany family, a sign of wealth in a former owner.

He clambered over the sill. Every move was as difficult as ever, yet he was propelled not only by curiosity, but by insecurity. The floor had been tiled with what looked like marble. As he moved, he nearly slipped on a patch of decayed vegetation. Here and there, an eerie bracken shoot had forced its way through a crack between tiles and soared upwards for light, while old dead bracken lay all round. One or two charred beams still remained, broken and tilted at odd angles. But most of the marble floor had survived, either cracked or calcified. Obviously, the place had succumbed to fire, and long ago, judging by the extent of the decay.

The sun was setting in a blaze of crimson, and he knew he must leave the ruin and move on. He was so tired, he found every move needed an effort of will, but he must get to the village if he was to test Frau Flood again. But even as he was fighting his way through the undergrowth, he was planning what might be done with the ruin, if his strength allowed.

The light in the sky and the emerging stars still guided him. He knew that unless he cleared a path through this tangle, he would be lost without the stars. Last night, his fight with this wilderness had been a blind, instinctive search for food, like some animal staggering towards highland pasture away from drought-stricken plains. His intention had been to steal, not to beg. To beg meant contact with people, and until he had assessed the situation, political and military (he was a German, and as far as he knew was technically still at war with Frau Flood's people), he would lie low so long as he could lay his hands on food. Frau Flood had been more than a surprise, she had been an angel, not only friendly, but a provider of the one thing that would keep him going – food. Keeping going was his only defence against the creeping despair he could so easily succumb to, and to be absent when Nelli and Dieter arrived was unthinkable.

In the purpling depths of the late summer evening, he negotiated the wall that seemed to mark the division between his wilderness and the world. Before him stretched rolling heathland, not unlike the open stretch of Lüneburg, with dark tree-clumps silhouetted against the dying northern sky. He recalled that the going was easy from now on, for the grass was closely cropped. He could see the twinkling lights of the village in the distance.

It was already familiar, the easy fence, just strong and high enough to keep stock out of her garden. He did not leap so much as roll over in his weariness. The other lights from the village were set apart – or rather, Frau Flood was set apart. That suited Zorn, who felt quite bold in Frau Flood's garden, shielded from the rest of the village by the house.

In the quarter-light, he was touched to see he was expected. There was a plate and a tall mug on the edge of the grass nearest to the house, as though left out for starving birds or some half-domesticated hedgehog. The plate was covered by a tea-cloth. There were two baps, ham-filled again, and under the saucer which covered the mug, steaming sweet tea, again laced with milk which made him nauseous. She must indeed have been waiting for him, for the tea was hot. Was he so clumsy that he could be heard while not hearing? He sat on the unkempt grass that mostly constituted the garden, this haven set apart from the unknown village, and ate solemnly, as by right.

He wiped the crumbs from his beard, which itched still. As things stood, he would have to put up with it, but it affected him in an odd way, imparting false years. He would not smile until it was gone. He sat on, sure of his welcome, and waited. If she had been good enough to expect him, perhaps her curiosity would bring her out again. He could hear her wireless behind the closed curtains, what sounded like a news bulletin. Certainly, he was curious.

Then the sound was switched off. He waited, but stood up. The thought occurred to him that it might be a trap, the food a bait and she about to bring out with her some official, some British Vogel. He was ready to bound off as he heard her drawing the bolts.

First she popped out only her head. Then, apparently satisfied, she came out, still armed with her poker.

'You're there again, so,' she said, keeping her distance.

'Ah, thank you, Frau Flood. It was very good. Thank you.'

He watched for a second figure, but she was alone. Hence the poker, whose office rather than menace disturbed him.

'Where've you come from, Mr Thorn? I was half-expecting you all day. I reckoned you'd come back – for more.'

He did not care to declare his demesne – not yet.

'Oh, over there.' He waved an arm vaguely. 'I sleep over . . . there.' It could be anywhere. His voice, she thought, sounded so much younger than he looked.

'Are you a foreign sailor or something?'

'Yes, yes – a sailor.'

It seemed to satisfy, even to intrigue her.

200

'Was there any more?'

'Any more?'

'Yes. Any more of you. Was you wrecked or something?'

'Yes. Wrecked.'

'And you the only one?'

'No – two more . . .' He choked on a crumb and coughed.

'And with you as well, then? Over there?'

'No. Only me.'

'Did they drown then?'

He found it difficult to keep up, to find words, but finally muttered: 'I wait for them,' and was glad of the dark as tears pricked his eyes.

'Ah, you poor man,' Frau Flood murmured, hazarding a thought for the closeness of shipmates on the high seas. 'How are you sleeping then? Are you sleeping rough or something?'

He considered this. It had implications. 'I sleep' was all he was prepared to say.

It was her turn to consider. The poker now hung limply at her side. Zorn wished he could see her face, but he could read only her voice and judged it right to declare that he was very hungry. She retreated at that, still banging the bolts home, but was soon back. There was no sign of fear in her as she came up close to him.

'You poor man. Here, take this.' She handed him a loaf and a half-pound package of butter. 'They'll keep you going – like. I'm only a poor body, a widow.'

Did this require some special response? Her tone indicated it.

'Widow?' he struggled with it. He was sure it was significant. 'Ah, yes . . .' he went on, too wrapped up in himself, she thought. 'Yes, yes, widow. I'm sorry, Frau Flood.' It was like steering through shoals. It was not a statement she seemed to accept – rather a badge to wear, a mark in her favour.

'Aye,' she sighed contentedly. 'A widow these four years.' It was established, but soon dismissed. 'And here,' she rabbited on, testing the ground all the time. 'You can have these

201

as well, but mind you, they're on tick. Not the bread and butter. They're as little as a body can give if you're as hungry as you say you are. But these' – she handed him two further tins – 'are on tick.'

She was trying to take him in, looking him up and down in the luminous dark. His whiteness glowed. Perhaps, if he had been dark, he might have frightened her more. But he noted that this time she had left the poker behind.

'Oh, and you'll very likely want these.' She handed him a box of matches.

'Thank you, Frau Flood. Oh, thank you – very much.'

Perhaps he was too effusive. 'Mrs' she corrected him, with a note of irritation. 'Mrs. Not Frau.'

'Ah yes. "Mrs Flood".'

'That's better.' She obviously enjoyed the role of instructress. Both giggled. She seemed satisfied, dared to lay a hand on his arm. 'It's time for a poor body to get to bed. Goodnight, Mr Thorn.'

'Zorn!' he corrected her in turn, the Z, Paterfamilias's ultimate letter, spat out almost like a threat.

'Mm?' was all she would say to that, and left him abruptly, shooting the bolts home behind her. He heard her switch on the wireless – dance music.

Jazz, he supposed. Though, like the milk in her tea, he found its smoothness cloying. He felt desperately alone, rammed his two tins and the butter into his capacious battledress pockets, and set off across the heath – 'over there' – clutching his bread inside his tunic.

It could not last. Either he must give himself up – the thought barely entered his head. As an option it was closed off. Or he would die. He knew how easily that happened, once the food stopped coming through. Even more unthinkable – to die before *they* arrived. Or he could place his complete dependence on Frau Flood. It took its own course, it could last, if he measured Frau Flood correctly. After ten days of it, each nightly journey and each day's rations assured, Zorn began to feel a return of vigour, to life itself, to looking forward rather than closing off memories. And with it came the burden of conscience.

'Frau – Mrs Flood. What is "tick"?' he asked one night, mumbling over his ham sandwich. He more than half-suspected, but wanted it from her own lips.

'"Tick"? Why, it's getting things today and paying for 'em tomorrow.'

It was as he thought. 'So I have to pay you – tomorrow?'

'Well, some time, yes. There's some would call it "never-never".' She tried to be offhand, not to frighten him away. She must not featherbed him, but he was – well, in some ways, she thought, he was all she had. She had been at the end of the village too long, kept apart by Flood's doubtful reputation and by her religion. Not that she had attended Mass for many a year. But that made no difference in a tight community like Nentend. So whatever this white man was, all skin and bones recovering under her care, her charity, he was all hers – or, at any rate, he was nobody else's.

He had appeared every night, and while the heatwave lasted, it was all right. He always set off back the way he had come, 'over there', but she could guess. He must be sleeping rough, and the good weather would not last for ever. Then what? The thought of Miss Willis crossed her mind. She felt disinclined to share him with anybody.

She had decided he was a foreign sailor, which might be daunting. He seemed anything but dangerous, though the hint, because he was foreign and a sailor, that he might be, added spice to this surge of companionship in her life. He was all right sitting there in her back garden. He depended on her, but she knew his question about 'tick' pointed to the next move.

The poker was never in her hand now. She waited, arms folded over her bosom and tucked under her pinafore against the chill of the late evening, waited for his next question – or answer. She had no idea what she should do, for this all showed signs of being more than she could handle. And off he would go, across the golf links, and 'over there'.

She had grown used to his nightly visits. Slyly, she looked across from her darkened upstairs window, and by sixth sense knew when he was approaching. But she still knew nothing about him, except his name, his surname she presumed, which she would always have difficulty with – and his whiteness. She could not read his mind. That was the problem. But she knew instinctively that he was not dangerous. She liked the way he always thanked her, effusively, and the way he had fallen in with the game of secrecy, that he was her secret as much as she was his. Her only concern was the weather. If he became ill, or died . . . it was the inadequacy of their arrangements that worried her. So she listened to Henry Hall's late-night programme and tried to keep the weather from her thoughts.

She had reckoned without Zorn's ingenuity. He was still sleeping in his tree root, but with growing strength his activity increased. Only so would he cease remembering for long intervals. The beach was his own. Between that broken wall and the beach, he sensed that nobody ever set foot but himself. Less and less he feared that the day might bring forth a Friday. The tideline was one great pile-up of wrack, weed, tins, bottles, but, above all, timber – timber of all shapes, sizes and varieties.

He had returned several times to the burnt-out hulk in the trees. He had found a broken barrel on the beach, and had stripped off the one remaining hoop, straightened it out, then detached a suitable length by bending it back and forth at the centre. With this he began to slash at the bracken and brier in the ruin. He was methodical, clearing it room by room, sweeping the rubbish together with a rough besom he had made of tree fronds. He tipped the sweepings outside, but resisted the temptation to burn them before nightfall. He did not dare to send up smoke signals, and there was always the danger of setting off a brush fire in this dry weather.

As he cleared the floor, he was surprised at its quality. He manhandled the surviving broken beams away, and at last had the whole floor cleared, a plan of the house. He paced what must have been the hall, then the more elegantly floored rooms of fractured and calcified marble. What seemed to him to have suffered least was the kitchen. He knew it must be the kitchen, for the sturdy quarry tiles had survived best of all, though broken here and there and occasionally raised by the growth of bracken and grass tufts. Here he had a floor to his own needs, and he smiled as he picked up cast-iron cooking utensils, some surprisingly still intact under a coating of rust. And another mess of rust, damp soot and moss was the kitchen range.

This area he would work on. The walls were a tangle of ivy, pennywort and hart's-tongue fern in the damper patches. At first he planned to use the walls, but abandoned the idea, for with the first rain those walls would be running with water and he would be worse off than under his tarpaulin in the tree root.

So he would use the floor and build from scratch within the walls. He would begin small, the merest hut, and all being well, he would spread outwards as need arose and time allowed. Need? Nothing but security, from what he never questioned. But he needed security. Time? So long as he was secure, he had all the time in the world, provided his arrangements with Frau Flood survived.

He hauled the best timber from the beach to the ruin. It was hard work, but the distance was short. Perhaps in its day the house had a view to the sea. He piled the timbers upright against the walls to dry out.

After a further week, he began to space out his nocturnal visits to Frau Flood. The 'tick' arrangement worried him. But the fresh air of the demesne and the provisions from Mrs Flood had restored him so much to a state of health and strength that he now had a home of his own making. It was barely more than a wigwam structure, the longest baulks of timber leaning against one another and lashed at the top, the covering made of odd bits of overlapping tarpaulin and plywood. He faced the entrance towards the still-intact kitchen stove, and at night, sitting in the door of his wigwam, he faced a glowing fire of twigs. As he cleared the floor of the house and then the immediate surroundings, he burned the debris in his stove at night.

He visualized the next stage, but for that he would need things the beach could not provide, principally nails, for although he had already devised a clawed tool for drawing out the less recalcitrant nails from his timber, it was a poor thing.

'Mrs Flood, how to pay "tick", please?'

By now she was so confident of him that she longed to see his face as he spoke, so that she might read it as he enunciated in his quaint way.

'Oh, don't worry about that, Mr Thorn. I can wait a bit longer.'

'But I cannot wait, Mrs Flood. It will be too much. How am I to pay?'

This, she guessed, could mean the end of their secret. Victor's little offerings 'off the back of a lorry' allowed her a margin to spare for Zorn, and as far as she was concerned, the arrangement could go on indefinitely. But she could sympathize with Zorn. In fact, she was touched by his concern, that in his straits the thought should even occur. There were one or two in the village to whom the thought would never occur, unless she pressed. But Zorn was a man. No man would allow himself to be dependent on a woman, she mused, though a rebellious question at the back of her mind said: 'Why not?' Because the world ordained otherwise? That was why she had to use the 'tick' formula. She would much sooner have declared he could have what little she had to offer, provided no one else knew. She might have enjoyed that arrangement, out of defiance, but she bowed to the world, as owing it a living.

'Well,' she began, feeling her way, 'you might get yourself a bit of work.'

'Work?' Was he eager or indignant? Men were so touchy. 'Work, Mrs Flood? But where is work for me?'

Yes, it would end their little secret. Whoever he was, he

would have to declare himself to the world to get work. That might have been that. Zorn quaffed his tea and felt he had now reached a stage when he might declare something.

'Mrs Flood. May I ask, please no milk in tea?'

Her head clicked sideways, it might be, with indignation.

'Well! Why didn't you say so in the first place? And me giving you the top of the milk out of consideration! Some of you people have such funny habits, how's a body to know?'

This 'body' again. He feared he had offended her, for already he had detected something disembodied about her 'body' whenever she used it.

'Can you bring me the coal in?' she said abruptly.

Such was the moon this summer evening that he was able to read her face at last: plain, homely, a sort of Berthe, but not without guile now as she switched the subject from tea to coal.

'Coal, Mrs Flood?'

'Yes. You want to work. All right. You carry the coal for me. I always find it a bit heavy.'

'So?' He followed her to the door, wondering why she needed a fire in such weather, not knowing it provided company and would be missed, however the temperature held. Still, she did not invite him across the threshold. She brought him a large scuttle, bade him follow her to the outhouse at the end of the garden. It was a small enough task. He filled the scuttle, carried it after her to the door. For a moment, she hesitated. He waited.

'Well, come on. Fetch them right in.' She held the door for him to pass inside.

It was the first house he had been in since . . . since leaving home for the *Luftwaffelazarett*. He had erased that brief incursion into the dead husk of his home in Welckmar. And the subsequent entries, first into Berthe's small house, then into Nelli's, were hidden behind a veil.

Dingy, lit only by the light filtering through the open door from her living room, and stacked untidily with boxes and crates of various provisions, it was no haven. His nose twitched – yeast, stale cheese, sauce and sour flour pervaded this back room. He put down the scuttle as directed.

'Thank you, Mr Thorn,' she said. 'That'll be all.'

A mistress's dismissal of a servant, his mother to Berthe. He was not to see that cosy room where the wireless and the fire of an evening were her habitual and only entertainment.

It was not much, carrying a scuttle of coal each evening, but it was an end to his life as a beggar. It marked an end – or a beginning. He had graduated from prisoner to beggar, and now it seemed he might move on to wage-earner. For that appeared to be her intention.

It was much easier than he had expected. He learned from Mrs Flood that the war with Germany was well over, and now Japan too had surrendered. He did not care to think how that left him, except that, technically, he and Mrs Flood were no longer enemies.

Mrs Flood extended his work. He had learned to sleep through the mornings and leave himself free for the evenings and such duties as she might devise. His first task was to start on the unkempt garden. Mrs Flood had ambitions there. He hacked and dug at night, for the sun was never far below the horizon at this time of year. But he was irritated by the want of light. Only so could he measure progress, both at home 'over there' and here, in Mrs Flood's garden. Hacking and slashing at things night after night, Zorn was impatient for more constructive work.

'There'll be no harm in coming after the shop closes, Mr Thorn. Why don't you come tomorrow after six?'

'But people will see me, Mrs Flood.'

'And what if they do? I'll tell them you're doing casual labour. Nobody'll take a penn'orth of notice, except for a bit of gossip. And God knows I'm used to that . . .'

He sensed it was heartfelt. 'But Mrs Flood . . .' Suddenly he was terrified.

'Nobody'll lay a finger on you, mark my word, provided you keep your nose clean.' Which worried him further. It was all so difficult to follow. As to the last, like old Stern, he had had to devise all sorts of little wipers for his proboscis, and keenly felt the impropriety.

'Casual labour?'

'Ay. I'll tell one or two of them. You can paint, can't you?'

'Paint?'

'Doors, windows, that sort of thing. Everything's been so neglected on account of the war. And the men still away.'

It was indeed all much easier than ever he would have believed. These people, he reflected as he tended Miss Willis's windows, ask so few questions. By the autumn, he had been quietly, even gratefully, accepted as their own shy hermit and casual labourer. He was not to know that they asked questions about him among themselves: how and where did he sleep; discreetly, was he even clean?

'Does all his own laundry,' Mrs Flood claimed. 'Like a new pin, every stitch on him.'

But nobody asked him any questions as he slung his bundle over his shoulder and set off homewards along the edge of the golf links. He always kept well away from the players. In his army fatigues, nobody thought to question him.

Only once did he make a mistake. He was skirting the edge of the links as usual, when a man some way behind had shouted: 'Fore!' It startled Zorn, who turned to see why a man should shout at him. 'Fore'? Then he saw why. A golf ball was hurtling towards him and came to rest just past him.

'Sliced the bloody thing!' he heard the man shout to his companion, and they laughed. Zorn went to pick up the ball, he had got so used to obliging, to return it to its owner.

'Hi, there!' the man called urgently. 'Put the bloody thing down and bugger off, whoever you are!'

Well, who *was* he? Zorn realized he had somehow caused offence. The man and his partner were speaking together. Were they discussing him? Zorn was relieved and grateful when he saw the game came uppermost and he was ignored thereafter, but it frightened him. He made a point of never traversing the links till the players congregated in their club-house.

Despite one or two such frights, Zorn established a way of life which was acceptable to the people of Nentend. Mrs Flood was the most discreet agent on his behalf. He earned wages: two shillings here, half-a-crown there, and in the longer 'contracts' like painting the Willis house, he earned three whole pounds. He and Mrs Flood had their reckoning. Though he was no longer dependent on her for his daily bread, he still liked to stay for his ham sandwich and tea at dusk, not least because he felt that she required it. He was in danger of supplanting the wireless of an evening, but he was never invited beyond that inner threshold. He now asked for what he needed and was able to pay, though he still had no idea of value, of how much his labours were worth, or the food he purchased with his earnings. Mrs Flood accepted his payments and fobbed off questions about prices.

'Oh, ten shillings would do,' she would say. With that he had to be content, and was.

Mrs Flood's agency gradually extended from finding casual jobs for Zorn to procuring one or two essential items for him. The wigwam saw him through to the autumn, but he was dissatisfied with it. He felt a keenness in the air in the evenings, and at last signs of rain above an innocuous summer shower. It had been difficult enough describing to Mrs Flood that he needed a saw – she seemed to draw the line at the hatchet she used for chopping kindling. What would he be needing one for? He was allowed to use hers, but not to possess one. Her husband had left tools behind, and she was quite content to pass them on. But not the hatchet.

It was the matter of the nails that was instrumental in this extension. When Zorn asked about nails (which took some explaining), Mrs Flood gladly passed on a two-pound jar of nails of all sizes and conditions. He was grateful, but far from satisfied. He had plans for the winter, he had timber, but needed the means to construct: nails.

'I'll see you get some more then,' she said huffily, implying by her tone that he was one of those who were never satisfied. But he was not to be put off, or down. He drew approximate sizes on a piece of paper. He, quietly persistent but cautious, she, equally dogged but quite reckless, they made perfect partners in crime – if his very presence was a crime, or an offence. He was no longer an enemy, but otherwise he had no identity – here.

But nobody asked questions. In their eagerness to recruit his services, the villagers were willing to turn a blind eye. A woman called Mrs Hartside had trouble with the ballcock in the water system in her loft. Since both husband and the local plumber were still in the forces, basking in the Canal Zone somewhere, she was delighted when Mrs Flood suggested she try Zorn.

Again, though Mrs Hartside presumably had asked Mrs Flood questions, she asked none of Zorn. He was guided through a labyrinthine house, up some stairs, then by step-ladder into the loft. Failure here could spell disaster for him, he felt. Mrs Flood's advocacy was all very well, but what if she forced him to bite off more than he could chew? Yet once declared a handyman, he was in no position to refuse. Either he was of use and therefore protected (from whom or what he was far from sure) – or he was useless and fit only to be handed over. Furthermore, this was the first time he had been inside a British house. Clean, yet how different-smelling.

In the loft, lit only by an electric torch, he searched out the source of the trouble. The ballcock was not turning the water off when the tank was filled, so an irritating overflow was pouring continuously over Mrs Hartside's backyard.

He had to succeed. But the whole apparatus was a mystery to him. He went over his physics. He lifted the ballcock manually, noted that the inflow of water ceased. So why did the ball not rise of its own accord, without manual assistance? As a hollow sphere, it should float up with the level of the water, but it didn't. He found that the ball screwed off its supportive arm, and he was able thus to dash the water out

211

of it. He did not know how to repair the tiny pin-point puncture in the ball, but asked Mrs Hartside for some '*Mastik*'. It was only by sign language that eventually she understood that he needed chewing-gum. She rushed to Mrs Flood, for it was not a commodity she would ever admit to possessing.

Zorn chewed and masticated, then pushed the gum into and over the minute puncture. That did the trick. Mrs Hartside gave him half-a-crown and asked no questions. As he was leaving, she pushed a bag of freshly baked scones into his hand.

He was too good to lose. Gardens were tidied, lawns cut and trimmed, blocked drains released, rain gutters cleared, a septic tank cleaned up (relatively), walls mended, doors and windows painted. He was so thorough, they declared, that husbands would henceforth be released from such chores – they never did the job properly, anyway . . . .

And never any questions asked, or, at least, none of potential menace. For Zorn was as nervous as ever over his status. The least threat of *unerwünscht* would . . . he would not let the thought develop.

They did not know about his demesne, his house-building there. What he failed to realize was that he was fulfilling a function, not only the material one of providing casual labour at a rate they could not quibble at, but also that of a hermit, their own hermit, living 'over there' on his own, and no harm to anybody.

A few of the more sophisticated (or was it not simply the better-off?) declared they found it 'rather sweet' that they had their own hermit, settled quite happily in the Gwildy, always ready to attend to any small chore that nobody else would touch. And the men were so slow to return from the forces.

Zorn was a blessing, and nobody asked questions – being British, they never would; not to his face. Mrs Flood kept finding him odd jobs, and each job generated another. Now that he could come out in daylight and look people in the eye, and read them, he knew how safe he was. He was 'handy', and such a quality was in great demand in a community still depleted of men. So Mrs Flood shopped for him, or at any rate had ways of getting his needs seen to. Husband Flood's tools were useful, but only a beginning.

By October, Zorn had spied out the land sufficiently to realize that the village was not the world, and that if he was to get any real tools, he would have to walk to the nearest town. Mrs Flood said it was only six miles up the road and that nobody would bother him.

He was not only testing Mrs Flood's confidence, but his own. That six-mile walk had its terrors, and when he saw a figure approaching, he had to steel himself not to turn back.

Crosstrees was hardly a town, more an enlarged version of Nentend, though it did have a number of shops around its square. Zorn had a few pound notes on him, the fruit of long hours of labour, and he dearly wanted a smoothing plane. Despite vocabulary difficulties, he had little trouble negotiating with a man in Fairclough and Sons Limited, until he was about to leave with the plane under his arm.

Mr Fairclough (or so Zorn presumed – the man was old, and there was no sign of 'limited' sons) looked kind enough. As he passed the change over the counter, he asked:

'You a released POW then, sir?'

'?'

'So sorry, sir . . . I thought perhaps . . .'

Zorn left with a beating heart. Yet he learned to tolerate their politeness. It was not as punctilious as the German kind, it was only more inscrutable. He found difficulty in assessing it, measuring its potential meaning and menace, if any. If they did question, they were ready to withdraw or forget the question if it appeared to embarrass. He had to learn that while they might be curious (his English, he feared, must be excruciating), they meant no harm. He would have preferred greater candour, to know what they really thought, of life, of himself. On the other hand, he had to admit he was less than candid himself. He was afraid to give himself away. His whole existence here was still a guilty secret, for while they seemed ready to accept him, even to welcome him, he was unsure if they would accept his status.

But as he walked back, calling in the dusk on Mrs Flood for his customary baps and tea (he was now allowed to sit in the back room among the crates, bags, spilled rice, with their attendant smells, and, he suspected, mice), he was learning all the time to move with the bland tolerance of these people and to accept his place among them.

Before winter set in, his second home was ready. The tools, bought or donated, and nails had helped him produce a hut of sturdy build, set on the quarry tiles of the old kitchen. He enjoyed ranging over the rest of the floor, but had no ambition beyond the kitchen. He cleared what had obviously been the garden round the house, uprooting tangled exotica and straying box-hedge. There lay his ambition.

Every day he brought up something new from the beach. There was even a mattress, sodden when he found it. He wrestled with it, dragged it above high-water mark, draped it over some tree boughs to dry out, then bundled it up the slope to the house. He placed it for two weeks before his fire, then decided that it was well dried out.

The first night he slept on it over a plank bed he had made for it, he could still smell the sea. But the sheer comfort confirmed in his mind that at long last he was free – FREE. And the mattress was large enough for two. From then on he kept a weather eye open for a mattress that would fit the little bunk he had prepared for Dieter.

So Zorn became established as the unquestioned hermit 'over there' and nobody bothered, not even the police at Crosstrees, whose general policy was that the less they heard of Nentend the better.

By his second summer he was so busy that it passed almost without his noticing. Now, as he wandered in the village, or on his rare visits to Crosstrees, people appeared not to notice him, or if they did, would greet him with a 'good morning'

214

or a nod. His material needs were attainable, and casual work was always available. He was so busy, he had little time to think, or at any rate to remember. For he did think, over his daily round of beachcombing, home-making, walking and casual labouring.

His graduation from forced to casual labour had changed his inner status – he was a free man, and exercising his freedom was a vocation that helped keep memories and loves at bay. If he felt almost mortally wounded by his wartime incarceration under Vogel, here in his new-found land he recovered daily under the uncanny tolerance of the village, which could call upon his latent craftsmanship for a variety of neglected and even newly conceived projects.

They were not to know of his healing, since what few questions they asked were too easily fobbed off. They might have preferred the mystery, out of gratitude for the benefits, for Zorn was thorough, he was *good*.

His inner and outer life centred round his demesne, its security, its sufficiency (for he had started a garden) and its comfort, in that order. If he needed the world inasmuch as he worked in the village and met people, nevertheless he was jealous of his privacy as expressed in his demesne. His going into the world depended on his freedom to return behind his wall into the wilderness as and when he wished it. It was his.

One day when he was fixing yet another pane of glass into a window, he heard a dog barking. The one thing he relied on was his safe seclusion, shared with birds and animals, and their noises. It was only one bark, then silence. But he rushed out into his garden to see. That one bark sent his mind reeling back. He listened. Then he heard a rustle. He had to see this out. He took up a stick and tried to locate the noise. He stalked to the edge of his cleared garden, slashed his way through the undergrowth towards the intermittent rustling.

He came out in a sweat as he saw the dog, crouched low in a menacing position. He had no idea what to do, but, like a moth to a lamp, approached with one wild rush, his stick held out threateningly before him. He had not the heart to hate this dog as he had hated others. It was the sort he had seen here in the fields, rounding up sheep or cattle, as often as not wall-eyed, and preferably to be avoided. He did not hate it, but resented its presence in his demesne. Frightened and determined, mindful still of some attendant Vogel, Zorn approached the dog with panic in his heart.

Then he saw. The dog was pointing a sheep tangled in a brier and, with each struggle, getting more badly enmeshed. With his stick always at the ready, Zorn reached for the sheep's fleece, but still flinched before the dog's lunges, until he realized it was the sheep, not himself, that the dog was interested in. He tore at the brier stems while the sheep lay supine, as though dead, only showing signs of life when the dog moved. Zorn's hands bled as he struggled, tearing loose wool from the fleece, until finally the sheep knew it was time to make its last lunge. It leapt free, trailing briers with it, and was gone, with the dog chasing it homewards towards the wall.

It was done, but the fact that his wilderness was not quite inviolable set Zorn back. He bathed his hands and wrapped the worst scratch in a rough dressing. But he could not move. For two nights he did not sleep properly, the vision of Vogel oddly alternating with that of his father before him.

On the third day, aware of an impending madness should he give way, he ventured out, his right hand still bandaged and extremely sore. For the first time since his arrival he felt ill, but he struggled to the wall, determined to seek reassurance in the unquestioning village, in Mrs Flood in particular, and thus to expunge his nightmare.

He saw sheep scattered over the golf links. It was dusk, the season was over, and a farmer was grazing his flock on the fairways. One errant ewe must have scaled a broken section of the wall and the farmer, obviously, had sent his dog after it. Zorn saw the logic of all this, but found little comfort in it. The incident with the dog had shown him that he was not wholly secure.

★   ★   ★

'What's the matter with your hand? And where've you been these three or four evenin's?' Mrs Flood's tone, if anything, was reprehensive.

'*Krank,*' he answered, lost for the English word.

'?'

He thought, then the word came. 'Ah, ill. Yes, ill!' he blurted out.

She seemed, as ever, satisfied, so long as she had some sort of retort. Its import would not matter, not after the first shock of his advent, when it really mattered and he looked, as she was fond of reporting, 'like death warmed up'.

It took him some time to recover. Yet no further invasion disturbed his sense of security. The sheep quickly nibbled the fairways to a carpet and left. He was alone again, as he would wish, ready to face the winter in comparative security, comfort even, waiting for his family, Nelli and Dieter.

The garden was beginning to supply him with vegetables all the year round. He could live for days without entering the outside world. When he did, nobody asked questions, except about his general state of health, over which he had learnt to reply as imprecisely and as briefly as was their custom. He was part of the landscape. Had he but faith, the village would feel bereft should he disappear from their midst for any reason.

By the third summer, his intermittent fright had softened into only the occasional nightmare. By day he moved with an easier confidence, performing his tasks as they came along. Since there was no joiner in the village, his craftsmanship was much appreciated, and one transformed kitchen or mended chair generated another. His entrée into various houses did nothing to entice him from his own. As evening came and he made ready to depart, his employer might push some tit-bit into his bag, and he was happy returning across the links, to scale the wall at his own secret spot and trace the path he had trodden through his wilderness. Enfolded in his chosen solitariness at night, with his fire going, he felt secure as he never felt outside.

He was building a new house. He decided he could use the old kitchen stove and its walls and chimney as one end of a more ambitious hut. The difficulty was to make a weatherproof bond between the old wall and his new roof, but with time, patience and a makeshift flashing of felt strip he managed it. He had restored one window-frame washed up on the beach, and with his now extended skills as carpenter had no difficulty making a door-frame and door.

However much timber he hauled up from the beach, each spring tide and storm brought more. He had devised a chariot of two old bicycle wheels he had found in a dump in the village, and it eased the job of getting the timber from beach to house. He talked to himself as he combed the wrack, mostly in his execrable English.

'That will make window fasten tight,' he would say as he unscrewed a delicately wrought brass fitting lost from some yacht in a squall and now washed up, still attached to its host plank of valuable teak. 'I file a bit here, and then it goes, so . . .' turning it over and rubbing the barnacles off with his rough fingers. When a piece of metal proved absolutely unusable, it was joined in any one of several ways (short of welding) to a structure he had begun idly one day at the end of his garden. It was so placed that he could view it through his own window and the original aperture of the kitchen window of the old house.

This structure, which he constantly addressed as 'a body' (for he was still unsure what Mrs Flood referred to, except that 'a body' seemed to be some sort of self at a remove, some *alter ego*), was at first amorphous, a sort of dustbin of useless metal. He would throw nothing away. Even Mrs Flood's tins were cut open, flattened, and if they did not serve a house purpose, were assigned to The Thing. This habit of joining bits of metal satisfied his tidy mind. Litter of any kind he abhorred, like the good German he was at heart, and sometimes he would fling savage oaths at the innocent sea for the mess it flung up on the tide.

Then 'a body' began to assume a shape of its own. As time

218

passed, Zorn found himself developing a complex, as though there were two quite distinct areas of his mind-life: one concerned with life's perennial practicalities, like subsistence, security, weatherproofing; the other concerned with providing for this structure, which made its own demands, and which could not be said to subscribe to any of his material needs. In some ways, it even impinged on his material life, in the sense that if he found he had to choose between performing some domestic task, like glazing a window, or fettling a new-found piece of brass for The Thing, he would choose the latter, and the glazing would have to wait. It was there, competing for his attention with the requirements of survival, fuel, food, garden, house improvement. Always at the back of his mind as he beachcombed or worked in some villager's garden, it was to be provided for, crying out for his attention, presenting its own peculiar problems of survival and, more, of growing. He came to love and to hate it: to love the sight of it from his window, framed in the old mansion's window aperture; but to hate its importunity. Its demands concerned both scale and intricacy, as well as technique and artistic decisions. If, after a more than usually arduous search, Zorn triumphantly brought a fine piece of metal home, 'a body' on occasion would refuse to accept it, rejecting it as not quite appropriate, as forced, as not sufficiently expressive, or even as the wrong colour. It was as though it were challenging him, speaking to him: 'Come on, Zorn, use your brain – or your heart, if you have either – and I sometimes wonder. Stop messing me about . . .'

Zorn could be quite irritable and might go so far as to kick at it irreverently, returning to his hut out of sorts for the rest of the day, muttering to himself, in an off-stage way which it was not meant to hear, but could if it cared to. For, of course, the fruit of so many hours of searching, carrying, straightening, hammering and fastening was bound to impose its own standards, to require quite different laws from ordinary, material living. It was highly acquisitive. It came to demand prior choice of any metal he found – aluminium,

219

brass, copper, steel, chromium plate, copper wire: all went to its making, some bright, some patinated by the sea. Sometimes it even demanded a sacrifice, as he found one day, when he levered off a finely turned brass piece from a teak plank. What it was he was not sure: the deck machinery of these yachts was so much more sophisticated than the old Baltic craft. He earmarked it for a lathe he was keen to make.

But The Thing demanded otherwise. It was now about three metres high, but as yet raw in detail. Zorn, obeying its aesthetic dictates, put aside his own material needs, and by careful wrapping with copper wire fastened the unit in its place. He found it deeply satisfactory. The lathe would have to wait on the tide's charity. And he smiled indulgently, perhaps with love, but with that mingling of patience when love is not easy.

Zorn could return to his conscience over more practical concerns. But not for long. Its appetite was insatiable, and somehow deeply personal. It was at the back of Zorn's mind day and night, and in his prowlings for metal, the demands of 'a body' superseded all others – she had enslaved him.

She rose higher and higher, requiring a ladder. From time to time, he had to reinforce her lower members to ensure stability, so that she was well staked to the ground and no gale would move her. She had limbs, wings, hollows and humps, all subscribing to a whole that breathed its own life. Each detail, each form was attached in such a way as to satisfy both her and Zorn. It was a dialogue in space and form – 'a body', in short, was autonomous, unique. She had insinuated herself into his life, had become his other half, even to the extent of nagging when she was dissatisfied with his latest attentions.

As the seasons followed one another, a viridian patina of ageing copper crept over the other metals, enhancing their red, white and umber oxides. The Thing now blended so well with her enfolding trees that Zorn would sit at his window, head this way, then that, admiring this combination of his own handicraft and her importunity. Although she was silent (except for a becoming metallic susurration when the wind got up and stirred her), Zorn would often talk to her, even more than to Mrs Flood. He took great satisfaction in the knowledge that this was his alone. No one had set eyes on her, or was likely to, until Nelli and . . .

He continued, winter and summer, to work in the village as he wished. He had no use for money, beyond what he required for his basic needs. His one difficulty was in his human contacts, for he still found it hard to trust anybody but Mrs Flood. A woman called Mrs Dinning had persisted with Mrs Flood. Mrs F. knew her customers, and Mrs D. was not among her favourites.

'Would Mr Thorn be able to put a shelf in for the TV?' Mrs Dinning asked one day in the shop.

'Oh, I don't think I could ask Mr Thorn to come for just a shelf,' Mrs Flood replied tartly. It was not so much the shelf as the TV she objected to. Mrs D. would be the first; the rest would now have to follow, no doubt. The expense! – for such rubbish, she had heard.

'What a pity,' Mrs Dinning said, off-hand of course, for there were ways with the like of Mrs F. 'It wasn't just the TV shelf, though that's important. I thought perhaps he could try making me a fitted wardrobe.'

'Try!' thought Mrs Flood. 'Try! Fitted wardrobe indeed!' What was a 'fitted wardrobe'? She was far from sure. Translating what she did not comprehend into language fit for Zorn's indifferent reception of English was a further problem. Explaining a 'whatnot' that Mrs Ludkin had ambitions to had been difficult enough. (Miss Willis had one as model, it was discovered, and the bother! Did Miss W. have the copyright to all whatnots?) The result had been beautiful. Only a perverse disinclination in Zorn had prevented a rash of whatnots spreading through Nentend. 'Fitted wardrobe'? The prospect was too intriguing to resist. Mrs Flood said she couldn't promise, but . . .

221

The TV shelf was so simple a project that Zorn completed it within two hours. Mr Dinning, who was a night-shift worker at the power station fifteen miles away and earned good money, sat throughout the process behind a newspaper, his feet sprawling in such a way that Zorn found himself constantly saying: 'Excuse, please,' while a quiet rage circulated in his mind. With immense relief, he brushed the shavings from around Mr Dinning's feet, wondering how or why he should find himself in such a position. He would have been glad to leave, but Mrs Dinning hovered and he awaited further orders.

She asked if he would care to take the measurements for her fitted wardrobe. Zorn, aware of glares in the wings, obediently followed her to the bedroom. He had some difficulty in following her specifications. Measuring-tape in hand, he kept bumping first into the double bed and then into Mrs Dinning. Aware that she was far from minding, Zorn crept about like a thief, anxious not to disturb the ominous figure below.

'Three metres forty-six,' he was muttering as he scribbled figures in his notebook, when he heard footsteps clumping up the stairs. Mr Dinning appeared in the open doorway. Mrs Dinning swivelled sharply towards the protective bottles and face lotions on her dressing-table.

'Out!' Mr Dinning shouted, pointing to the stairs. 'Come out! No bloody foreign tramp's going to mess about in my bedroom. Out now – and quick!'

Zorn looked to Mrs Dinning for help, but frantically she riffled through her bottles and showed only her back. Zorn snatched up his pencil and notebook and brushed past Dinning-Vogel as though propelled by a rocket. His instinct was to strike the man, not for the words, but for his manner, which in this country of unspoken questions was too near the bone. But he ran down the stairs, had the presence of mind to collect his tool-bag below, and made for the door. He heard the Dinnings shouting abuse at each other upstairs. He slammed the door behind him and sped towards his demesne, skirting the golf links, over the wall and through the Gwildy at a run.

He stayed at home for a week, eating very little, drinking far too much black coffee, sleeping hardly at all, and trying to restore his equilibrium by fiddling with 'a body' and being constantly rejected by her.

His only call after that was on Mrs Flood at night. The bap and tea was understood, as ever, to be between friends, but he was so out of joint and unable to work that he ran up quite a bill 'on tick'.

After three weeks, only conscience forced him out to work. Falsely, he had hoped he had been cured. But he was wrong. He stuck to wood-chopping, gardening and hedge-clipping, outside jobs that kept his body just this side of exhaustion and his mind in an acceptable state of torpor. He was afraid of fear.

It was with a sense of triumph that Mrs Flood announced to him one night that Mrs Dinning had left her husband. She inferred that, like TV, it was a trend that might catch on.

Zorn settled in more and more as he built, cultivated, washed, sowed, arranged, sewed and forever tidied – waiting, waiting with an ultimate patience as the welcome for Nelli and the boy achieved a completion that never quite satisfied him.

He was now more conscious of the seasons. The Baltic, in a memory that he allowed to patinate like 'a body', seemed to have had only two: the sun and green dyke banks of summer, the chill and grey monotone of winter. But here there were four seasons, and quite distinct. Winter might envelop him briefly in a covering of snow, and 'a body' would shudder ever so slightly under the weight, and with disdain shake down a dusting of white crystals. But snow never lasted. The sea's proximity kept the worst rigours at bay. Wood was plentiful, though Zorn forbore ever to chop down a living tree. Enough had been blown down, or matured and fallen, like his first shelter. He kept warm, worked when necessary for food, accepted clothing without the condescen-

223

sion with which it was offered, constantly improved his house, and watched over 'a body', perhaps by way of exorcism. For ghosts still surrounded him as he continued to wait. So the winters passed, as near as humanly possible in a state of animal hibernation.

When the sun came out and touched the tacky buds sufficiently to induce some movement, he would put up a ladder against 'a body' and touch up anything faintly damaged by the ravages of winter. He turned the garden, raked and prepared it, mulched it with abundant leaf-mould, sowed it, then waited and watched.

He explored the Gwildy endlessly. As late as his eleventh spring, he came across the melancholy remnants of a dogs' cemetery. He had passed the spot many times, but ivy, leaf-mould and the ubiquitous brier had camouflaged it. He detected the dressed stone and a vestige of lettering, and pulled away the tangled ivy. Painfully, he read:

Dear Dog Jim
Once a Stray

For the earnest expectation of the Creature Waiteth for the Manifestation of the Sons of God.
For the Creature was made subject to Vanity, not willingly, but by reason of him who hath subjected the same in Hope.
Romans 8: 19, 20

Like Nelli; he might not get the meaning, but he understood the drift.

There was a single line at the foot of the stone, and he ran his finger along it, removing the lichen and leaf-mould: 'Erected at the Proper Cost and Charges by Miss Furnival'.

Who? No taint of 'tick' about that, and he felt the lady's mild reproof. She must have loved her hounds, he mused. But WHO? How many more had joined Jim in that final conflagration that had provided him, phoenix-like, with his present home? For the humpiness of the ivy-clad terrain

224

indicated more if he cared to explore by tearing at the clinging stems and foliage.

The largest hump revealed another. It appealed to him, spoke to him in more personal terms. He needed company, so he read:

Miss Furnival's
Beloved Dog
CLORAGH

How are the Dead raised up
And with what body do they come?
God giveth it a body as it hath
pleased Him, and to every seed
his own body: All flesh is not
the same. Corinthians I Chapter 15
So also is the Resurrection of the Dead.

It all fitted. He would not uncover more. It was enough. He returned to 'a body' with renewed energy and impatience at its occasional recalcitrance. Miss Furnival had bequeathed enough to assume for Zorn a presence, so that Miss Pfeiffer and Nelli Furnival fused, elements of a fluid past and future subsumed into his fixed present.

Towards late June each year, the forest floor would be a blood-red carpet of spilt blossom, the exotica, unlike dear Cloragh, giving up their aerial life for earthy compost, an inverse resurrection that affected Zorn more than he would care to admit. For he loved everything in his wilderness, and when autumn touched the foliage to gold and crimson fire, and the earth tightened in anticipation of winter sleep, Zorn felt the state of mourning fall over him like a shroud, and it was difficult to get any work out of him. He did things, they said to one another, he did things over there in the Gwildy, but never specified what, for none would trespass on the golf links.

★ ★ ★

'How are the Dead raised up, And with what body do they come?'

But ebbing and flowing as he did, nevertheless on one thing he was constant. His possession of his demesne, both of place and of time, was complete. THIS – not home, *domus* in Paterfamilias's sense, where his mother and father had wrestled in words with each other and excluded him even at the very end – THIS was theirs, Nelli's and his – and the boy's, of course. THIS would be sanctified and blessed by Nelli's ultimate presence, all sweetness and light, untainted by any doubts or guilt, and certainly beyond reach of all that had once impinged and hurt. It would be loving (he was so besotted) – loving and being together.

'Have you not told them anything about us?' she had asked, and he had confessed that he had told nothing, because there was THIS yet to find and possess, their own place, away from . . .

He gathered strands of a past he dreaded and a future he did not recognize into the thread of a fixed present. The clock might persist in ticking, but the hands had stopped, pointing to Nelli and the boy. This future of coping with English and odd, incomprehensible people, had to be endured, even exploited in the name of a perpetual present with . . . with his own family. There would always be these caesurae in the middle of his ponderings and activities, like a prompter to an actor who ignores him and proceeds with lines of his own making. It was the future asserting its presence, or the past reminding him of its imperfections. But this, *their* present, persisted.

There were difficulties, as when Mr Dinning had dislodged some granules of corrosive rust whose calloused carapace protected his eternal present, threatening to expose him to the ever-beckoning future. That was why he kept his distance, trusting only Mrs Flood. Difficulties there were, but could be laid aside with time, whatever that was, is, will be.

What never arose now was despair. It was not in the nature

of things, for did not Nelli affirm and nourish life, even from off-stage? His chief ally was Mrs Flood, who seemed only too content to keep things as they had begun, he calling most evenings but never entering her house, she asking no questions beyond the barest minimum.

Mrs Flood had her own problems over neighbourliness, or its lack, and Zorn provided a pair of ears, even if he did not always comprehend. Listening she required, comprehension she could live without, at least some of the time, so long as he was there. He was a foreign shipwrecked mariner, who had lost something, probably all, did she but know. But she did not wish to know particularly, for she too connived at that perpetual present of their initial encounter. Any forays she arranged through her agency into work and activity were to be merely vehicles of preserving that mutual initial present. Not that he ever disabused her about the awful cataclysmic disaster at sea, that it was not 'shipmates' in her sense, but . . .

There was a wiliness in his response to any passing probes Mrs F. might make, usually the gentlest, most oblique of probes, for she too could be wily – after all, there he was, on his own, so how did he feel about . . . well, didn't he ever feel the need of . . .?'

'Shipmates' therefore sufficed, and though he might frown momentarily over the word 'gone', as she used it, he let it stand and never, in his own wily way, allowed the subject to expand into anything that might be construed as historic fact.

His disembodiment was almost complete. What he looked like he had almost forgotten. All the petty, daily vanities had gone. For years, he had shaved his blond beard every other day, without a mirror. Except for glimpses of his head as he passed the polished window surfaces of his hut, he had lost all true image of himself. His own reflection was the last thing he wanted to see. His eyes were directed rather towards the hidden treasure in the ever-changing beachwrack, towards the work it induced – his garden, his hut, 'a body'.

Then one day, after eighteen years, he was combing the

227

beach after a storm when he saw a flat surface of what was unmistakably mahogany, its brown-pink hue too precious to pass by. He picked it up. As he brushed off the dust, he saw it was a beautiful frame, with rounded corners, in dark polished mahogany. He turned it over, and amid the nodules of adhering sand, he suddenly saw himself, white-polled as ever, with eyes of flecked hazel, eyebrows and lashes paler than he remembered. He was fascinated. It was a stranger. Beyond the hair and eyes, it bore no resemblance to the boy who had left home twenty-one years ago. He brushed off the sand and saw a middle-aged man with firm jaw, cheeks hollowed by life's sheer effort, the temples hard and bony, the brow high and bare. He did not carry the thing home. He laid it down in the safety of that first uprooted tree that had offered him shelter so many years ago. He would not have the mirror in the house. But neither would he destroy it. He laid it carefully among the dead leaves. It was for reference only. And the day would come when she would comb her blond tresses before it.

Zorn swam in the sea throughout the season, from mid-April, when it hurt, to the end of October, when it was still bearable. But he could never shake off ghosts. He would plunge into the breakers, and once past them and into the smoother swell, would swim parallel to the shore, never committing himself wholly to the sea. It was his habit, day-in day-out, rain or fine, to swim the length of the bay, then walk back.

Summers varied so. While during one he might be soaked as much by rain as by the sea, in another he would be so drenched by the sun that he would take on that bleached aspect he had when first he had beached like a stranded dolphin on this shore. His hair would go absolutely white, contrasting with his sunburnt brown body. But even there, a white down on chest, arms and legs would give the impression of patination, like the oxidization on 'a body'. He achieved a rare health of body, but still would not venture beyond the breakers. It was not so much want of physical strength or courage, as caution about trespassing on the privacy of Nelli's present world . . . and the boy's.

So, punctiliously, beyond the thrashing water of the rollers, he would swim his length of the bay parallel to the shore, his head bobbing up and down in the swell, with occasional seals as company. He was so familiar, they were more curious than frightened. And though sometimes one might beckon him out a little, he never went more than a couple of yards beyond the rollers. For only between the sea and that wall into the world was he truly at peace. What the sea had kept from him the world beyond the wall could never replace.

Even after twenty-five years, Mrs Flood always stood, arms folded under pinafore, at the doorway into her living room when she entertained Zorn of an evening. While he, even more punctiliously, polished the chair she provided with his lean backside in the scullery among the raisins, caster sugar and Mars bars, and their attendant predators. He had entered many other houses by way of work, but had never crossed the threshold into her living room where she always leaned against the door jamb. Any work she might require of him was always outside, always the coal, the garden as need arose, and repairs to her fence abutting on the golf links.

It was understood, from the beginning and throughout the years, that that was how it would be. She, being a widow, must be circumspect about having a man in the house – 'A body can't be too careful these days, there's all sorts about,' she would muse, implying that while he was not one of those, nevertheless she must be seen to be careful, respectable.

Inevitably, there were whisperings in the village, for the shopkeeper is a public figure, and public figures are for talking about. But with a canny judgment, Mrs F. allowed Zorn into the store-room and no farther. It was a respectable limbo for all weathers. There she chatted, while he, a man of few words, chewed his bap and sipped his tea, and listened. She was his eyes and ears on to a world he could not wholly accept, but which still left him curious. For if he was never sure of being

229

wholly alive, what Mrs F. reported was very much so, by the sound of it.

Their ritual was unfailing, their mutual limbo inviolate. Then, one evening, when the first autumn winds were tearing the leaves off the trees, she was waiting for him, as ever, holding the coal scuttle, but with a load of concern on her face. She had these faces, depending on the news: 'They say on the wireless the balance o' payments is terrible. I reckon the whole country's on tick' would warrant screwed lips, but not as seriously as 'Did you hear? Old Mrs Fenton's gone – my, she suffered, poor soul, if anybody did . . .'

This was serious, he could tell at once. He went down the garden to fill the scuttle. But when he returned to the scullery to hand it over, she was at the living-room door, beckoning him to bring it further and follow her. It startled him. He was loath to break their unwritten law. But she was quite firm:

'Fetch it right through, Mr Thorn.' And suddenly, he was over the threshold, into her sanctum, where a television set flickered madly in pride of place at the side of the hearth. She bade him sit in the one easy chair before a low table, where she had laid out his supper. She drew up a dining chair and poured his tea, then a cup for herself. The crazy flicker of the TV set disturbed Zorn. His heart was thumping at this sudden break in their ritual. Twenty-five years, and now this. He longed to be back in his old chair out in the scullery. The fire blazed merrily; he took in the framed photograph on the mantelshelf – ('That's Mr Flood, as was') – the patterned wallpaper, the trinkets – ('A present from Bridport' was surely not acceptable, he thought) – the geraniums on another table in front of the drawn curtains, and a picture of a shepherdess over the fireplace, one hand holding up her skirt to cross a stream barefoot, the other carrying a pail – made of wood, he noticed and wondered how one made such things. His hand shook as he took up his tea and waited for the next move in this terrifying departure from the norm.

230

'Mr Thorn, you'll have to do without your sup o' tea for a bit . . .'

'I'm sorry, Mrs Flood. Is it trouble for you?'

'Oh no, it's not that. It's just that the doctor says I have to go in for an operation.'

'Go in?'

She had hoped the word 'operation' would have registered more.

'Go in, why yes. You can't have an operation without goin' in. Stands to reason, surely.'

He was used to this form of correction, but still could not register the full import of what her face, in ghastly contortions, was saying.

'The knife,' she went on, more graphically – a matter of life and death, her face said. He was both relieved and alarmed. She was his link with the world. It had worked, their system. She had always been the agent in his day-to-day arrangements. He understood it, the village understood it.

'Miss Willis'll manage the mornin's for me while I'm away. And Mrs Watkin's girl'll be doin' the afternoons,' she said, little finger crooked at her cup out of respect for company.

She sensed his misery. 'They reckon I'll be back as right as rain in a fortnight. You can manage while I'm away, can't you?' Then added lightly, for the gravity was now all on his side: 'D'you want anything on tick before you go?'

But he was hardly listening. If you live as solitarily as he, then the world is indeed centripetal. It was not that he came every evening. Indeed, he had left many a gap in the past, either for weather outside or anguished mental hurricanes inside. But she had always been there. There had never been a gap on her side.

'I will miss you,' he said, touchingly she thought, even if he did look shrivelled, even frightened. He had not touched his ham roll.

'Eat up now, Mr Thorn. I can't abide waste.'

'Thank you.' He nibbled disconsolately, finished his tea, and then almost dived out.

231

Hum! If that's the way he feels, she thought, and went upstairs to search out a nightgown she had kept for emergencies. It was white with frilly pink facings.

She looked forward to the wearing of it, but with regret to the loss of two whole weeks in the shop. Miss Willis she could trust to hold the fort, if not to advance the cause, but the Watkin wench was an unknown quantity. As for Thorn, he'd better be keeping out of the way. As usual, the feeling uppermost was that he was her business, and most certainly nobody else's.

After two weeks, Zorn was low on rations. He had enough potatoes and vegetables to offer some for sale, or for barter, but without Mrs Flood that was unthinkable. As the third week approached, he had not eaten bread, meat, butter or cheese for ten days, and a good Baltic man is not easily contented on vegetables alone.

He had hardly any money, having stayed at home over the two weeks of Mrs Flood's absence. Would she be back yet? He could have gone to the shop, but should she still be detained, the thought of arranging 'tick' with anybody but Mrs Flood frightened him. Miss Willis he knew well enough as a casual employee (was she mornings or afternoons?), but he suspected that she would not be acquainted with the 'tick' arrangement. The Watkin girl he did not know. She could be any of the maidens round the village, a face he might know. But the idea of approaching her, talking to her in his (as ever) excruciating English, above all asking for 'tick' was more than he dared face.

Mrs Flood had said two weeks. After three weeks, and by now subsisting on a wholly vegetable diet, mostly potatoes, he plucked up courage by climbing his long ladder to the top of 'a body' to fix that glass sphere he had first picked up on landing twenty-five years before. He knew where it was to go. The tentacles of copper wire were already fixed firmly, waiting to be folded round the sphere. It satisfied him that nearly six metres up, there was no sign of swaying. From

232

now on, it needed only the most refined embellishments.
When he descended, he knew that 'a body' was just as
satisfied as he. And now he had the courage. He made his
way through the wilderness, over the wall and across the
links as darkness descended.

There was a light at her window, and he climbed the fence,
paused to see if, as usual, she would open the door for him.
She always heard. But she did not come. The acidity from a
day of nothing but potatoes afflicted him. He broke wind
audibly and, though giggling weakly, was ashamed that she
might have heard. Something to eat was urgent. But there
was no sign of her. He returned to his very first signal and
noisily tipped an empty plastic carton into the dustbin. He
was irritated with himself. He had one friend whom he could
trust in all things, one friend in the whole world, and here he
was, rattling a dustbin lid to announce his arrival after an
absence of three weeks. It took decisive courage to knock,
and when she still did not answer, he tried the door. It was
bolted. Suddenly he was desperate. It was not so much the
food he needed. He had been more desperately hungry. It
was that he needed to see her. Why the bolted door?

He approached the window and tapped. 'Mrs Flood. It is
Zorn.'

He heard the chair creak. But she still did not answer.

'Mrs Flood. I need food . . . please.'

The curtains parted, lighting his stricken face. He looked
in at the shadowed figure, searching for reassurance.

'Ah! Mrs Flood!' he cried. 'I am so happy to see you. Are
you well now?'

'Shsh!' she warned him, with finger to lips. He could just
hear her. 'I'll come to the back door. But you can't come in.
Just stay where you are, or I won't open!'

He heard her drawing the bolts. Obediently, he stayed by
the window while she opened the door slightly. He could
just discern her face in the dusk and made to step forward.

'Don't! Don't come any nearer,' she hissed. 'Just stay where
you are.'

'But why, Mrs Flood? It is so long. I am very hungry. I need food, please.'

She kept the door open a mere chink. 'Have you been up to any mischief, Mr Thorn?'

'Miss Chiff?' He searched for the word, but to no avail.

'Yes. Mischief. What've you been up to while I've been poorly? I've been home a week and no sign of you.'

As when they first began, all those years ago, he found himself straining to read her face – or what was visible, for she kept the door almost closed, only one eye and the tip of her nose showing.

'I am at home. Eating only potatoes. Not good.' Again he moved, but she was ready with the door. It slammed.

He retreated, in despair, his hand running frantically over his brow. '*Ein Alptraum*,' he muttered, recalling the too-frequent nightmares in his double bunk. Then he shouted: 'It is good, Mrs Flood. I am with the window. Please. I need food. Nothing but potatoes all week. Not good. You understand?'

The door opened just enough to show the whole of her face. 'Have you been seein' anybody lately?' she whispered.

'I am at home all the time. Please, bread and ham, yes?' Only so, as on that first occasion, would she understand and come out with the usual benison, he thought, and he wanted just that now, just herself, standing before him. Food could wait.

'You've seen nobody?'

'You need coal, Mrs Flood? I get coal for you, yes?'

'You never came to the shop, not once? – to see Angie Watkin?'

'Angie?' He could just smile at the thought. A simple affair of female jealousy?

'Yes. Angie Watkin. You're in trouble, Mr Thorn. All the men are.'

There was a note in her voice that terrified him. The wall was no obstacle, the wilderness was open. A world was falling apart. If only he could approach her, sit on his chair among the cartons with the friendly mice and eat his bap, drink his tea.

'Mrs Flood. I am at home,' he pleaded. 'All the time, eating only potatoes. I see nobody.'

'You know nothing about Angie Watkin?' He had never experienced that sternness in her voice. 'You've not been near the place since I went in? You haven't touched Angie, have you now?'

Was it she who was pleading now?

'Touched, Mrs Flood? I do not touch people. I am at home.'

'Are you sure?'

'Sure? I cannot ask for "tick", you understand? Only you I can ask – for "tick". I am at home. I wait for you.'

The way he said it touched her. She opened the door just a little wider. He moved a step nearer, but again she told him to stay where he was.

'Mr Thorn. There's a horrible business in the village. Police is all over the place. You'd better watch out.'

'But why, Mrs Flood? I am at home – till now. I come now, to see you.'

It was she now who sought to read his face in the gloom.

'Stand back by the window,' she said sharply, 'where I can see you.'

He retreated to the window, his eyes searching hers as she opened the door wider. She paused, the better to see him. Then: 'Somebody's murdered Angie Watkin. The girl I had in the shop. They found her just over an hour ago. A man. They're after a man, bound to be. Are you sure you know nothing about it?'

He was on his knees, out of the light from the window, his hands over his eyes.

'Murdered?' He knew the word, knew it only too well. '*Mord – Mord?* Mrs Flood, I do not understand.'

Seeing him on his knees, just like that first time when only his whiteness was visible, affected her.

'Yes, Mr Thorn. Strangled, poor little soul, and her only

235

eighteen yesterday. They'll want to see all the men. They'll want to see you, Mr Thorn. You'd better be at home.'

He was bent low over his knees, perhaps weeping. She could not see clearly, but his silence caused her to open the door wide. She came out, approached him, put her hand on the white poll.

'You didn't do it, Mr Thorn, did you?'

But it was only reassurance she needed. She could not believe it.

He was weeping, she was sure of it.

'Murder?' he moaned on. 'Ach, Mrs Flood. Only once . . .'

And she was gone. The bolts slammed home. He rose slowly, walked dejectedly down the garden, leapt the fence. He gathered pace across the links, clambered over the wall, tore his way through the wilderness, past the house and 'a body', and down to the beach. He walked straight into the breakers, plunged in, and this time did not swim parallel to the shore. He swam strongly, despite the clinging of his scanty clothes.

He swam on and on, out and out, beyond the mouth of the bay, on and on, keeping a strong breaststroke. And on, and on . . .

'Nelli!' he shouted with what strength he had left. 'Nelli! *Es gibt nur eine Einsamkeit . . .*'

And on . . . and on . . .

VI

'The moving waters at their priestlike task
Of pure ablution of earth's human shores.'

John Keats

Sergeant Helliwell traversed the Gwildy once again, this time with only one constable in attendance. What was to be done about the hut, the house, was undecided. There was no precedent that anybody could unearth as yet, and no Furnival apparent to refer to. The customary legal searches would take months, perhaps even years. This sort of thing was a staple for lawyers, depending upon the reward, if any. So many small wildernesses remain so for the sole reason that nobody wants to own them, whereas large ones must always be worth something to somebody. As for the Gwildy, nobody was sure yet whether it was still nominally a Furnival estate. So the house, Zorn's house, would remain untroubled for the time being.

But on one point Sergeant Helliwell's superiors were adamant – that mast, whatever it was, would have to go. That, the sergeant suggested, was more easily said than done. The man had made a solid job of it, he reminded them, it was well secured in every part, and stable. It was no easy task even getting to the site through all that tangled vegetation. Besides – but this he did not suggest aloud – it did seem a pity to destroy the thing. Corporal Alley, who was an

237

expert, had confirmed that it had no function beyond being something to look at – so why . . .?

But once a word is floated – ('Mast, did you say?') – authorities have a way of bearing down on an objective. Reasons are surplus to requirement. The thing simply should not be there; somebody might be to blame; the man, whoever he was, or had been, had no right to be there in the first place. And since on this point Sergeant Helliwell felt a certain unease, who was he to argue? But if 'why' could not be queried, 'how' could be.

On this, the authorities did have a precedent. Corporal Alley had proved efficient on the first occasion. They would send him in again. He knew the thing better than anybody.

'But,' the sergeant protested, 'it'll take him days to dismantle it.' What would he use: his bare hands, hammer and chisel, pliers, what?

They bore with him patiently, sensing his irritation. It had been a rough assignment, everybody agreed. Because a mast was so very reprehensible in such a secret place, the authorities would spare nothing to demolish it. They would send a welder and a portable welding kit along with Corporal Alley in the helicopter. That would settle it. It would be done in a couple of hours.

The word 'vandalism' crossed Sergeant Helliwell's mind, but he kept his peace. When he arrived at the house, he was just about all in. He would not enter the man's house. By now, he felt a certain irreverence about such an act, so he sat on a log that Zorn had placed on the terrace for just such a purpose, lit a cigarette and waited, while his constable wandered admiringly in the vegetable patch.

Then the old chopping and hum of the helicopter disturbed the peace; the same hovering, with Corporal Alley descending on the winch cable, then the welding kit, and finally a wide-eyed stranger, the welder.

'Pity,' was all Corporal Alley had to say to the sergeant. He could see the sergeant was completely at a loss. This was

238

so patently a home, a little estate of its own set in a wilderness and giving nobody any trouble until . . .

'Well, it's got to go; that's all there is to it,' Helliwell replied. 'They've decided against the damned thing. Though if you say it's useless, I can't think why they're so bloody determined . . .'

The welder was soon busy, connecting leads to his battery, fixing a rod in his torch, and scratching his head about where to begin.

'Because it's there, I suppose,' Alley declared. 'Authorities can't stand things being there, not if they're not under jurisdiction, if you see what I mean.' He turned to the bewildered welder: 'Just topple the thing from the bottom, eh! And then chop it up.' What are two stripes for if not for decision? He mooned about idly, in no mood to talk to the sergeant, who stubbed his cigarette underfoot and did not give it a second thought.

The welder soon had sparks flying, and after a quarter of an hour, the 'mast' began to lean and then crashed gracefully among some raspberry canes.

'Timber!' shouted the welder, who was innocent of details and might be excused.

'I'll take this, I think,' Alley said to the welder, who nodded. Welders behind their weird visors are men of few words. Alley took up the glass ball as a memento. Whoever the bloke is – was – he thought, this mast and the house are worth remembering.

'What d'you want a thing like that for?' Sergeant Helliwell asked him.

'Souvenir, that's all,' Alley answered, not without a note of irritation. 'I know I'd have liked the guy,' he continued lamely, for policemen, he thought, do rather make a thing of being unsentimental.

'Yeah,' the sergeant conceded, 'he must have been a nice fella, I suppose, judging from this shack – and that, whatever it was . . .' pointing to the fallen structure. 'Yeah, maybe he was . . .' the sergeant rabbited on, for he still had nagging

239

reservations – that double bed, the cot. He still did not feel they had got to the bottom of this case.

'A pity he had to get mixed up in the Watkin affair,' Alley said in a tone which could be construed as attaching blame.

Sergeant Helliwell went immediately over to the defensive. 'Don't blame us,' he said. 'We don't listen to village gossip. Nothing more unreliable. We had nothing particular on this Thorn fellow. Until the boyfriend broke down and confessed, we were just keeping tabs on every man in the district, that's all, routine.'

Alley just gazed at the green glow of the glass ball in his hands, as though for divinations. But none came.